"King Sivo's not here. He's gone to his people for the summer. Who's called Prince Vakar of Loti—

Throne of Horror

The music stopped and Prince Vakar lurched toward Queen Profia's throne, carved from some olive-colored stone in the form of a huge serpent. He fell into the stone embrace just ahead of the Queen, who landed in his lap with a playful squeal that changed to a shriek of terror.

Vakar echoed the scream as he realized in one horror-struck flash that he was sitting on the coils of a giant, live snake. There was an explosive hiss as the head and neck reared up to stare down at the two humans, a forked tongue flicking. A loop, thicker than Vakar's thigh, whipped around them.

The coil tightened. His ribs creaked; it was like being squeezed to death by a live tree trunk.

The snake hissed louder. . .

The
Tritonian Ring

L. SPRAGUE DE CAMP

A Del Rey Book

BALLANTINE BOOKS • NEW YORK

A Del Rey Book
Published by Ballantine Books

ISBN 0-345-25803-7-150

Manufactured in the United States of America

First Ballantine Books Edition: March 1977

Cover art by Vincent Di Fate

TO FRITZ LEIBER

Contents

AUTHOR'S NOTE

Alert readers will note resemblances between some of the names in this story and the names of persons and places in ancient history and mythology. Thus my "Euskeria" is cognate both with Scheria, the land of the Phaeacians or kingdom of Alkinoös in the *Odyssey,* and with *Euskara,* the Basques' name for their anomalous language. The story, however, has nothing to do with my serious opinions on such subjects as lost continents, human prehistory, and the origins of civilization, for which see my book *Lost Continent* (Ballantine Books).

Pronounce these names as you please. The letters *ö* and (preconsonantal) *y* are meant for vowels like German *ö* and *ü* (or French *eu* and *u*) but may be rendered by the vowels of "up" and "it" respectively, rhyming *Söl* and *Ryn* with "hull" and "in." The characters *â, ê,* and *ô* stand for long *ah, eh,* and *oh* sounds in French. *Awoqqas* may be rhymed with "caucus." The X in *Ximenon* is meant for a *ks* sound as in "box," but you may simplify it to *z* or *s* if you prefer.

L. Sprague de Camp

I

The Gorgon God

WHEN THE GODS OF THE WEST WERE GATHERED IN their place of assembly, Drax, the Tritonian god of war, said in his ophidian hiss:

"Events will take a deadly turn for us in the next century, unless we change this pattern."

The assembled gods shuddered, and the vibration of their trembling ran through the universe. Entigta, the sea-god of Gorgonia (a kingdom so ancient that it had withered to mere myth when Imhotep built the first pyramid for King Zoser) spoke in his bubbly voice out of the midst of his tentacles:

"Can you not tell us the true nature of this danger?"

"No. The only further clue my science gives is that the trouble centers in the continent of Poseidonis, in the kingdom of Lorsk. There is something about its being caused by a member of the royal family of Lorsk. I believe my own folk are also involved, but I cannot be sure. Since King Ximenon got that accursed ring, I can no longer get through to them."

Entigta turned to Okma, the god of wisdom of Poseidonis, or Pusâd to use the more ancient form. "That, colleague, would be in your department. Who are the royal family of Lorsk?"

Okma replied: "There are King Zhabutir and his sons Kuros and Vakar, and the infant children of the former. I suspect Prince Vakar, whose spiritual obtuseness is such that I cannot speak directly to him."

Entigta's tentacles writhed. "If we cannot communicate with this mortal, how shall we deflect him from his intended path?"

"We might pray to *our* gods for guidance," said the

1

small, bat-eared god of the Coranians, whereupon all the gods laughed, being hardened skeptics.

Drax hissed: "There is another way. Set other mortals upon him."

Okma said: "I object! Vakar of Lorsk, despite his defect, has been a faithful votary of mine, burning many fat bullocks upon my altars. Besides it might be true that such patterns of event are laid down by an inflexible fate, not to be altered even by a god."

"I have never subscribed to that servile philosophy," said Drax, his forked tongue flicking. He turned his wedge-shaped head towards Entigta. "Colleague, of all of us here, you command the most warlike worshippers. Send them to destroy the royal family of Lorsk and all of Lorsk if need be!"

"Wait!" said Okma. "The other gods of Poseidonis—" (he looked around, noting Tandyla with all three of her eyes shut and Lyr scratching his barnacles) "—and I ought to be consulted before such devastation is loosed upon our own—"

The rest of the gods (or at least those not of Poseidonian provenance) shouted Okma down. Drax concluded:

"Waste no time, squid-headed one, for the peril is imminent!"

In Sederado, the capital of Ogugia in the Hesperides, Queen Porfia sat in her chambers with emeralds in her night-black hair and eyes as green as the emeralds, consulting with her minister Garal. The minister, a short, stout, bald man who deceptively appeared to radiate bluff good humor and sterling worth, rolled up a sheet of papyrus and said:

"Come, come, madam. You are not consulting your best interests in refusing to marry the king of Zhysk. Why should you boggle at the mere detail of his present three queens and fourteen concubines when—"

"Mere detail!" cried Queen Porfia, looking too young for a widow. "While Vancho was no god, at least while he lived I had that fat slob to myself. I do not care to wed one-seventeenth of any man, however royal."

"One-eighteenth," corrected Garal. "But—"

"Besides, who would run Ogugia whilst I languished in gilded durance in Amferé?"

"Perhaps you could spend most of your time here, where young Thiegos could comfort you."

"And how long before King Shvo found out and slew us both? Moreover, despite his fair promises to respect our independence, he would soon send some grasping Zhyskan governor to squeeze you dry as bones."

Garal gave a slight start, but said calmly: "You must remarry some time. Even your supporters murmur over the lack of a man at the head of the state. They would take even Thiegos . . ."

"I do not see it. The island flourishes, and Thiegos, while amusing as a lover, would be quite impossible as king."

"My thought also. But since you must eventually have a consort, you could hardly ask for one better situated than Shvo of Zhysk. Or is there some other man . . . ?"

"Not unless you count . . ."

"Whom?" Garal leaned forward, eyes bright with interest.

"Just a foolish idea. When I went to Amferé as a girl ten years ago, for that wedding of Shvo's daughter, one young princeling took my fancy: Vakar of Lorsk. Though no great beauty or mighty athlete, there was something about him—an irreverent wit, a soaring fancy, a keenness of insight, unlike most of his lumpish compatriots—Oh, well, he will no doubt have collected a dozen women by now and have forgotten the awkward Porfia. Now about this rise in harbor dues . . ."

Zeluud, king of the Gorgon Isles, slept after his midday meal, lying on his back upon his ivory-legged couch. With each inhalation his paunch rose, and with each exhalation the paunch sank while the silken handkerchief that covered his face rose in its turn with the force of the king's breath, which issued from his hidden features with a mighty snore. A Negro dwarf, kidnapped years ago from Tartaros by Zeluud's corsairs,

tiptoed about the chamber with a flyswatter of reed
and shredded palm-frond, lest any noxious insect disturb the king's rest. And the king of ancient Gorgonia
dreamed.

King Zeluud dreamed that he stood before the wet
black basalt throne of Entigta, the squid-headed sea-
god of the Gorgons. The king knew from Entigta's
dark coloration that the god was in no affable mood,
and from the rapidity with which the color-patterns
chased each other over Entigta's mottled hide, Zeluud
further inferred that the god was in a state of ungodly
agitation.

Entigta leaned forward on his sable throne, his slimy
hands gripping the arm-rests carven in the likeness of
sea-dragons, and fixed King Zeluud with his cold wet
eyes. His voice bubbled out of the parrot beak in the
midst of the octet of tentacles that served Entigta for a
face, like the gaseous products of decay bubbling up
through the slime of one of the somber swamps of
Blackland. Entigta said:

"King, do you obey me?"

"As always, God," said Zeluud, beginning to shake
in his sandals, for he was sure that Entigta was about
to impose some outrageous demand upon him.

"Well, trouble comes upon us from the North, and it
is your place to deal with it. Trouble not merely for the
Gorgades, but also for the entire race of the gods."

"What trouble, Lord?"

"The exact nature thereof we know not. I can but
tell you it centers in the royal family of Lorsk in Poseidonis."

The king replied: "And what, God, shall I do?
Lorsk lies far from here, with its capital well inland, so
that it is not vulnerable to a sudden raid from my corsairs."

Entigta's tentacles writhed impatiently. "You shall
follow two courses. First you shall send my priest
Qasigan to deal with these princes in person. He is well
qualified, being hardy and discreet, widely travelled,
and devoted to my interests. Moreover, he has two able
non-human helpers."

"And the other course?"

"You shall prepare to conquer Poseidonis."

Zeluud, aghast, took a step back. "God! The Gorgades are but three small islands, whereas Poseidonis is a great land whose people outnumber ours fifty to one and are famed for their athletic prowess. Moreover, bronze is so common there that they even use it for arrowheads. How in the seven hells do you expect . . ."

Zeluud fell silent as Entigta turned an ominous black.

"Is your faith then so fragile?" gurgled the squid-god. "By whose help have you long raided with impunity the coasts of Poseidonis and the mainland, and the rich commerce of the Hesperides?"

"Well then—what am I to do?"

"Seize Lorsk and the rest will fall, for Lorsk is the strongest of the Pusadian states, among whom there is no unity but only mutual hatred and suspicion. Your warriors are the world's mightiest, and even if they were not, my priests have the world's deadliest weapon: their captive medusas. With your warlike people and the mineral wealth of Lorsk, you can conquer the world! And I," murmured Entigta, "shall be sea-god not merely of the Gorgades . . ."

"Still—" began Zeluud doubtfully, but Entigta said:

"There is another point of attack against Lorsk. King Zhabutir has twin sons, Vakar and Kuros. Vakar, being the younger by a quarter-hour, is heir according to their old system of ultimogeniture. Now Kuros, who mortally hates his brother, might serve your interest in return for a promise of the throne, even as a tributary of yours. And once in control you can slay all three of them."

"How can I deal with this Kuros? He is too far for messengers, and the Pusadian sea god would not let you communicate with one of his votaries."

"I can handle Lyr. There is a Gorgonian fisherman on the west coast of Poseidonis, in the Bay of Kort. In accord with the pact between Lyr and myself, I visit this fisherman in dreams as if he were back in Gorgonia. You can therefore speak to Kuros through this man."

"Mightiest of gods though you be, not even gods

know all, or you would know more of the doom over-hanging you. What if we fail?"

"Then the reign of the gods is ended, unless Posei-donis be sunk beneath the sea."

"What?"

"Know you not the continent settles, the water round its shores having risen three feet in the last century? We can speed this process so that in a few centuries nought would show above the waves save the tallest peaks." The god's slit-pupilled eyes stared into space. "The outlines of land and water would be altered from the swamps of Blackland to the snows of Thulê. Nor would this be all. Without the copper of Poseidonis, men might even forget the metal-working art and return to stone. But even that is preferable to the other doom, for without the gods to guide you, how could you poor weak mortals survive? Return to the waking world, then, and set about your allotted tasks."

Entigta dissolved into a swirl of slime. The king awoke, threw the handkerchief off his sweating swarthy face, and sat up on his gold-knobbed couch. He shouted:

"Khashel! Go to the temple of Entigta and tell the priest Qasigan to come to me at once!"

II

The Sinking Land

ON AN EARLY SPRING EVENING MONTHS LATER, THIR-teen hundred miles north of the Gorgades, on the continent of Poseidonis, in the kingdom of Lorsk, in the capital city of Mneset, the king of Lorsk held council. A cold wind roared through the streets of Mneset, whipping tatters of scud across the pocked face of the moon and rattling the shutters of the houses. Inside the castle of King Zhabutir, the wind swayed the wall hangings and made cressets flare and lamps flutter. Outside in the castle courtyard, the pigs huddled together to keep warm.

In the king's council room, the light of the central hearth fire flickered upon the walls of massive cyclopean stonework and the ceiling of rough-hewn oaken beams. Four men, wrapped in cloaks against the drafts, sat around the council table listening to a fifth: Söl the spy, a thickset, commonplace-looking fellow with quick-shifting eyes.

As these eyes flickered across the table, they first passed over, on the left, Ryn the magician, peering vaguely through watery eyes over a stained beard like an elderly and absent-minded billygoat. A hunched back added to the grotesqueness of his appearance. Next sat the king's elder son Kuros, square-jawed and broad-shouldered, nibbling on a wedge of cheese. Then came King Zhabutir himself, in the chair of pretence at the head of the table, looking with his high-bridged nose and flowing white beard like the serene embodiment of justice and wisdom, although his nickname of "the Indecisive" belied his looks. His golden crown glowed redly in the firelight, and little gleams from his uncut stones, polished by the black craftsmen of Tartaros, chased each other about the walls when he moved his head. A great shaggy wolfhound lay across his feet.

On the king's left sat his younger son Vakar, the twin (but not the identical twin) brother of Kuros, looking a bit vacuous (for age and experience had not yet stamped his features with character) and a bit foppish. The jewels on his fingers shone as he nervously cracked his knuckle joints. He had a narrow hatchet face, which swept back from a long, forward-jutting nose, which had been straight until a fall from a horse had put a slight dog-leg in it. Instead of the normal Pusadian kilt, he wore the checkered trews of the barbarians, and (another fad) copied the barbarian custom of shaving all the face but the upper lip. He was small for a Lorskan, a mere five-ten, with the swarthy skin and thick black hair of most Pusadians. Deepset dark eyes looked out of his narrow face from under heavy brow ridges and thick black brows into those of Söl, who said:

"I couldn't get to the Gorgades myself, for their system of public messes serves to check all adult men, and they'd soon see through any disguise. Since the land lives by robbery, the ships of other nations have no peaceful occasion to touch there. I did, however, spend a month in Kernê and there learned that the Gorgons are preparing a great expedition somewhither."

Kuros said: "Pff. The Gorgons' ferocity has been exaggerated by distance and the envy of their neighbors. If we knew them at first hand, we should find their intentions as peaceful as anybody's."

Prince Vakar shifted his gaze from the smoking wood fire to the pocked face of the spy. His tight-drawn lips betrayed his inner tension as he spoke:

"Certainly their intentions are peaceful, like those of the lion for the lamb. The lion wishes only to be allowed to devour the lamb in peace. But, Master Söl, if the Gorgons have no peaceful contacts with other nations, how could such news reach Kernê?"

"The Gorgons' isolation isn't so perfect as they pretend. They carry on a small secret trade with certain merchants in Kernê for things they can neither make, grow, nor steal. Although the Kerneans hang or head any man they catch in this traffic, such are the profits that there's always someone to take the chance. A Kernean would brave the seven hells for a profit."

Ryn the wizard blew his nose on his robe and spoke: "Was there any indication of the Gorgons' direction?"

The wind blew a gout of smoke into Söl's face as if trying to stop him from replying. When the spy got over coughing and wiping his eyes he answered:

"Nothing definite, but the shadow of the echo of a whisper that said 'Lorsk'."

"No more?"

"No more, sir. I had it from a harlot of the town who said she'd learned it from a sailor who worked for a trader who'd heard . . . and so on."

Kuros swallowed the last of his cheese, dusted the crumbs off his fingers, and said: "That's all, Söl."

Vakar wished to hear more, but before he could protest Söl had glided out and Kuros said:

"Very interesting, but let's not work ourselves into a sweat over the shadow of an echo of a whisper—"

"Is that so?" said Vakar sharply. "With due respect, my brother wishes us to take the attitude of the man in the story who went to sleep on the skerry thinking he had a spell that would hold back the tides. You remember:

> *"Shoreward they shouldered   with crests ever-*
>   *curling,*
> *The waxing waves   washed higher and higher—"*

"For Lyr's sake don't start one of those!" said Kuros.

Vakar shot a dagger-glance at his brother and continued: "Where there's shadow there's more often than not a substance to cast it. And the words of so reliable a spy as Master Söl should not lightly be thrown aside. The Gorgons—"

"You have Gorgons on the brain," said Kuros. "Suppose they did sail against us? They must pass Tartaros and Dzen, sail west through the Hesperides, land upon the coast of Zhysk, and march through that land to come to grips with us. We should have ample warning, and one Lorksan's worth three Gorgons—"

"As I was saying when the yapping of a mongrel interrupted me," said Vakar. "The Gorgons don't even fight fair. I've been reading—"

"As if any real man ever learned anything from marks on papyrus," put in Kuros.

"Those who can't read can't judge—"

King Zhabutir said: "Boys! Boys! I forbid this dreadful quarreling. Go on, Vakar."

"You know how we fight: in loose groups, each led by a lord or champion followed by his kinsmen and liegemen and friends. We usually start out with challenges to single combat from our champions to the foe's, and sometimes the whole day is occupied with such duels. Moreover, our men go equipped as they like: with swords, spears, axes, halberds, berdiches, war clubs, and so on."

"What other way of fighting is there?" said Kuros.

"The Gorgons equip all their men alike, with helmets, shields, and weapons of the same pattern. They align their men in a solid mass, every man having a fixed place despite rank or kinship. They waste no time in challenges but, at a signal, all move upon the foe, every man keeping his place in the whole. Such a mass goes through an army like ours like a plow through sand."

"Fairy tales," said Kuros. "No true warriors would submit to be so forced into a single rigid mold . . ."

As usual the argument went round and round, with Vakar (whose disposition it was to take a gloomy view of things) arguing against Kuros while the other two remained mute. Kuros began to press the king:

"You agree, don't you, Father?"

Zhabutir the Indecisive smiled weakly. "I know not . . . I cannot decide . . . What thinks Master Ryn?"

"Sir?" said the magician. "Before sending my opinions forth across the chasm of surmise, I prefer to wait until they're provided with a more solid bridge of fact. With your permission I'll call upon witch Gra for counsel."

"That old puzzel!" cried Kuros. "We should have hanged her . . ."

Ryn began his preparations. From his bag he produced a small bronze tripod, which he unfolded and set over the guttering fire. The fire threw a streamer of smoke at him as if to keep him off, but at the mutter of a cantrip it drew in upon itself. At the first syllable, the wolfhound jumped up, gave a faint howl, and trotted out with its tail between its legs, its claws clicking on the stone.

Ryn poked the fire and added sticks until it blazed up again. With a piece of charcoal, he drew a circle around the hearth and added lines and glyphs whose meaning Vakar did not know. Ryn rose to his feet and prowled around the room, extinguishing the wobbling flames in the little oil lamps. His hunched shadow reminded Vakar of that of a great scuttling spider—for all that Vakar esteemed the man who had tutored him as a boy. Ryn then went back to the hearth, and into the miniature cauldron at the apex of the tripod he sprinkled powders, whose smell made the others cough.

He resumed his stool facing the fire and spoke in a language so ancient that even the scholarly Vakar (who could read over a thousand pictographs) could not understand a word, all the while moving his hands in stiffly geometrical gestures.

Vakar told himself that it was mere illusion that the room became even darker. A plume of smoke arose from the cauldron, and although the wind still sent drafts whistling through the chamber, the air within the circle seemed quite still. For instead of diffusing and dispersing as it rose, the column of smoke held together and twined itself snakelike into knots at the top of the column. Vakar (who would have nourished magical ambitions himself but for his peculiar disability) held his breath, his heart pounding.

The smoke thickened and solidified and became a simulacrum of a tall, heavy woman, clad in a wolfskin tied over one shoulder and belted around her thick waist with a thong. She was seated, half-turned so that she seemed to be looking past the four men without seeing them. In one hand she clutched a bone from which she was gnawing the meat. Vakar realized that it was not the woman herself, for the substance of which she was made was still smoky-gray in the semidarkness, and he could see the tripod and the fire beneath it through her massive legs and feet.

"Gra!" called Ryn.

The woman stopped gnawing and looked at the men. She tossed the bone aside, and as it left her hand it vanished. She wiped her fingers on the wolf hide and scratched under her exposed breast. Her voice came in a far-off whisper:

"What wish the lords of Lorsk with me?"

Ryn said: "Word has come of threatening movements by the Gorgons. We are divided as to what to do. Advise us."

The witch stared at the ground in front of her so long that Kuros squirmed and muttered, until Ryn hissed him to silence. At last Gra spoke:

"Send Prince Vakar to seek the thing the gods most fear."

"Is that all?"

"That is all."

Ryn spoke again in his archaic speech, and the phantom of the witch turned to mere smoke, which wafted about, making the spectators sneeze. Ryn took a burning stick from the fire and relighted the lamps.

Vakar viewed Gra's message with mixed feelings. If the very gods feared the thing that she had spoken of, what business had a mere mortal pursuing it? On the other hand, he had never been to the mainland and had long wished to travel. While Lorsk was a fine rich land, the real centers of culture and wisdom lay eastward: Sederado with its philosophers, Torrutseish with its wizards, and who knew what other ancient cities?

Kuros said sourly: "If we were fools enough to believe that harridan—"

Vakar interrupted: "Brother, since you always seem so eager to discredit warnings against the Gorgons, could you have a motive other than simple skepticism?"

"What do you mean, sir?"

"Such as—let's say a little present from King Zeluud?"

Kuros jumped up, reaching for his knife. "Are you calling me traitor?" he yelled. "I'll carve the word on your liver . . ."

Ryn the magician reached up to seize Kuros's arms, while King Zhabutir laid a hand on Vakar's shoulder as the latter, too, started to rise. When they had pacified the furious Kuros, he sat down, snarling:

"All that effeminate bastard does is to stir up trouble and enmity amongst us. He hates me because he knows if the gods hadn't fumbled, I should be heir and not he. If we followed the sensible mainland custom of primogeniture . . ."

Before Vakar could think of a crushing reply, Ryn spoke: "My lords, let's sink our present differences until the matter of the foreign threat be resolved. Whatever you think of Gra or Söl, I've had confirmation of their tale."

"What?" said the king.

"Last night I dreamt I stood before the gods of Poseidonis: Lyr and Tandyla and Okma and the rest. As usual I asked if they had advice for Lorsk."

"What did they say?" asked Kuros.

"Nothing; but it was the manner of their saying it. They turned away their eyes and faces as if ashamed of their silence. And I recalled where I'd seen that expression. Many decades ago, when I was a young fellow studying magic in mighty Torrutseish—"

"Gods, he's off on another of those!" muttered Kuros.

"—and one of my friends, an Ogugian youth named Joathio, got excited at a bullfight and made indiscreet remarks about the city prefect. Next day (though the remarks had been nothing dreadful) he disappeared. I asked after him at the headquarters of the municipal troop, and those tough soldiers turned away from me with that same expression. Later I found Joathio's head on a spike over the main gate. Not a pretty sight for one still young and soft of soul, heh-heh.

"I therefore infer that something's impending in the world of the gods, unfavorable to us, against which our own gods are for some reason forbidden to warn us. In view of Söl's news, it could well be a Gorgonian invasion. Therefore let's send Prince Vakar on his quest. If he fail—"

"Which he will," put in Kuros.

"—no harm will be done, whereas if he succeed, he may save us from an unknown doom."

King Zhabutir said: "But the gods—how can we oppose them?"

Vakar said: "It were cowardly to give up before the fight has even begun, merely because we might face odds. If the gods fear something, they can't be all-powerful."

"Atheist!" sneered Kuros. "When do you go? While I can't understand sending Vakar Zhu on a supernatural quest, Gra did name you and not me."

"Tomorrow."

"As soon as that? You'll miss the games of the vernal equinox, but that'll be small loss as you've never won a prize."

"Anything to get away from your brags and boasts," said Vakar.

Kuros had always boasted his superiority in sport: He could out-run, out-jump, and out-wrestle his brother. He had also annoyed Vakar by stressing the sobriquet "Zhu" which meant, not exactly "fool" or "deaf one," but "one who lacks supernatural perceptions." For Vakar had the unenviable distinction of completely lacking normal powers of telepathy, prescience, or spirit communication. Not even did the gods visit him in dreams.

"When you return," said Kuros, "you'll have thought up such a fine assortment of lies about your adventures that I, who must depend upon my known accomplishments, shall be quite outclassed."

"Am I a dog, that you call me a liar?" began Vakar with heat, but his father interrupted.

"Now, boys," said King Zhabutir in his vague way, then to Ryn: "Are you sure she meant Vakar? It does seem a challenge to the gods to send the heir to the throne on a wild chase for who-knows-what."

Ryn said: "There's no doubt. Say your farewells and sharpen your bronze tonight, Prince."

"Whither am I bound?" asked Vakar. "Your lady consultant was as vague in her directions as my brother is about the paternity of his wives' children."

"You—" began Kuros, but Ryn interrupted the outburst:

"I know of nothing in Poseidonis answering Gra's description. I advise you to go to lordly Torrutseish, where the greatest wizards of the world make their dwelling."

"Do you know any of these wizards?" inquired Vakar.

"I haven't been there for decades, but I recall that Sarra and Nichok and Vrilya and Kurtevan were preëminent."

"How many shall I take with me? A troop of soldiery and—let's say—a mere dozen or so of servants?"

A faint smile played about the corners of Ryn's old mouth. "You shall take one—possibly two persons with you. One body-servant, let's say, and one interpreter—"

"I have the interpreter for him," chuckled Kuros. "A fellow named Sret with the most marvelous gift of tongues—"

"What?" cried Vakar in honest amazement. "No bodyguard? No women? By Tandyla's third eye!"

"Not one. For your kind of search you'll go farther and faster without a private army."

"Who'll know my rank?"

"Nobody, unless you tell them, and usually you'd better not. Princes have been known to fetch fine ransoms."

Kuros threw back his head and laughed loudly while the king looked ineffectually anxious. Vakar glared from one to the other, his knuckles itching for a good smash into his brother's fine teeth. Then he pulled himself together and smiled wryly, saying:

"If the hero Vrir in the epic can run all over the world alone, I can do likewise. I go to procure a beggar's rags, suitably verminous. Think kindly of me when I'm gone."

"I always think kindly of you when you're gone," said Kuros. "Only you're not gone enough."

"It's time we were in bed," said King Zhabutir, rising.

The others bid their respects to the king and departed, Vakar towards his chambers, where his mistress Bili awaited him. He dreaded telling her of his plan, for he disliked her scenes. He would not be altogether displeased to be leaving her, for not only was she ten years his senior and fast fattening, but also her late husband had with good reason referred to her as "Bili the Bird-brained." Moreover, he would have to take a wife or two one of these days, when matches with the daughters of rich and powerful Pusadian lords could be organized, and such matters were more easily arranged without the complication of a concubine already at home.

He shouted: "Get out!" and kicked at one of the royal goats, who had somehow wandered into the castle.

"Prince Vakar!" said a low voice from the shadows.

Vakar whirled, clapping a hand to his hip where his sword hilt would have been had he been armed. It was Söl the spy.

"Well?" said Vakar.

"I—I couldn't speak out in council meeting, but I must tell you that . . ."

"That what?"

"You guarantee my safety?"

"You shall be safe though you tell me I'm the son of a sow and a sea demon."

"Your brother is in league with the Gorgons—"

"Are you mad?"

"By no means. There's proof. Go ask—*urk!*"

Söl jerked as if he had been stung. The man half-turned, and Vakar saw something sticking in his back. Söl gasped:

"They—he—I die! Go tell . . ."

He folded up upon the stone flooring, joint by joint. Before Vakar could have counted ten, the spy was huddled motionless at his feet.

Vakar stooped and pulled the dagger from Söl's back. A quick examination showed the spy to be dead, and also that the dagger had been thrown so that the point had stuck in the muscle covering the man's right shoulder blade: a mere flesh wound. Holding the dagger, Vakar moved quickly down the corridor in the direction from which the weapon had come, his moccasins making no sound. He neither saw nor heard anyone and presently turned back, cursing himself for not having run after the assassin the instant Söl fell.

He returned to the victim, whose eyes now stared sightlessly up, reflecting tiny highlights from the nearest lamp. Vakar held the dagger close to the lamp and saw that the bronzen blade was overlain with a coating of some black gummy substance, covering the pointward half of the blade. This stuff was in turn coated by a faint film of blood for a half-inch from the point.

Vakar, his blood freezing, pondered his predicament. Could Kuros be playing so deadly a double game? Somebody had shut Söl's mouth just as he had been about to reveal matters of moment. If Söl were right, what could Vakar do? Accuse Kuros publicly? His woolly-headed father would scoff, and his brother would ask whether he, Vakar, hadn't murdered Söl and then invented this wild tale to cover the fact. Whatever the proof Söl had spoken of, Vakar had no access to it now.

At last Vakar wiped the dagger point—lightly, so as not to remove the substance under the blood—on the edge of Söl's kilt and tiptoed away. As he entered his outer chamber, he heard Bili's voice:

"Is that you, my lord and love?"

"Aye. Don't get up."

He picked up the lighted lamp from the table and held it close to the row of daggers and axes and swords that hung upon the wall. He took down one of the daggers and tried the murder weapon in the sheath. He had to go through most of the collection to find a sheath that fitted.

"What are you doing?" came the voice of Bili, whose curiosity must have been aroused by the snick of blades in their sheaths.

"Nothing. I shall be along presently."

"Well, come to bed! I'm tired of waiting."

Vakar sighed, wondering how often he had heard that. Much as he esteemed Bili's lectual accomplishments, he sometimes wished she would occasionally think of something else. He replaced the dagger sheaths on their racks, hid in a chest the dagger in whose sheath he had placed the murder weapon, and went into the bedchamber.

III

The Sirenian Sea

BEFORE DAWN, VAKAR WAS AWAKENED BY A KNOCK ON his door and a voice: "Prince Vakar! There's been a murder!"

It was the captain of the castle guard. His noise partly awakened Bili, who stirred and reached out. Vakar eluded her embrace, tumbled out of bed, and pulled on some clothes.

They were all standing around the body of Söl, even that fisherman whom Kuros (normally more rank-conscious than Vakar) claimed as a personal friend to be entertained at the castle. King Zhabutir said:

"Terrible! Do—do you know anything about this, Vakar?"

"Not a thing," said Vakar, and looked hard at Kuros. "You, brother?"

"Nor I," said Kuros blandly.

Vakar stared into his brother's eyes, as if in hope of seeing through them into the brain behind, but could make nothing of the man's expression. He turned away, saying:

"Perhaps Ryn can make something of this. I have to collect my gear for departure."

He went back to his chambers, but instead of packing at once he took down the murder knife from the wall rack, hid it in his shirt, and went down into the courtyard. The East was pale with the coming dawn, and the wind whipped Vakar's cloak. A dozen swine lay in a mud wallow, huddled for warmth, chins resting on each other's bristly bodies. An old boar grunted and showed his tusks. Vakar kicked him out of the way and grabbed a half-grown shoat, which burst into frantic struggles and squeals.

With a quick look around, Vakar drew the murder dagger from his shirt. He clamped his teeth upon the sheath, drew the blade, and pricked the pig's rump with the point to a depth of a quarter-inch. Then he released the animal, which raced across the court. Half-way across it began to slow down. Before it reached the far side, its legs gave way under it, and it lay twitching for a few seconds before it died.

Vakar stared thoughtfully at the dagger as he sheathed it and hid it in his shirt. If the venom worked so fast upon a beast notoriously resistant to poison, there was no doubt of what it would do to a man. He started to return to his chambers, then paused as another thought struck him. It would not do to have this poisoned porker fed to the castle's dogs, or even more so to have it unknowingly fried up for the royal breakfast. Vakar walked over to the pig, picked it up, and carried it to the outer gate. There the usual pair of guards leaned on their zaghnals or dagger-halberds: pole arms with knifelike triangular bronze blades.

"Which of you is junior?" he said. When that question had been answered, he handed the shoat to the startled young man, saying:

"Get a shovel from the tool house and take this pig outside the city and bury it: deeply, so no dog or hyena shall dig it up. And don't take it home for your wife to cook, unless you wish a sudden death."

At that instant Drozo, King Zhabutir's treasurer, appeared at the gate on his way to work. Vakar went with him to pick up a supply of trade metal. Drozo gave him gold rings and silver torcs and copper slugs shaped like little ax heads, then handed him a semicircular piece of bronze, saying:

"If you get to Kernê and are pressed for funds, go to Senator Amastan with this. It's half a broken medallion whereof he has the other half, and will therefore identify you."

Vakar went back to his room. Bili called from the bedchamber:

"Aren't you coming back to bed, Vakar? It's early—"

"No," said Vakar shortly, and began rummaging through his possessions.

He took down one dagger for which he had rigged a harness of two narrow strips, so that the sheath was positioned in front of his chest. He switched this harness to the sheath that now housed the poisoned dagger, took off his fine linen shirt, strapped the harness around his torso, and donned the shirt again.

Then he began collecting garments and weapons. He assembled his winged helmet of solid gold with the lining of purple cloth; his jazerine cuirass of gold-washed bronzen scales; his cloak of the finest white wool with a collar of sable. He looked over his collection of bronze swords: slender rapiers, heavy cut-and-thrust longswords, short leaf-shaped barbarian broadswords, and a double-curved sapara from far Thamuzeira, where screaming men and women were flayed on the altars of Miluk. He picked the best rapier, the one with the gold-inlaid blade, the hilt of sharkshin and silver with a ruby pommel, and the scabbard of embossed leather with a golden chape at the end . . .

At this point it occurred to Vakar that while he would no doubt make a glittering spectacle in all this gaudery, it would be useless to pretend that he was but a simple traveler of no consequence. In fact, he would need a bodyguard to keep the first robber lord who saw him from swooping down with his troop to seize this finery.

One by one he returned the pieces to their chests and pegs and assembled a quite different outfit. As the rapier would be too light to be effective against armor, he chose a plain but serviceable longsword; a plain bronze helm with a lining of sponge; a simple jack of stiff-tanned cowhide with bronze reinforcings; and his stout bronze buckler with the repoussé pattern of lunes: work of the black Tartarean smiths. Nobody in Lorsk could duplicate it.

He was pulling on a pair of piebald boots of shaggy winter horsehide when Fual, his personal slave, came in. Fual was an Aremorian of Kerys who had been seized by Foworian slavers and sold in Gadaira. He was a slender man, more so even than Vakar, with the light skin of the more northerly peoples and a touch of red in his hair that suggested the blood of the barbarous Galatha. He looked at Vakar from large melancholy eyes and clucked.

". . . and why didn't you call me, sir? It isn't proper for one of your rank to work for himself."

"Like Lord Naz in the poem," grinned Vakar:

Slavishly swinking,   weary and worn . . .

"If it makes you unhappy, you may complete the job."

They were stuffing extra clothing into a goatskin bag when Bili, scantily wrapped in a deerskin blanket, appeared in the doorway, looking at Vakar from brown bovine eyes. She said:

"My lord, as this will be the last time—"

"Don't bother me now!" said Vakar.

He finished packing and told Fual: "Get your gear too."

"Are you taking *me*, sir?"

"And why not? Get along with you. But remember: You shall steal nothing except on my direct order!"

Fual, who had been a professional thief before his enslavement, departed looking thoughtful. It now occurred to Vakar that once they touched the mainland, Fual could easily run away. He must try to learn more of what went on in the mercurial Aremorian's mind; Fual's attitude towards him might make the difference between life and death.

A snuffling from the bedroom attracted Vakar's attention. Bili huddled sobbing under the blankets.

"Now, now," he said, patting her awkwardly. "You'll find another lover."

"But I don't wish—"

"You'd better, because there's no knowing when I shall return."

"At least you might . . ." She rolled over, throwing off her blankets, and slid her plump hands up his arms.

"Oh, well," sighed Prince Vakar.

They paused as they topped the pass to look out over the irrigated plain on which stood sunny Amferé. The spires of the city shone distantly in the afternoon sun on the edge of the blue Sirenian Sea. The capital of Zhysk was laid out as a miniature of mighty Torrutseish, with the same circular outer wall, the same sea canal running diametrically through it, and the same circular harbor of concentric rings of land and water at the center.

Vakar twisted on his saddle pad to look back at his convoy of two chariots, one carrying Fual and the interpreter Sret, the other the baggage. They were all splashed with mud from fording streams swollen by the melting of the snow on the higher peaks. Vakar rode horseback instead of in a chariot because, in a day when equitation was a daring novelty, it was also one of the few physical activities wherein he excelled. This was not entirely to his own credit but was due in some measure to the fact that the average Pusadian, standing six to six-and-a-half feet, was too heavy for the small horses of the age. Although Vakar was small for a Lorskan, his boots cleared the ground by a scant two feet.

"Shall we be there by sundown?" he said to the nearest charioteer, who replied:

"Whatever your highness pleases."

Vakar started down the slope, slowly, for without stirrups not even an accomplished rider can gallop downhill without the risk of being tossed over his mount's head. Behind him, the bronze tires of the vehicles ground through the gravel and squished in the mud. Vakar smiled wryly at the reply, reflecting that if he asked them if the tide would obey him they would no doubt say the same thing.

They drew up to the walls of Amferé at sunset, to wait in line behind an oxcart piled with farm produce for the last-minute rush before the gates were closed. The people were lighter in coloring than those of Lorsk, lending support to the legend that a party of Atlanteans had settled Zhysk some centuries back.

When Vakar identified himself, showing his seal ring, the guard waved him through, for there was peace at the moment between Zhysk and Lorsk. Vakar rode for the citadel at the center of the city, meaning to sponge on the King of Zhysk. The citadel comprised an island surrounded by a broad ring of water. The palace and other public buildings stood on the island, and the outer boundary of the ring formed the harbor, instead of three concentric rings as in Torrutseish.

When Vakar arrived at the bridge across the oversized moat (a bridge that had been the wonder of all Poseidonis when built, as the continent had never seen a bridge longer than the length of a single log) he found that the guards had already stretched a chain across the approach for the night. A guard told him in broad Zhyskan dialect:

"King Shvo's not here. He's gone to Azaret with all his people for the summer. Who's calling?"

"Prince Vakar of Lorsk."

The guard seemed unimpressed, and Vakar got the impression that the fellow judged him a liar. He tugged his mustache in thought, then asked:

"Is his minister Peshas here?"

"Why, didn't ye know? Peshas lost his head for conspiracy two months gone. Eh, ye could see it on its spike from here, rotting away day by day, but they've taken it down to make room for another."

"Who is the minister then?"

"Himself has a new one, Lord Mir, but he's gone home for the night."

Under these circumstances, it would be more trouble than it was worth to try to talk his way in. Vakar asked:

"Where's the best inn?"

"Try Nyeron's. Three blocks north, turn right, go till ye see a little alley but don't go in there; bear left . . ."

After some wandering, Vakar found Nyeron's inn. Nyeron, speaking with a strong Hesperian accent, said that he could put up Vakar and his party for six ounces of copper a night.

"Very well," said Vakar and dug into his scrip for a fistful of copper, wondering why Nyeron had looked surprised for a flicker of an eyelid.

After the usual period of weighing and checking, they found a small celt of just over six ounces.

"Take it and never mind the change," said Vakar, then turned to one of the charioteers. "Take this and buy a meal for all of us for Nyeron to cook, and also fodder. Fual, help with the horses. Sret . . ."

He paused to notice that Sret was speaking in Hesperian to Nyeron, who replied with a flood of that tongue, in the dialect of Meropia. It seemed that Sret, a small man with a long apelike upper lip, had once lived in Meropia and that he and Nyeron had acquaintances in common. Although he had never visited the Hesperides, Vakar had a fair acquaintance with their language by virtue of having had an Ogugian nurse. However, being tired from his day's ride, he said impatiently in his own tongue:

"Sret! Haul in the baggage and see that nobody steals it until we're ready to eat. And not then, either."

Sret went out to obey, while Nyeron shouted for his daughter to fetch a washbasin and a towel. A handsome wench appeared lugging a wooden bowl and a ewer, in one door and out another that led into the dormitory. Vakar followed her with an appreciative eye. Nyeron remarked:

"A fine piece of flesh, no? If the gentleman wishes, she shall be at his disposal . . ."

"I've had all the riding I can manage in the last ten days," said Vakar. "Perhaps when I've rested . . ."

He went back to the dormitory for the first turn at the washbasin and found Fual beside him. Vakar, scrubbing the grime off his hands with a brush of pigskin with the bristles on, said:

"How are we doing, Fual?"

"Oh, very fine, sir. Except . . ."

"Except what?"

"You know it's unusual for one of your rank to stop at a vulgar inn?"

"I know, but fortune compels. What else?"

"Perhaps my lord will excuse my saying he hasn't had much experience with inns?"

"That I haven't. What have I done wrong?"

"You could have got lodging for three ounces a night, or at most four, if you'd bargained sharply."

"Why the boar-begotten thief! Am I a dog? I'll knock his teeth—"

"My lord! It wouldn't become your dignity, not to mention that the magistrates would take a poor view of the act, this being not your own demesne. Next time let me haggle, for my dignity doesn't matter."

"Very well; with your background I can see you'd make a perfect merchant."

Vakar handed over the washing facilities. By the time the last of the party had washed, the water and towel were foul indeed. They ate from wooden bowls with the dispatch and silence of tired and hungry men, washing down great masses of roast pork and barley bread with gulps of the green wine of Zhysk and paying no heed to a noisy party of merchants clustered at the other end of the long table.

When they turned in, however, Vakar found that the chatter of the merchants kept him awake. They seemed to be making an all-night party of it, with a flute girl and all the trimmings. When the flute girl was not tweetling, the men were engaged in some game of chance with loud boasts, threats, and accusations.

Vakar stood it for a couple of hours until his slow temper reached a boil. Then he climbed out of bed and knocked aside the curtain separating the dormitory from the front chamber of the inn.

"Stop that racket!" he roared, "before I beat your heads in!"

The noise stopped as four pairs of eyes turned upon him. The stoutest merchant said:

"And who are you, my good man?"

"I'm Prince Vakar of Lorsk, and when I say shut up—"

"And I'm the Queen of Ogugia. If you foreigners don't like it here, go back—"

"Swine!" yelled Vakar, looking for something to throw, but Nyeron, cudgel in hand, intervened:

"No fighting here! If you must brawl, go outside."

"Gladly," said Vakar. "Wait while I fetch my sword—"

"Oh, it's to be swords?" said the stout merchant. "Then you must wait while I send home for mine. As it's drunk the blood of several Gorgonian pirates it shouldn't find a Lorskan popinjay—"

"What's that?" said Vakar. "Who are you, really?" His initial burst of rage had subsided enough for his ever-lively curiosity to come into play, and he realized that he was making himself look foolish.

"I'm Mateng of Po, owner of three ships, as you'd know if you weren't an ignorant—"

"Wait," said Vakar. "Are any of your ships leaving shortly for the mainland?"

"Yes. The *Dyra* sails for Gadaira tomorrow, if the wind holds."

"Isn't Gadaira the nearest mainland port to Torrut-seish?"

"It is."

"How much—" Vakar started to say, then checked himself. He stuck his head back into the dormitory and called: "Fual! Wake up; come out and haggle for me!"

Next morning, Vakar was collecting his crew to ride to the docks when he found that Sret was missing. Back in the inn, he found the interpreter chatting with Nyeron.

"Come along!" said Vakar.

"Yes, sir," said Sret, and as he started out called back over his shoulder in Hesperian: "Farewell; I shall see you again sooner than you think!"

Then he came. They rattled down to the harbor, where Vakar stopped at the temple of Lyr to sacrifice a lamb to the sea god. While he did not take his gods too seriously (as they never visited him), he thought it just as well to be on the safe side. Then, by questioning all and sundry, he located the *Dyra*. Mateng was ordering the stowing of a cargo of copper ingots, bison hides, and mammoth ivory.

"Waste no time in getting home!" Vakar told the charioteers, who clattered off, leading the horse he had ridden. Vakar sauntered up to the edge of the quay and stepped aboard the ship, trying not to show his excitement. Fual and Sret staggered after under their loads of gear and food for the trip.

Mateng called: "Ruaz! Here's your passenger! He's all paid up, so take good care of him."

"A prince, eh?" said Captain Ruaz, laughing through his beard. "Well, keep out of the way, your sublime highness, if you don't want an ingot dropped on your toe."

He bustled about directing his men until, after a long wait, they got the last goods stowed and the hatches closed and cast off. The crew manned four sweeps, which they worked standing up, maneuvering the ship out from its quay. They plodded around the annular harbor to the main canal, Vakar craning his neck this way and that to see all he could of Amferé from the water.

As they entered the canal, they picked up speed, for a slight current added its impetus to the force of the oars. Soon they passed through the outer city wall, where a great bronze gate stood ready to swing shut across the channel to keep out hostile ships. Then down the canal half a mile to the sea.

At the first roll of the *Dyra* in the oceanic swell, Sret curled up in the scuppers with a groan.

"What ails him?" said Vakar.

"Seasickness, sir," said Fual. "If you don't suffer a touch also, you'll be lucky."

"Like what happened to Zormé in the poem?

> *With eyeballs aching*   *and hurting head,*
> *Sunk in the scuppers*   *the hero huddled*
> *Loathing life*   *and desiring death?*

"I'm not so badly off as that yet."

Fual turned away with a knowing look. After a few minutes of tossing, Vakar did experience a slight headache and queasiness of stomach, but not wishing to lose face, he stood proudly at the rail as if nothing was wrong. The four sailors hauled in the oars, lowered the steering paddles until they dipped into the water, and hoisted the single square scarlet-and-white striped sail. The west wind sent the *Dyra* plunging toward the Hesperides. Vakar now saw the reason for the high stern, as wave after wave loomed up behind and seemed about to swamp them, only to boost them forward and up and slide harmlessly underneath.

He staggered to the poop, where Ruaz held the lever, which operated the yoke that connected the two steering paddles, and asked: "What happens when you wish to sail back from the mainland to Amferé and the wind is against you? Do you row?"

"You wait and pray to your favorite sea god. In this sea, the wind blows from the west four days out of five, so you must wait for the fifth day. I've sat in port at Sederado a month awaiting a fair wind."

"That sounds tedious. What if some other sea captain is praying for the wind to blow in the opposite direction?"

Ruaz's shoulders and eyebrows went up in a great shrug. Vakar looked past the poop towards Amferé, now fast dropping out of sight behind the bulge of the ocean. He felt a lump rise in his throat and wiped away a tear. Then for a long time he stared at the water: although normally nervous and impatient, quickly bored by inactivity, he found that he could watch the soothing sight of the endless series of crests riding by.

But something nagged him, filling him with a vague feeling of incongruity and unease. In the late afternoon, they skirted a mountainous coast.

"Meropia," said Captain Ruaz.

By nightfall, Sret had recovered enough to eat. Afterwards Vakar, though monstrously sleepy, got little sleep because of the moonlight, the motion, and the ship noises. Next day, they left Meropia behind in the afternoon and sailed eastward over the empty sea. Ruaz explained:

"We don't see other ships because we're the first out of Amferé after the winter layup. We're taking a chance on a late storm, to get higher prices in Gadaira before the competition arrives."

Vakar wondered at his continuing unease, until the sight of Sret chatting with Ruaz gave him a clue. He remembered Sret's saying to Nyeron he'd be back sooner than expected. Why? Did he think that Vakar would lose heart and turn back, or get killed in a brawl? Or . . .

Vakar felt like kicking himself for not having seen it sooner. Kuros, acting in concordance with the Gorgons, could have sent Sret along to murder him and then go home with a story of how his master had been eaten by a monster. Sret had spoken to Nyeron in Hesperian in ignorance of the fact that Vakar knew that tongue. Vakar fingered his hilt and glanced narrowly to where Sret huddled under his cloak, the hood pulled up over his head, swapping jokes with the captain. He thought of walking up to the fellow and striking off his head. Still, he might be wrong in his suspicions, and at best the killing would be embarrassing to explain.

Vakar wondered whether to take Fual into his confidence. He asked:

"Fual, who *is* Sret? I never knew him before this journey."

Fual shrugged. "I think he's part Lotri, but I never knew him either."

If true, that made it unlikely that both Sret and Fual were in on the plot. After the evening meal, Vakar told Fual that they should keep watch-and-watch through the night in case of foul play. Fual looked startled and produced a handsome silver-inlaid dagger.

"Ha!" said Vakar. "Where did you get that? You stole it at Nyeron's! I ought to beat you ... But perhaps 'tis a lucky theft for once. Go to sleep while I take the first watch."

Shortly before midnight, Vakar was aroused by Fual's shaking him. The valet whispered:

"You were right, sir. They're gathered aft, whispering."

Vakar rolled over and peered aft from the bow, where he and Fual lay. Before the lower edge of the sail he could see the whispering knot of men in the light of the just-risen gibbous moon.

He slowly drew his sword and whispered to Fual: "Get your knife ready. Keep close to me and cover my back."

His shield was still in the duffelbag, but for fighting on an unsteady deck, one needed a free hand to grab things.

"You—you're going to attack six men?" quavered Fual.

"Lyr's barnacles! Should I wait for them to cut my throat?"

"But six—"

"Our only hope is to rush them. If it makes you any happier I'm frightened too, but I prefer a small chance to none."

Fual's teeth chattered. Vakar inched caterpillarlike along the deck aft, hoping to get close enough to overhear before the crew noticed him. As he neared the mast, he found that he could make out the separate figures. Sret was talking in low tones to Ruaz, who turned a leaf-shaped broadsword this way and that so that the moon glimmered dully upon it. Sret was saying:

". . . not an experienced fighter, though he's been in brushes with hill robbers. But he's young and no giant; one quick rush while he sleeps . . ."

"Come on," breathed Vakar, rolling to his feet.

IV

Queen Porfia

VAKAR DUCKED UNDER THE LOWER YARD AND RAN TOwards the group. With a shout the sailors leaped apart, drawing knives. Vakar bore down upon the nearest, feinted once, and ran the man through. The man's scream pierced the rising clamor. As Vakar stepped back to pull out his blade he glanced over his shoulder. Fual had hardly finished ducking under the sail.

Damn the coward! thought Vakar, setting his teeth. As his victim fell, he faced Ruaz, Sret, and two sailors, plus one other on the poop steering. Sret and Ruaz were shouting:

"Forward! Kill him! Get in close! Rush him!"

Vakar leaped over the body on deck, slashing right and left. His sword clanged against Ruaz's blade and bit flesh and bone, and then he was through them. As he whirled to face them again, his back to the poop, he saw that they were all still on their feet. As Fual finally came closer, a sailor turned and closed with him rather than face the sword. Now the twain were staggering about in a deadly waltz, each gripping the other's wrist.

The three facing Vakar closed, Ruaz in the middle. Vakar cut and thrust at the captain, who parried while Sret and the other sailor closed in from the sides. Vakar, wishing he had a light rapier against these agile unarmored foes, had to leap back until he backed into the high step up to the poop and almost fell.

They came on. Vakar slashed wildly, only his superior length of blade keeping them from finishing him. He could not quite reach them, for if he moved far enough towards any one the others would get him in the back. They moved on the swaying deck with catlike ease, while he reeled and staggered. One got close enough to send a stab home, but the point failed to pierce Vakar's leather jack.

A shout came from behind: the steersman encouraging his mates. Vakar wondered what a ship would do without a man at the helm. He leaped back up on to the poop, turning as he did so, and swung a mighty blow at the sailor. The sharp bronze sheared through the man's neck. The head thumped to the deck, rolled off the poop, and continued its bloody course forward towards the mast while the spouting body collapsed beneath the steering-yoke.

Vakar turned to face his three antagonists on the main deck, but as they confronted each other, the *Dyra* slewed to starboard and heeled far to port, so that water poured over the port rail.

Vakar found himself sliding down the steep deck towards the black water. He threw up his free hand and snatched at the night air for support—and to his infinite relief caught a mast stay. As the ship continued to heel, Vakar found his feet dangling over the water while he gripped the stay in a death-grasp.

He glanced forward in time to see a figure that he took for Sret go over the side into the smother of foam while the others, sprawling or sitting on the deck, snatched at the ropes and each other for purchase.

As the wind spilled out of the sail, the *Dyra* began to right herself. When his feet were firmly on the slanting deck again, Vakar let go his stay to creep forward on knees and knuckles. Captain Ruaz was also on all fours, groping for his sword. Vakar rose as he neared the captain and brought his sword down on his head. Down went Ruaz.

One sailor clung to the rail, which was just emerging from the water. Vakar struck at the gripping hand, missed, and struck again. This time the edge hit home and the seaman disappeared.

Up forward Fual lay upon the deck, holding the mast with his arms while his antagonist, the remaining sailor, clutched Fual's legs to keep from going over the side with the roll of the ship. Only a few heartbeats had elapsed since the ship had started to right herself and roll in the opposite direction. Vakar ran forward and, as the sailor rose crying a word that might have meant "mercy," he struck. The man threw up an arm, yelped as the blade bit into the bone, and an instant later collapsed with a split skull.

Fual started to rise, then clutched the mast as the ship rolled in the other direction. Vakar, staggering over to the starboard rail, cried:

"How do you straighten this damned thing out?"

"The steering lever," said Fual. "You—you keep the ship's—that is—"

Without waiting for more explicit directions, Vakar, the next time the ship righted herself, bounded aft and seized the lever arm. He hung on until the wind caught the sail and the *Dyra* began to pick up way on her former course. When she was straightened out and running free again, Vakar examined the steering mechanism. He experimented so that the ship yawed wildly until he got the hang of steering. Fual said:

"My lord, I've never seen anything like the way you slew those four men! Just one—two—three—four, like that!"

"Luck," growled Vakar. "Must we always sail exactly with the wind?"

"No, I think one can sail at a small angle to it, or sailors would never reach home."

"I wish I knew whither we were headed. What land did Ruaz expect to sight next?"

"I don't know, sir. I believe Eruthea and Ogugia and Elusion lie somewhere ahead of us."

"In what order?"

"That I don't know."

"I once met the present Queen of Ogugia; a gangling child, but she'd be a grown woman now."

"Has Ogugia a king, sir?"

"Had; Porfia married a Lord Vancho, who was said to have been an amiable nonentity. He died of some pox, and as the Hesperian throne descends in the female line she'd still be queen."

"What sort of place is it?"

"Ogugia? I know little, save that it's called the Isle of Philosophers. I've always wished to ask those sages some simple questions, say about the origin of life and the immortality of soul and so on. Oh, Fual! Since you're no more mariner than I, throw these bodies overboard."

"Including this one without his head, sir?" said Fual with such a pronounced grimace of distaste that Vakar could see it in the moonlight.

"Especially that one. They clutter the deck."

Fual went to work, first stripping each corpse. When he had finished, he came back to the poop with Ruaz's broadsword, which he had found in the scuppers, saying:

"May I carry this, sir? If we're to meet such perils, we can't be too well armed."

"Surely, surely." Vakar turned the helm over to Fual while he straightened the kinks out of his own sword and smoothed down the nicks in the blade with his pocket hone.

Towards morning, Vakar sighted another land ahead and said: "Let's follow this coast around to the right until we come to a port."

"What will you do with the ship, sir?"

"I hadn't thought." Vakar looked around. "If somebody sees the blood they'll make trouble. Clean it up, will you?"

"And then what?" said Fual, hunting for rags.

"How does one sell a ship?"

"One finds a merchant who wishes to buy. Unless somebody recognizes it as belonging to Mateng of Po."

"How could we disguise it? When you finish with the blood, see if you can remove that image of Lyr at the stern."

Thus about noon, a somewhat altered *Dyra* came in sight of a harbor full of tubby merchantmen and rakish fifty-oared war galleys, with a fair city lying behind it. Vakar said:

"How do we steer this ship into the harbor without the wind at our backs?"

"I think one lowers the sail and rows in."

"And how—oh, I see! One unties that rope that runs from the upper whatever-you-call-it, that long stick, and lowers it until it rests upon the bottom one."

He meant the upper and lower yards, for the ship had yards at both the top and bottom edges of the sail. A tackle of ropes confined the sail and kept it from spilling over the deck when lowered. Vakar steered the ship as far into the port as it would go. Then Fual unhitched the halyard; but, as the upper yard and the sail were heavier than he, they sank down into their tackle, hoisting the little Aremorian into the air. The spectacle so doubled Vakar up with mirth that, despite Fual's yells, it was some time before he came forward to pull his servant back down to the deck.

They got out the sweeps and pushed the ship shoreward. It was a long row for only two oars, and Vakar, though his hands were hard from weapon practice, had begun to develop blisters before they reached the shore. Along the waterfront, men were unloading ships and hauling their cargoes away in ox-drawn sledges and truckle carts. As the *Dyra* neared the quay, a small knot of loafers gathered to gaup: dark men smaller than those of Poseidonis. Vakar said:

"Get ready to leap ashore with the stern rope."

As they drifted against the quay, Vakar sprang ashore with the painter and belayed the rope to one of the row of posts, while Fual did likewise astern. Vakar caught the eye of the nearest loafer and called in Hesperian:

"What place is this?"

"Sederado, the capital of Ogugia."

Vakar said to Fual: "Let's hope Queen Porfia remembers me . . . I know! As we can't drag this whole cargo with us, I might jog her memory with a portion of it and dispose her to help us on the next leg of our journey. Ho, you people! I wish four strong porters to carry a load to the palace. Fual, pick the four and make an arrangement with them for their wage. You with the nose! Is copper mined in Ogugia?"

"Yes," said the man addressed.

"Do you have mammoths or bison?"

"No mammoths, though there are a few bison in the royal park."

Vakar turned back to Fual. "Ivory is the thing she'll best appreciate. Help me get these hatch-covers off."

In a few minutes, Vakar had his porters lined up, each with a great curling mammoth tusk over one shoulder. He was about to order them to march when he noticed that the people on the quay were staring seaward.

Vakar saw another ship drawing up to the adjacent wharfage space: a low, black thirty-oared galley, much larger than the *Dyra*, with a crew of a dozen besides the rowers and three passengers. The ship had a beak of bronze jutting out at the waterline forward, and a pair of eyes painted on the bow so that, sailors believed, she could see her way. No device or insigne, like the mermaid of Ogugia or the octopus of Gorgonia, variegated her plain brown sail, nor did any pennant or banderole betray her origin.

One of the passengers was a man of medium height, with a small round cap perched on his shaven poll, a small, pointed gray beard, and a loose robe to his ankles. The other two, who wore no clothes, were not really human. One was a pigmy about four feet high, with huge membranous ears like those of an elephant in miniature, and covered all over with short, golden-brown fur. The other was eight feet tall, with a low-browed apish countenance and coarse black hair all over. He carried a great brass-bound club over one stooping shoulder, while his other arm embraced a large wooden chest with bronze clamps.

"By all the gods, what are those?" said Vakar. "Some kind of satyrs? The large one looks like the giant in the *Lay of Zormé:*

> *Grimly glowering   and fearsomely fanged*
> *The monster menaced   the vulnerable virgin . . .*

"Eh?"

Fual said: "The larger I don't know, but the smaller is a Coranian."

"A what?"

"A native of the northern isle of Corania. It's said they can hear any word uttered for miles around."

The second ship tied up as their own had done, and its people climbed ashore and set out in various directions. Vakar said:

"We can't wait around all day; I'm for the palace. You stay here to dispose of the stuff . . ."

Just then, the shaven-headed man pushed through the spectators towards Vakar. After him came the giant apeman and the Coranian.

"You are for the palace, sir?" said the man in strongly accented Hesperian. "Perhaps you will permit me to go with you, for my errand takes me thither also and I am not familiar with Sederado. And while I have never met you, something tells me I ought to know you. My name is Qasigan."

"And whom have I the honor of addressing?" said Qasigan, smiling pleasantly as he fell into step beside Vakar. His leathery skin was even darker than Vakar's, and his broad head bore a round, blunt-featured face. He stooped slightly and shuffled rather than walked.

"My name is Vakar."

Vakar happened to be looking at the man's face as he spoke, and observed the pleasant smile vanish and flicker back again.

"Not Prince Vakar of Lorsk!" said the man.

Vakar tended to take a dour and suspicious view of untried strangers—especially queer-looking ones who traveled about in their own war galleys with inhuman assistants and showed an egregious interest in his identity. He shook his head.

"Merely a relative. And what, sir, do you know of Lorsk?"

"Who does not know the world's greatest source of copper?"

"Indeed. Where do you come from?"

"Tegrazen, a small city on the mainland south of Kernê."

"You have unusual servitors. The first, I understand, is a Coranian?"

"That is correct. His name is Yok."

"And the other?" said Vakar.

"That is Nji, from Blackland. The Blacks caught him young, tamed him, and sold him. He can speak a few words, for he is not the great ape of Blackland—the gorilla—but another and rarer kind, intermediate between apes and men."

Vakar fell into a wary silence until they arrived at the palace. He gauped like a yokel at the rows of gleaming marble columns and the gilded roof, for this was the first two-storey building that he had ever seen.

He sent in the four tusks, with word that Vakar of Lorsk would like an audience. After a half-hour's wait, he was ushered in, leaving Qasigan staring pensively after him.

"Prince Vakar!" cried Queen Porfia, stepping down from her audience throne and advancing upon him. She kissed him vigorously. "I thank you for your splendid gift, but you need not shower me with wealth to assure your welcome! Did you think I had forgotten when we won the dance contest in Amferé ten years ago? What brings you so far from the bison-swarming plains of windy Lorsk?"

Porfia, Vakar thought, had certainly developed into a splendid-looking woman. Though she was not large, her proud carriage gave her a deceptive look of tallness. Lucky Vancho! He said:

"I am on my way to mighty Torrutseish, madam, and could not pass by Ogugia without renewing so pleasant an acquaintance."

She looked at him keenly from emerald-green eyes. "Now how, I wonder, does it happen that you and one servant put into the harbor of Sederado navigating a small merchant ship all by yourselves in most thwart tyronic fashion? Are you running away from Lorsk to become a corsair? Perhaps to sail under the octopus banner of the accursed Gorgons?"

"You seem to have learned a lot in a short time."

"Oh, I watch my kingdom's commerce, and was getting a report on you while you waited. Well, what happened? Was all the ship's company but you washed overboard, or snatched by a kraken?"

Vakar hesitated, then gave in to his instant liking for Porfia and told the story of Sret's treachery.

"So," he concluded, "being as you have said no barnacled mariners, we propose to sell this ship and continue eastward on the next merchantman that passes that way."

"How much cargo have you?"

"By Tandyla's third eye, I do not know!"

"Well then. Elbien!" A man came in and Porfia told him: "Go to the waterfront, board Prince Vakar's ship, and reckon up the value of the cargo." As the man bowed and left she turned back to Vakar. "I will give you your ship's fair value in trade metal. If Mateng squeals, we will remind him that as owner he is responsible for the murderous attack upon you. And what do you know of that odd fish who came in with you? The one who arrived in his private galley?"

"He claims to be Qasigan of Tegrazen, but beyond that I know no more than you, Queen. He is certainly as peculiar as a flying pig, though courteous enough."

"So? The description of him sounds like one of the Gorgonian race, though that proves nothing because Tegrazen lies near the Gorgades on the mainland, and the people of those parts are much mixed. But tell me how things go in Lorsk: the land of warriors, heroes, and athletes, with hearts of bronze and heads of ivory?"

Vakar laughed and plunged into small talk. A man of few friends, he felt that at last he had found someone who spoke his language. They were chattering away some time later when Porfia said:

"By Heroé's eight teats, I have spent the whole morning on you, sir, and others await me. You shall stay at the palace, and we will have a feast tonight. You shall meet my minister Garal and my lover Thiegos."

"Your—" Vakar checked himself, wondering why he felt a sudden pang of annoyance. It was none of his affair if the Queen of Ogugia kept a dozen lovers; but the feeling persisted.

She appeared not to notice. "And I think I will have this Master Qasigan too if I like him. He seems like a man of position, and we should at least get some rare tales of far lands."

"Queen," said Vakar, "I told Qasigan my name but denied being the scion of Lorsk, and should therefore prefer to be known simply as Master Vakar, a simple gentleman, while that fellow in the long shirt is about."

"It shall be done. Dweros! Take Pr— Master Vakar to the second guest chamber in the right wing and provide for his comfort."

Vakar saw no more of Porfia until evening but spent a lazy day sleeping, being washed and perfumed, and reading a Hesperian translation of the Fragments of Lontang in the library while his dirty clothes were being washed and dried. As the writing of the time was largely pictographic, the written languages of Ogugia and Lorsk differed much less than their spoken tongues. However, the symbols for abstract ideas differed widely. Vakar asked a dignified-looking oldster copying a roll of papyrus in the corner:

"Can you tell me what this means, my man? This skull-and-crescent thing?"

"That, sir, signifies 'mortality.' It combines the skull, which symbolizes death, with the inverted crescent, which represents the abstract aspect of the moon, to wit: time. Therefore the meaning of the passage is:

Though germinate generations	*of mortal man*
In thousands of thousands	*while in dwellings divine*
A god grows his eye-teeth,	*yet time taketh all:*
Even the gods so glorious	*must march at the last*
Down the dim dusty road	*to death the destroyer.*

"Is Lontang trying to tell us that even the gods must die?"

"Yes. His theory was that the gods are created by the belief of men in them, and that puissant though they be, in time men will forsake them for others and forget them, and they will fade away and vanish."

Vakar said: "You seem a knowledgeable man in such matters. May I ask your name?"

"I am Rethilio, a poor philosopher of Sederado. And you . . . ?"

"I am Vakar of Lorsk."

"Curious," mused the man. "I have heard your name . . . I know! Last night I dreamt I witnessed an assembly of the gods. I recognized many of ours, such as Asterio, and some of those of other nations like your Okma. They seemed to be rushing about in agitated fashion, as if dancing a funeral dance, and I heard them ejaculate 'Vakar Lorska'!"

Vakar shuddered. "As I never dream of the gods, I can shed no light on this matter."

"Are you remaining here long, Prince?"

"Only a few days. But I should like to return to Ogugia some day to study its famed philosophies."

Too late, Vakar realized that he should have at once denied his principate; by failing to do so he had confirmed Rethilio's guess as to his true identity. Rethilio said:

"Many of my colleagues believe that if only kings would study philosophy, or the people would choose philosophers as their kings, the world would be a less sorry place. In practice, however, kings seem to lack either time or inclination."

"Perhaps I can combine the two."

"A laudable ambition, though broad. The gods grant that you achieve it."

"I see no difficulty. I have many ambitions and, I trust, many years to fulfill them."

"What are these ambitions, sir?" said Rethilio.

"Well . . ." Vakar frowned. "To be a good king when my time comes; to master philosophy; to see far places and strange peoples; to know loyal and interesting friends; to enjoy the pleasures of wine, women, and song . . ."

He stopped as Rethilio threw up his hands in mock horror. "You should have been twins, Prince!"

"I am—or rather my brother Kuros is my twin. What do you mean, though?"

"No man can compress all that into one lifetime.

Now it seems life is endless and you can sample all experience while attaining preëminence in any careers that suit your fancy. As time passes, you will discover you must make a choice here and a choice there, each choice cutting you off from some of these many enticing possibilities. Of course there is the hypothesis of the school of Kurno, that the soul not only survives the body but is subsequently reincarnated in another, and thus a man undergoes many existences."

"I do not see how that helps if one cannot remember one's previous lives," said Vakar. "And if that be so, how about the gods? Are their souls likewise reincarnated?"

They were at it hammer and tongs when Dweros appeared to tell Vakar that his clothes were ready.

"I hope I shall see you again before I leave," he told Rethilio.

"If you are here tomorrow at this time, we may meet. Good-day, sir."

V

The Serpent Throne

THE BANQUET HALL WAS SMALLER THAN THAT OF THE castle at Mneset, but of more refined workmanship, with plastered walls on which were painted scenes from the myths of Ogugia. Vakar was particularly taken by the picture of the seduction of an eight-breasted woman by a bull-headed man of egregious masculinity.

He met the plump minister Garal and his wife, the latter a pleasant but nondescript woman of middle age; and Thiegos, a tall, clean-shaven young man wearing splendid pearl earrings, who looked down a long nose and said:

"So you are from Lorsk? I wonder how you endure the winds and fogs. I could never put up with them!"

Though not pleased by this comment, Vakar was amused when, a few minutes later, Qasigan came in and Thiegos said to him: "So you are from the South? I wonder how you endure the heat and the flies. I could never abide them!"

Another youth came in, whom Thiegos introduced as his friend Abeggu of Tokalet, who had come from far Gamphasantia to Sederado to study philosophy under Rethilio. The newcomer was a tall, slender fellow, very dark and quiet. When he spoke, it was with an almost unintelligible accent. Vakar asked the conventional question:

"How do you find these northerly lands?"

"Very interesting, sir, and very different from my home. We have no such towering stone buildings or lavish use of metal."

"Still, I envy you," said Vakar. "I have met Rethilio and wish I had time to study under the philosophers of Ogugia. What have you learned?"

"He is discoursing on the origin of the world-egg from the coiture of eternal time and infinite space . . ."

Vakar would have liked to hear more, for philosophy had always fascinated him, though it was little cultivated among the palaestral nations of Poseidonis. But Queen Porfia sat down and signalled to the servitors to pass a dry wine for an aperitif. She poured a libation from her golden beaker on to the floor and said a grace to the gods, then drank.

Vakar was doing likewise when a startled exclamation from Garal's wife drew his attention across the ivory tables. Where Qasigan's golden plate had lain, there now stood a plate-sized tortoise, peering about dimly with beady eyes. Qasigan laughed at the success of his feat of thaumaturgy.

"It is quite harmless," he said. "A mere illusion: It bites nobody and is housebroken. Are you not, tortoise?"

The tortoise nodded, and those around the tables clapped their hands. Vakar drank deeply and looked again. Where the tortoise had been, he saw only the snub-nosed magician making passes over his plate, though from their comments he inferred that his fellow-diners still saw the reptile. He was about to boast of his ability (which he had long been aware of) to see through magical illusions when stimulated by drink, but forebore. He still harbored suspicions of Qasigan and thought it imprudent to give the fellow any advantage.

He looked to where Porfia sat in her chair of pretence. This was a most unusual throne, carved from some olive-colored stone in the form of a huge serpent. The head and neck of the snake formed one arm rest, and a loop of its body the other. The rest of it was wound back and forth to form the back and seat down to the ground.

"It is unusual," said Porfia, whose pale flesh showed through the sheer sea-green robe she wore. "It was brought from Lake Tritonis, where such serpents are sacred, in the time of my grandfather. They say it was carried across the Desert of Gwedulia slung between two curious beasts used in those parts, taller than horses and having great humps upon their backs. The legend is that it is a real serpent paralyzed by enchantment, and—"

"Of course," broke in Thiegos, "we as a civilized people do not believe such silly tales." He dug at the carving with a thumbnail. "See for yourself, Master Vakar. This artistic monstrosity is nothing but stone."

Vakar touched the arm of the chair, which certainly felt like good solid chert.

Thiegos continued: "Still, my dear, you would do well to drop it into Sederado harbor and get another, not for superstitious but for esthetic reasons. What is to eat tonight?"

Ogugian custom called for a circle of chairs, with a small table in front of each. Servitors placed the food on golden plates in front of each of the small tables. Vakar thought the stuffed grouse excellent, but found the bread peculiar. He asked:

"What sort of bread is this, pray?"

Thiegos said: "You Pusadians would not know. It is made from a new kind of grain called wheat, which was brought from the mainland in the queen's father's time." He turned to Porfia, saying: "Really, madam, you must sell your cook before we all turn into swine from eating garbage!"

The wine was strong stuff, even better than that of Zhysk. Vakar drank deep and said:

"I beg to differ, sir. I find Ogugia's food the most delicious, its wine the headiest, and its queen the most beautiful—"

"You speak a fine speech, but you do not deceive anyone," said Thiegos, who had also been drinking hard. "You seek by flattery to wheedle favors from Porfia. Now, so long as these comprise such matters as trade metal or ships or slaves, I do not care. Should you, however, seek those of a more intimate kind, you must deal with me, for I—"

"Thiegos!" cried Porfia. "You have already become a pig, if manners are any indication."

"At least," said Thiegos, "I know how to eat and drink in civilized fashion, instead of tearing my meat like a famished lion and swilling my wine in great gulps." He looked down his nose at Vakar, who colored, realizing that by Ogugian standards his provincial table manners left much to be desired. "So I am merely warning this mustachioed barbarian—"

"Shut up!" cried Porfia, half rising out of the serpent throne, green eyes blazing and oval face flushed.

Vakar said in a tone of deadly calm: "He merely wishes to set himself up as palace pimp, do you not, Siegos?" He gave the fancyman's name the Lorskan mispronunciation on purpose to vex him.

"Boar-begotten bastard!" shouted Thiegos. "I will cut off your—"

"Down, both of you!" cried Garal with unexpected force. "Or I will have in the guards to whip you through the streets with leaded scorpions. Slaves, clear away these remnants!"

The servitors took away the plates and brought more wine. Abeggu of Tokalet looked shocked and bewildered; evidently he was unused to royalty with its hair down. Vakar, realizing that he was getting drunk, pulled himself together and said:

"Can one of you explain this?"

He pointed to the seduction-scene on the wall. Garal explained:

"Why, that illustrates the third book of *The Golden Age,* and represents the forest-god Asterio about to engender the first human pair on the earth-goddess Heroé. In the original it goes:

> *Painting with passion   the slavering satyr*
> *Supine on the sward   hurled helpless Heroé . . ."*

Thiegos interrupted: "You cannot do it justice without singing it," and he burst into a fine clear tenor:

> *The rose-colored robe   by the dawn-goddess*
> *dighted*
> *He savagely seized   and tore from her trunk . . .*

"Curse it, even I cannot perform properly without accompaniment. Shall we get in the flute girl?"

"I do not think that will be necessary," said Qasigan. "I have here a small instrument wherewith I while away empty hours."

He produced a tootle pipe out of his bosom and played an experimental run. "Now, sir, how does this tune of yours go? Ah, yes, I can manage. Sing!"

With the pipe ululating, Thiegos stood up and roared out the rest of the story of the Creation. When he finished, Vakar said:

"Sir, you may be a pimp and several other things I will not shock our hostess by mentioning, but you have the finest voice I have ever heard. I wish I could do as well."

"That is nothing," said Thiegos, staggering back to his seat. "The song does have a certain crude barbaric vigor, but now we are more refined. For instance, I at least do not take all this mythology serious—*uk!*"

An attack of hiccups ended the speech. Porfia called upon Vakar:

"Now, sir, contribute your part! What can you do?"

"I can tell you what I cannot do," said Vakar, counting on his fingers. "Once I thought I could sing, but now I have heard Thiegos I know I can only caw like a carrion-crow. I can dance when sober as the queen remembers, but just now I am not sober. I know a few stories, but not the sort a gentleman would repeat in such company—"

"Forget you are a gentleman, old man, old man," giggled Garal. "I have heard livelier tales from the lips of the queen herself than any you are likely to know."

"Very well; do any of you know the tale of the hunchback and the fisherman's wife? No? It seems that . . ."

They all laughed heartily; in fact, Garal's wife got into a fit of hysterics and had to be pounded on the back. Vakar told a couple more, and then Queen Porfia said:

"You claim you once thought you could sing; let us hear this crow's voice!"

"But really, Queen—"

"No, I insist. Master Qasigan shall accompany you."

"Then do not say I failed to warn you. Qasigan, it goes da de-de da de-de . . ."

When the tune had been straightened out, Vakar gave them the *Song of Vrir:*

> *Vrir the Victorious   rode to the river*
> *His scabbard of silver   shining in sunlight . . .*

When he had finished, Porfia clapped, crying: "Magnificent! While I do not understand Lorskan, you sing even better than Thiegos."

"I have heard no singing," growled Thiegos, who had got over his hiccups, "only the croaking of bull-frogs."

"What do you think?" said Porfia to Garal. "Vakar is the better, is he not?"

"They are both very good," said the minister with the adroitness of the practiced politician, and turned to Qasigan. "Pray, play us one of the tunes of your native country."

Qasigan played a wailing tune. Thiegos said: "By Asterio's arse, that sounds like the tune of our dance to the moon goddess!"

"How would you know, since men are strictly forbidden near when the maidens dance it?" said Porfia.

"You would be surprised. Here, Porfia, you are the best dancer in Ogugia; dance it for us! Qasigan can play."

"It would be blasphemous . . ." said the queen, but the others shouted her down.

At last she stood up and, with Qasigan playing, began a slinking dance. Being unsteady from the wines she repeatedly stepped on the hem of her thin trailing robe until she burst out:

"Curse this thing! How can I . . ."

She unfastened the robe, slipped out of it, and threw it across the serpent throne.

"Move those damned tables out of the way," she said, and continued her dance naked save for her jewelled sandals.

Vakar found the room swimming in a delightful fog. It seemed that the flames of the wall lamps swayed in time to the weird music, and that the frescoes came alive so that the bull-headed god appeared to get on with his protogenic project.

Vakar felt an urge to leap up and seize the swaying white figure of Porfia in imitation of Asterio, for though small, she had a form that practically demanded rape of any passing male. But at that moment the queen tripped and fell across Garal's knees. The minister raised a hand as if to spank the royal rump but reconsidered in time. The sight sent Vakar into such a convulsion of laughter that he could hardly keep his seat.

"That is enough of that!" said Porfia, reeling back to her throne, where she struggled to don the robe and got wonderfully tangled in its folds until Thiegos came over to help. "Who knows something else?"

"We have a game in Tegrazen," said Qasigan, "called 'Going to Kernê.' A number of stools are set in a circle, the number being one less than that of the persons present. Music is played and the persons march around the chairs. The music is stopped suddenly and all try to sit down, but one fails and is counted out. Then one chair is removed and the march repeated until there are but two players and one chair left, and whichever of these gains the chair wins. Now, suppose I play while the rest of you march, for I am a little old for such athletics."

"A childish sort of game," said Thiegos. "I fear we shall be bored—"

"Oh, you sneer at everything!" cried Porfia. "Vakar, Garal, move that chair back to the wall. Master Qasigan, sit here in the center and tootle. Great gods, look at him!" she pointed to Abeggu of Tokalet, who had quietly curled up in a corner and passed out. "Wake him up, somebody."

Vakar said: "How any man with blood in his veins could sleep through the spectacle we have just witnessed . . ."

"It means nothing to him," said Thiegos. "They go naked all the time in Gamphasantia, he tells me. Ho, Lazybones, wake up!"

He kicked the sleeping man. When Abeggu had been aroused and briefed on the game, they began marching unsteadily around the circle. When the music stopped, all plumped on to the seats except Garal's wife, who being fat was slow on her feet. She laughed and went over to the wall to sit while Vakar lugged another stool out of the circle.

"Begin again!" said Qasigan.

His music became more and more exotic. The whole room seemed to Vakar to writhe in time with the tune. He wondered what was wrong, for he had been prudently holding down his consumption of wine since his quarrel with Thiegos.

The music stopped and Thiegos this time was left standing.

"Oh, well," said the queen's lover, "I do not find these antics very amusing anyway," and went over to sit by Garal's wife. Out went another chair.

At the next halt, Abeggu of Tokalet was out.

This time the music seemed to go right through Prince Vakar, to make his teeth and eyeballs ache. The lamps darkened; at least he could not see clearly. The music shook him as a dog shakes a rat . . .

Then it stopped. Vakar took a quick look and

lurched towards a dark shape that he fuzzily identified as Queen Porfia's imported serpent chair, which as a seat of office was the only one in the room with arms and a back.

He half-spun and fell into its stone embrace just ahead of Porfia herself, who landed lushly in his lap with a playful squeal that changed to a shriek of terror.

Vakar echoed the scream with an animal noise, half grunt and half shout, as he realized in one horror-struck flash that he was sitting on the coils of a giant live snake. There was an explosive hiss as the head and neck reared up and back to stare down at the two human beings, its forked tongue flicking. At the same instant a loop, thicker than Vakar's thigh, whipped around both of them, preventing them from rising.

Vakar vaguely heard screams and the sound of running feet as the coil tightened. His ribs creaked; it was like being squeezed to death by a live tree-trunk. He had no sword and his left arm was pinned between Porfia and the snake; his right was still free.

Vakar frantically ripped open his shirt and pulled out the envenomed dagger that had slain Söl. With all his strength he drove it into the scaly hide, again and again . . .

The snake hissed louder, but the pressure of the coil relaxed an instant. With a tremendous effort Vakar freed his other arm. The snake's entire body was writhing convulsively around him. He got a foot against the coil in front and pushed. The coil gave, and he and Porfia were out of the monster's embrace. Vakar half-dragged the queen across the room out of harm's way, then looked back at the expiring snake.

They were alone in the room.

Vakar put away his dagger and held the queen in his arms until she stopped trembling. She put her face up for him to kiss, but when he would have gone on with a full course of lovemaking, she pushed him away.

"Not now," she said. "Is the monster dead?"

Vakar stepped forward to see, then jumped back as the scaly body twitched. "It still moves! What does that mean? We do not have these creatures in Poseidonis."

"They die as a frog swallows a worm, by inches, but

I do not think this one will harm us any more. Evidently the legend at which Thiegos sneered is no empty fable. And speaking of Thiegos, what a fine pack of poltroons I am served by! Not one stayed to help, save you."

"Do not give me too much credit, madam. I was caught in the same scaly embrace as yourself, and could not have fled were I never so timorous. But why should our cold-blooded friend here come to life just as we sat upon him? Do you suppose our extra weight was more than he could bear, and he showed his displeasure by awakening from his sleep of centuries?"

"No, for I have often cossetted in that same chair with that craven Thiegos. There is malevolent magic in this, Vakar, and we must solve the riddle before the clues are scattered by the winds of time. But where *is* everybody? Elbien! Dweros!"

No answer. She led Vakar about the palace, which proved entirely empty, except for a trembling knot of guards in the front courtyard who pointed their spears at Porfia and Vakar as they approached.

"What is that?" she said. "Do you not know your own queen?"

A man in a cuirass of gilded scales stepped out and said: "You are no ghost, madam?"

"Of course not, Gwantho!"

"May I touch you to make sure?"

"Of all the impertinent nonsense ... Very well, here!"

She held out a hand with a regal gesture. The officer took it and kissed it, then said to the men:

"She is real, boys. Your pardon, Queen, but the clamor of those that fled the palace so perturbed my men that but for me they would have bolted likewise."

"It would have gone hard with them if they had. Next time you hear I am in danger you might try to help instead of thinking of nought but your own hides. Now back to your posts!"

As the guards slunk off, Porfia said to Vakar: "That was Gwantho, the legate of the commandant of the city garrison. Are there no brave men outside the epics and legends? The runagates must have spread terror through the palace as they fled. What do you make of it?"

"I suspect our queer friend Qasigan," said Vakar judiciously. "On the other hand, he is a stranger, as is Abeggu of Tokalet, while Garal and Thiegos, being among your familiars, might harbor some hidden rankling resentment."

"I doubt that last. Neither is of royal blood and therefore neither could cherish regal ambitions."

Vakar smiled. "That is no sure barrier. How do you suppose most dynasties were founded in the first place?"

"Well, neither have I quarreled with either lately— unless you count my refusal to follow Garal's counsel to wed Shvo Zhyska."

"He so advised you? Hang the hyena! I know Shvo well, being his cousin. He is as grasping as a Kernean and as perfidious as an Aremorian."

"I am not likely to follow Garal in this matter. But we are not even sure the serpent came to life by human agency, instead of in the course of the natural termination of the enchantment that bound it ... Fetch your sword and cloak while I likewise dress for the street."

"Where are we going?"

"In such perplexities, I consult a wise woman nearby. Hasten, and meet me here."

Vakar went. When he returned with the hood of his cloak pulled up over his helmet, he found a very different Porfia, with peasant's cowhide boots showing under her short street dress, a hood pulled over her head likewise, and a scarf masking her face below the eyes.

Porfia led Vakar out the front entrance, where he took a torch from a bracket. She guided him into the stinking tangle of alleys west of the plaza in front of the palace, where not even the starlight penetrated.

Porfia made a sharp turn and stopped to rap with a peculiar knock on a door. They waited, and the door opened with a creak of the door post in its well-worn sockets.

They were ushered in by a small bent black figure, whose only visible feature was a great beak of a nose sticking out from under her cowl. Inside, a single rush-candle lent its wan illumination to a small cluttered room with a musty smell. A piece of papyrus, on which were drawn figures and glyphs, lay on a three-legged table with one leg crudely mended.

The witch mumbled something and rolled up the papyrus. Porfia said:

"Master Vakar, this is my old friend Charsela. I need not tell her who you are, for she will have already discovered that by her occult arts."

The witch raised her head so that Vakar could see the gleam of great dark eyes on either side of the beak.

"Now do you know," quavered the crone, "I cannot tell you one thing about this young man? It is as if a wall against all occult influence had been built around him at birth. I can see that he is a Pusadian, probably of high rank, and that he is by nature a quiet scholarly fellow forced by his surroundings to assume the airs of a rough predacious adventurer. That much, however, any wise person could have inferred by looking at him with the eye of understanding. But come, child, tell me what troubles you this time. Another philtre to keep that sneering scapegrace true?"

"No, no," said Porfia hastily, and went on to recount the strange tale of the serpent throne.

"Ha," said Charsela and got out a small copper bowl, which she filled with water and placed on the table.

She lit a second rushlight, placed it in a small metal holder, and stood the holder on the table. She rummaged in the litter until she found a small phial, from which she dropped one drop of liquid into the water. Vakar, looking at the bowl, had an impression of swirling iridescence as the drop spread over the surface. Charsela put away the phial and sat down on the side of the table opposite the flame, so that she could see the reflection of the flame on the water.

Charsela sat so long that Vakar, standing with his back to the door, shifted his position slightly, causing his sword to clink. Porfia frowned at him. Somewhere under the junk, a mouse rustled; at least Vakar hoped that it was a mouse. He shifted his gaze from the motionless wise woman to a large spider spinning a web on the ceiling. At last the witch's thin voice came:

"It is strange—I can see figures, but all is dim and confused. There is some mighty magic involved in this, mark my word. I will try some more . . ."

She put another drop from the phial into the bowl and fell silent again. Vakar was watching her sunken face in the rushlight when the door burst open behind him with a crash.

Vakar saw the witch and Porfia jerk their heads up to stare past him and started to turn his own head, when a terrific blow clanged down upon his helm and sent him sprawling forward.

He fell against the table, which overturned with a clatter as the bowl and the rushlight struck the floor. Charsela and Porfia both shrieked.

Finding himself on hands and knees with his head spinning, Vakar by a desperate effort sprang to his feet, whirled, and drew his sword all at once. He got the blade out just in time to parry another overhand cut at his head. By the light of the remaining candle he saw that three men had burst into the room, all masked.

VI

The Black Galley

VAKAR THRUST AT THE NEAREST, THE ONE WHOSE CUT he had just parried. As the man stepped back, his foot slipped on the wet floor, where the water from the upset bowl had run around the table and made the worn planking slippery. Before he could recover, Vakar drove his blade past the fellow's awkward attempt at a parry, deep into the folds of the man's clothing. He felt his point pierce meat.

"Get her out, Charsela!" yelled Vakar, not daring to turn his head.

The man whom he had stabbed fell back with a gasp, clutching his side with his free hand. Behind him, Vakar became dimly aware of a yammering from the witch and an expostulation from Porfia, and the sound of a back door opening and banging shut again. Meantime he was engaged with the other two, who were stumbling around among the junk and trying to get at him from two sides. Blades clanged as the two bravoes drove Vakar, fighting a desperate defensive, back into a corner. With a shield and the advantage of left-handedness, he might have handled them, but he had no shield and did not dare stoop for the witch's stool.

Instead he reached into his shirt and pulled out the poisoned dagger that had already saved his life once that night. The poison, he thought, must have pretty well worn off by now, but at least it might furnish a diversion. He threw it at the shorter of the two men.

The man tried to dodge. The knife struck him anyway, but butt-first, so that it clanged harmlessly to the floor. The man's attention had however been distracted, and even the other man let his eyes flicker from Vakar to the flying dagger.

Instantly Vakar threw himself forward, and his ferocious *passado* went through the throat of the tall assassin. At that instant he felt a heavy blow and the sting of a cut on his right arm. The shorter man, recovering from his attempt to duck the knife, had thrown a backhand slash at the Lorskan.

As Vakar, withdrawing his point from the tall man, half-turned to face his remaining assailant, that one skipped back out of reach before Vakar could get set for a blow. The tall man dropped his sword, clutched at his throat, gave a gurgling cough, and began to sink to the floor. The man whom Vakar had first wounded was hobbling towards the door, but now the unhurt man turned, knocked the wounded one aside, and dashed out.

Vakar leaped over the body on the floor and made for the wounded man, meaning to finish him with a quick thrust. The wounded man had been knocked down by the one who fled and was now just getting up, crying: "Quarter!"

The man's mask had come off in the fracas, and just before he sent the blade home Vakar jerked to a halt at the sight of a familiar face. A closer look showed that the man was Abeggu of Tokalet, the foreign friend of Thiegos at the rowdy supper-party at the palace.

"Lyr's barnacles!" cried Vakar, holding his sword poised. "What are you doing here? It will take uncommon eloquence to talk yourself out of this!"

The man stammered in his thick accent: "Th-thiegos told me I w-was to help thwart a plot against the queen. He never—never told me you were involved, and when I found out, it was too late to ask for explanations."

"Thiegos?" said Vakar, and bent to jerk the scarf from the face of the dead man.

Sure enough, the corpse was that of Thiegos, Queen Porfia's paramour.

Prince Vakar whistled. Either Thiegos had been in on the serpent-throne scheme, or had been smitten with jealousy of Vakar Zhu because of the latter's attention to the queen and had gathered a couple of friends to do the traveller in. Luckily they had not known that Vakar wore a helmet under his cowl, or he would have been choosing his next incarnation by now.

He looked at his wounded arm. The bloodstain was still spreading and the arm was hard to move. The hut was empty; Charsela must have pushed Porfia out the back door.

"Well," said Vakar, "this is the first time a man has tried to kill me because of my singing! What else do you know of this attentat?"

"N-nothing, sir. I am ashamed to admit that, when the snake came to life, I fled with the rest. Thiegos and I went to my lodgings near the palace to drink a skin of wine to steady our nerves and collect our wits. Then Thiegos left me to return to the palace. A little later, just as I was going to sleep, he came back with another man, saying for me to come quickly with my sword." Abeggu gulped.

"Go on."

"I—I do not know how to use the thing properly, as we Gamphasants are a peaceful people. I bought it merely as an ornament. When we entered here, they pushed me forward to take the first shock; a fine friend *he* was! This is all most confusing and unethical; I hope the people back in Tokalet never hear of it. Was there in sooth a plot against the queen?"

"Not unless your friend Thiegos was hatching one. I am probably foolish to let you go, but I cannot butcher one who comes from the rim of the world to seek philosophy. Go, but if you cross my path again . . ."

Vakar made a jabbing motion, and Abeggu, still bent over with pain, hurried out.

Vakar looked out the door after him, but except for the wounded Gamphasant nobody was in sight. If any neighbors had heard the clash of arms, they had prudently kept their curiosity in check.

Should he go back to the palace? Much as he liked Porfia, he was not sure that when she learned that he had slain her lover she would not, in a transport of emotion, have him dispatched out of hand. She might regret the action later, but that would not help him if his head were already rotting on a spike on the palace wall.

No, a quick departure would be more prudent. He took a last look at the corpse, recovered his dagger, and hurried out in his turn.

Down at the waterfront of Sederado, he found the *Dyra* with Fual asleep with his back against the mast and his broadsword in his hand. Fual awoke and scrambled up as Vakar approached, saying:

"I hope it's all right about those men who came aboard the ship during the day, my lord. They pawed all through the cargo, saying they were sent by the queen, and there were too many for me to stop. I don't think they stole much."

"It's all right," said Vakar. "We're putting to sea at once. Help me tie up this arm and cast off."

"You're hurt, sir?" Fual hurried to fetch one of the cleaner rags for a bandage. The cut proved about three inches long but not deep.

Vakar silenced the valet's questions, and presently

they were laboriously rowing the *Dyra* out into the sea-way. They got their ropes fouled up in hoisting the sail, and the ship took some water before they got her straightened out to eastward, with Vakar steering as best he could with one arm and Fual bailing water out of the hold with a dipper. Vakar said:

"I didn't see Qasigan's black galley at its place on the waterfront. Has it gone?"

"Yes, sir. Earlier in the night a party appeared on the wharf and boarded the black ship in haste. I recognized the ape-man by his stature even in the dark. There was some delay while the captain sent men ashore to drag his rowers out of the stews, and then they pushed off and disappeared out into the bay. What happened at the palace?"

Vakar briefed Fual on their situation, adding: "If I remember the teaching old Ryn beat into me as a boy, we pass another one or two of these islands and come to the mainland of Euskeria. What do they speak there?"

"Euskerian, sir; a complicated tongue, though I know a few words from the time I spent in Gadaira waiting to be sold."

"There should be a law compelling all men to speak the same language, as the myths say they once did. Too bad we couldn't have cut off Sret's head and kept it alive to interpret for us, as the head of Brang was kept in the legend. Teach me what you know of Euskerian."

During the rest of the night, Vakar's arm bothered him so that he got little sleep. The next day, the Ogugian coast faded away to port, and later another great island loomed up ahead. They coasted along this until, towards evening, Vakar noticed an unpleasantly hazy look in the sky and an ominous increase in the size of the swells that marched down upon them from astern. He said:

"If this were Lorsk, I should guess a storm were brewing."

"Then, sir, shouldn't we run into some sheltered cove until it blows over?"

"I daresay, save that being so green at seafaring we should doubtless run our little ship upon the rocks."

The night passed like the previous one except that Vakar suffered a touch of seasickness from the continuous pitching. His arm ached worse than ever, though he changed the bandage and cleaned the wound. The wind backed to the south so that it was all they could do to keep the *Dyra* from being blown on to the dark shore to port.

With the coming of a gray dawn, Fual glanced astern and cried: "Sir, look around! It's the black galley!"

Vakar froze. A galley was crawling upon their wake like a giant insect, a small square sail swaying upon its mast and its oars rising and falling irregularly in the swells. Vakar hoped that it was not Qasigan's ship, but as the minutes passed and the galley neared, he saw that Fual had been right. He could even make out the figure of Nji the ape-man in the bow. He assumed that their intentions were hostile. Presently the ape-man confirmed his guess by producing a bow twice normal size and sending a huge arrow streaking across the swells, to plunk into the water a few feet away. Qasigan and the little Yok were standing in the bow with Nji.

"They mean us to stop, sir," said Fual.

"I know that, fool!" fumed Vakar, straining his eyes towards the ever-nearing galley.

He wondered how they had traced him. This must be that strong magic spoken of by Charsela. Was Qasigan then the author of the bizarre episode of the serpent throne?

Why should this strange man try to hound Vakar Zhu to his death? Who would benefit by his removal? His brother, perhaps. Who else? He, Vakar, was trying to thwart the impending aggression of the Gorgons against Lorsk by seeking the thing that the gods most feared. Therefore either the gods, or the Gorgons, or both, might be after him.

"Sir," said Fual, "if a mighty magician pursues us, shouldn't we give up now, before we inflame him further by our futile efforts to flee?"

"You rabbit! The chase was hardly begun, and I know he couldn't cast a deadly spell at this distance, from a tossing deck, in this stormy weather. A spell requires quiet and solitude."

"I'm still afraid, sir," mumbled Fual. "Do something to save me!"

Vakar muttered a curse upon his servant's timidity and searched his memory for what he had heard of the Gorgons. It was said that their wizards had the power to freeze anybody within a few paces into a rigid paralysis, by some means called a "medusa," though Vakar did not know what a medusa was. In dealing with Gorgons, then, the thing to do was to keep away from them. As for the gods . . .

Vakar rolled an eye towards the lowering sky and shook a fist. If it's war you want, he thought, you shall have it!

At that instant thunder rolled, away to the north. The wind, which had veered back to the west, blew harder. Rain began to slant across the deck.

A voice came thinly across the waves: "Prince Vakar! Heave to!"

Vakar called to Fual: "Come back here and take cover!"

Vakar himself crouched down in the lee of the single high step up to the poop, holding the steering-lever at arm's length. In this position he was shielded by the sheer of the high stern.

Another arrow whipped by, close enough for its screech to be heard over the roar of the wind, and drove its bone point into the deck. Vakar said:

"So long as we keep down they can't reach us—"

"Beg pardon, sir!" said Fual, who had snatched a look aft. "They're drawing abreast!"

"Oh." If they did that, the pair on the *Dyra* would no longer be protected, and Qasigan could have them either shot down or sunk by ramming. As Qasigan had called Vakar "Prince," the man had evidently not been fooled by Vakar's denial.

Vakar took a look around, shielding his eyes from the rain with his hand. Sure enough, the dark nose of the pursuing ship was creeping up to the *Dyra*'s port quarter.

Vakar felt of his sword. He had no illusions of being able to leap aboard the galley and clean it out single handed, even with Fual's dubious help. For though he downed one or two sailors, he could hardly dompt the weapons of the rest, the ape-man's club, and Qasigan's Gorgonian magic all at the same time.

Closer came the bow of the galley, its bronze ram-spur bursting clear of the water each time the ship pitched. Vakar shifted his steering lever a little to starboard, sending the *Dyra* plunging off to southward, away from the shore, though at that angle the merchantman heeled dangerously with a horrible combination of pitch and roll. The galley swung its stem to starboard to follow.

The wind waxed further and the rain became an opaque, level-blowing mass, mixed with spray from the wave tops. The *Dyra* rolled her port rail under and dipped the corner of her sail into the crests. Vakar was sure that she would capsize.

"Help me!" he shouted, and he and Fual strained at the steering lever until the ship swung back on a straight down-wind course. The mast stays thrummed, and the slender yards whipped dangerously, but at least the ship stayed on an even keel.

Vakar said: "You may let go ... Take another look for the galley."

Fual tried but reported back: "I can't, my lord."

"Can't what?"

"Can't see. It's like thrusting your face into a waterfall."

Vakar fared no better. Clinging to the yoke, they held the ship on her course, though Vakar expected momentarily to hear the galley's ram crunch through their stern. When the squall abated, Vakar left the helm to take another look.

There was no galley.

Vakar's heart leaped up with the thought that their pursuers had swamped and drowned. But another look showed the big black craft still afloat in the distance and making for shore. Peculiar bursts of spray rising up from the galley's deck puzzled Vakar until he realized that they were caused by the sailors of the galley bailing for dear life.

Fual asked: "Why did they leave us?"

"Couldn't take the blow. With her low freeboard, the galley is even less suited to rough water than we are, and her skipper decided to call it quits and lie up in a cove."

"The gods be praised! It's like in that poem when your hero Vrir was best on all sides, and—how does it go, sir?"

Vakar declaimed:

> *Down to the deck*   *livid with lightnings,*
> *Scaly and seaweed-clad,*   *Lyr thrust his trident.*
> *Where the spear struck*   *rose there a rufous*
> *Ring-fence of fire,*   *helping the hero . . .*

The galley became invisible with rain, distance, and the loom of the shore. Vakar held his course, the ache in his right arm running through him. In wrestling with the helm, he had started his wound bleeding again. Soaked and wretched, he wondered if even the forlorn chance of saving Lorsk from the Gorgons was worth his present misery.

Wind and rain continued all day, though never with the severity of that first squall that had all but sunk both the *Dyra* and her pursuer. The wind moderated but veered to the north, so that Vakar had to hold the ship at an uncomfortable angle to the wind to avoid being swept south out to sea. During the night he got only a few nightmarish moments of sleep and faced the dawn feeling feverish and light-headed. His arm hurt so that every time it was touched or jarred he had to set his teeth to keep from yelling.

The rain petered out and the wind turned colder. The cloud cover thinned until Vakar had an occasional glimpse of the sun. He took a good look around the horizon—and stopped, his jaw sagging in horror. A couple of miles aft, the galley's small sail swayed upon its mast.

Vakar was overwhelmed with despair. With

Qasigan's magical powers tracking him down, how could he ever shake off the fellow? He was in no condition to stand and fight.

He pulled himself wearily together. Somewhere over the horizon ahead lay the mainland, and from what he had heard it also projected eastward to the south of him in the peninsula of Dzen. Therefore if he angled off to the right, the way the wind was now blowing, he should fetch up against the mainland. He would be taking a terrific chance, for out of sight of land an overcast that hid sun and stars would leave him utterly lost, and if the wind swung round to the east he would be blown out to sea without knowing it. On the other hand, the ship would sail faster and with less of this torturous rolling . . .

Vakar pulled his steering lever to the left, so that the *Dyra* swung to starboard. The galley followed.

As the hours passed, the island sank out of sight and the galley drew closer, though the water was still too rough for the latter to use her oars efficiently.

"Ah me!" said Fual. "We shall never see our homes and friends again, for this time we are truly lost."

"Shut up!" said Vakar. Fual wept quietly.

In the afternoon, another coast appeared ahead. As they drew nearer, Vakar saw a wooded hilly region with a hint of towering blue mountains in the distance. He wondered if this were the Atlantean range of sinister repute. Behind him the galley was almost within bowshot again.

"What do you plan now, sir?" said Fual.

Vakar shook his head. "I don't know; I seem no longer able to think."

"Let me feel your forehead," said Fual, and then: "No wonder! You're a sick man, my lord. I must get you ashore and put a cow-dung poultice on that wound to draw out the poison—"

"If I can get ashore, I'll take a chance on the wound."

Close came the shore and closer came the galley. Fual cried:

"Breakers ahead! We shall be wrecked!"

"I know it. Get our gear together and prepare to leap off the bow when we touch."

"Too late! They'll ram us before we can reach the beach!"

"Do as I say!" roared Vakar, straining his eyes ahead.

A glance back showed that the galley was over-hauling them faster than they were nearing the strand. Vakar gripped his steering lever as if he could thus squeeze an extra knot out of the *Dyra*.

Behind, the galley gained; Vakar heard the coxswain exhorting his rowers. Ahead, a line of rocks showed between waves, a score of paces short of the beach. As the combers toppled over, they struck these rocks and sent up great fountains of spray, then continued on to the beach with diminished force. If he could guide the little ship between these rocks they might escape, but if he struck one they would drown like mice . . .

Crash! Vakar staggered as the galley's bow struck the stern of the *Dyra*. Fual tumbled to the deck, then rolled over and sat up with a despairing shriek. Under the whistle of the wind, the roar of the breakers, and the shouts of the men on the galley, Vakar fancied he heard the gurgle of water rushing into the *Dyra*.

He recovered his balance and looked ahead. They were headed straight for one of the needles of rock. Vakar heaved on the yoke to swerve the *Dyra*, which heeled and scraped past the obstacle with timbers groaning and crackling. The change in the slope of the deck told Vakar that the ship was settling by the stern. The galley had withdrawn its beak and was backing water furiously to keep off the rocks.

"Get ready!" Vakar screamed to Fual, who blubbered with terror.

Then the deck jerked back under him as the ship struck the beach. Vakar staggered forward and stopped himself by grabbing the mast. He ducked under the lower yard to find that Fual had already tumbled off the bow into knee-deep water and was splashing ashore, leaving the bag containing their possessions on the deck.

With a curse that should have struck the Aremorian

dead, Vakar threw the bag ashore and dropped off the bow himself, the pain of his arm shooting through him like red-hot bronze. He picked up the bag with his good arm and caught up with Fual, to whom he handed the bag, and then hit him across the face with the back of his hand.

"That'll teach you to abandon your master!" he said. "Now march!"

Staggering, Vakar led the way straight inland, up the grassy side of a knoll that rose from the inner edge of the beach. At the top he looked back. The galley was still standing off the rocks, while the *Dyra* lay heeled over on the edge of the sand, her sail flapping and water pouring in and out of her great wounds. As the galley did not appear to possess a ship's boat to send a search party ashore, Vakar felt secure for the time being—until Qasigan found a safer landing place and took up his pursuit ashore.

Vakar led the weeping Fual down the back slope of the knoll until he was out of sight of the sea, then turned to the left and walked parallel to the beach.

They had tramped for an hour or so when a sound brought them up short: a fierce barking and snarling as of the dog that guarded the gates of the hells. They went forward cautiously, hands on swords, and over the next rise found a wild-looking shepherd clad in sheepskins tied haphazard about his person. In one hand he grasped a wooden club with stone spikes set in the thick end, while the other clutched the leash of a great dog, which strained to get at the travellers. The sheep huddled baaing in the background.

Vakar held out his hands. The shepherd shouted.

"What does he say?" asked Vakar.

"To go away or he'd loose the dog on us."

"A hospitable fellow. Ask where there's a settlement."

Fual spoke in broken Euskerian. After several repetitions, the shepherd waved his club, saying:

"Sendeu."

"That's a village," explained Fual.

"Tell him there's a wrecked ship back that way, and he's welcome to it."

Vakar began a detour around the surly shepherd and his flock. As they passed out of sight, the man was gathering his sheep to drive them south along the coast.

Vakar's arm hurt with an agony he had never known before. He muttered:

"I'll never sneer at others' sicknesses again, Fual ..."

Then the universe went into a whirling dance, and Vakar lost track of what was happening.

VII

The Satyr of Sendeu

VAKAR ZHU AWOKE TO THE SOUNDS OF DOMESTIC BUS-tle. He was lying on a rough bed in the corner of a log hut, which seemed, at the moment, to be entirely full of children and dogs.

The cabin had a door at one end, partly closed by a leather curtain, and no windows. On the walls hung the family's tools: a fishing spear barbed with sharks' teeth, hoes made from large clamshells, wooden sickles set with flint blades along their concave edges, and so on. Animal noises from beyond the wall opposite the door told Vakar that this wall was a partition bisecting the cabin, the other half being used for livestock. At one side of the room, a husky-looking peasant girl was working a small loom, whose clack-clack furnished a rhythm under the barking of the dogs and the cries of the children. A sweaty smell overhung the scene.

Fual was sitting on the dirt floor beside him. Vakar raised his head, discovering that he was weak as water.

"Where am I?" he said.

"You're yourself again, my lord? The gods be praised! You're in the hut of Juten, a peasant of Sendeu."

"How did I get here?"

"You walked, sir, but you were out of your head. We stopped at the first likely-looking hut, and you told Juten you were emperor of the world and he should order out your chariotry to attack the Gorgons. He didn't understand, of course, and after much struggle with the language I explained to him that you were a traveler who had taken sick and needed to lie up a few days. He was suspicious and unfriendly, but when I paid him out of your scrip he finally let us in." Fual looked around the hut with lifted lip. "Hardly people of our class, sir, but it was the best I could do."

"How long ago was this?"

"The day before yesterday." Fual felt Vakar's forehead. "The fever has left you. Would you like some soup?"

"By all means. I'm hungry as a spring bear."

Vakar moved his right arm, wincing. Still, it was better than it had been. Fual brought the broth in a gourd bowl.

As the day wore on, Vakar met Juten's wife, a very pregnant woman with lined peasant features. She began speaking to him while going about her chores, undeterred by the fact that they had only a dozen words in common, so the rest of the day Vakar was subjected to a continuous spate of chatter. From its general tone, he guessed that he was not missing anything by lack of understanding.

The people were tall, light-haired, round-headed Atlanteans, who never bathed to judge by their looks and smell. The girl who ran the loom was Juten's eldest daughter. Vakar never did get the names of all the children straight, but a little girl of six named Atsé took a fancy to him. When he pointed at things and asked their names, she told him, making a game of it and finding his mistakes a great joke. By nightfall he had a fair household vocabulary.

Then Juten came in, thickset and stooped, with dirt worked deeply into the cracks of his skin. He gave Vakar a noncommittal look and spoke in broken Hesperian:

"Lord better now?"

"Yes, thank you."

Supper was a huge loaf of barley bread, milk, and a strange golden fruit called an "orange." Juten pointed apologetically to a jug in the corner:

"Beer not good yet."

Next day Vakar, now well enough to move around, continued his fraternization with Atsé. He encouraged her to talk, stopping her every few words for an explanation. She got bored and went out, but then a rainstorm drove her in again.

"What do you do for fun?" he asked, shaving the three days' stubble from his chin with his bronze razor.

"I play with the others and I visit the tailed lady."

"The what?"

"The lady with the tail. She lives in the hills over that way." Atsé gestured eastward. "I call her with this."

She produced a tiny whistle tied around her neck with a string of grass and blew on it. Vakar, hearing nothing, asked:

"How can she hear you when that thing makes no noise?"

"Oh, but it does! A magical noise that she alone can hear."

Vakar tried blowing on it himself, with no result save that the two dogs who happened to be in the hut both howled. Later, when Atsé had gone out again, Vakar asked Juten's wife about the tailed woman.

"She told you that?" cried the woman. "I will tan her hide! She knows she should not . . ."

"Why? Many children make up imaginary playmates—"

"Imaginary! Would that she were! This is a satyr of Atlantis who has settled near here and entices the children into stealing our food and taking it to her secretly. The men have hunted her with dogs, but her magic baffles them."

Vakar, who had understood only about half of what the woman had said, dropped the subject of the satyr to take a snooze. That evening, after supper, Juten mumbled something about a village meeting and went out into the sunset. Vakar dozed until aroused by Fual's shaking him.

"My lord!" said the valet. "We must flee or they'll murder us!"

"Huh? What are you talking about?"

"I spied upon the village meeting, which was called to discuss us. Egon, the headman, urged that we be killed and persuaded the others."

"Lyr's barnacles! Why?"

"From what I could understand, they seemed to think that all foreigners are evil, and that we have wealth on our persons which the village could use. Moreover, their witch-doctor said he could insure a year's prosperity by sacrificing us to their gods. They sacrifice people with torture, and the shaman claimed his gods had appeared to him in a vision to demand our lives. Juten and one or two others wished to spare us, but were outvoted."

"What's their scheme?"

"They'll wait until we're asleep and rush in. They dare not attack us openly for fear of our swords."

Vakar glanced to where Juten's wife sat placidly in the doorway, milling barley with a hand quern. He thoughtfully twirled his mustache. Feeling sure that she would not have understood the conversation in Lorskan, he said:

"Is all our gear in the bag?"

"Nearly, sir. I'll pack the rest now."

Vakar got up, stretched, and put on his cloak. He bent over the children's beds until he located Atsé, whose single garment was wadded up to make a pillow. Vakar explored gently until he found the tiny whistle and withdrew it. He did not like robbing a child, but had little choice. He dropped the whistle into his scrip and said to Juten's wife:

"Your pardon, madam, but we are going out for a walk."

"Are you strong enough, sir?" she said, rising to make way for the pair of them.

"I think so, thank you."

Vakar led the way, Fual following with the bag on

his back. Vakar walked toward the corner of the hut. Just before he reached it, the woman called after him:

"Sir, why are you carrying your belongings? Are you leaving us?"

Pretending not to hear, Vakar swung rapidly around the corner of the house and headed eastward between it and the next hut. They ·passed a couple of store sheds, detoured a pig pen and a paddock containing horses, and strode through a plowed field, their boots sinking into the mud and coming out with sucking noises. Vakar felt a little weak and his arm was sore, but otherwise he seemed to be active again. He asked:

"This is the first I've seen of the neighborhood since recovering my senses. Can you lead the way?"

"No, sir. Except for a few glimpses of the main street of the village, I know hardly more about it than you. Where are you taking us?"

Vakar told about the female satyr, adding: "I know not whether she's real or a peasant superstition, but I brought the child's whistle along to try. She might conceivably help us, being of the third class of friends."

"What's that?"

"There's your friend, and your friend's friend, and your enemy's enemy. She seems to be of the last kind."

He blew experimentally, whereupon there was an outburst of barking from the village.

"For the gods' sake, my lord, don't do that!" said Fual. "There must be some sound emitted by that thing, even though we mortal men can't hear it. You'll have all those devils on our trail." He glared back at the village and muttered Aremorian curses upon the Sendevians.

They tramped in silence until they passed out of the fields and entered the zone of wild grass and scrubby forest. The stars came out, although the moon, being past full, had not risen. Somewhere in the hills a lion roared. They were stumbling their way up a draw between two of the smaller foothills of the Atlantean Mountains when Fual said:

"Sir, listen!"

Vakar halted and heard, far behind them, a murmur

of voices and a chorus of barking. Looking back he saw a tiny glimmer as of a swarm of fireflies. That would be the men of the village setting out with dogs and torches to hunt them down.

"Oh, hurry!" said Fual, teeth chattering.

Vakar hurried. One or two peasants he would have faced, but if all the able-bodied males of Sendeu caught him, emboldened by numbers, stone axes and wooden rakes and pitchforks would do him in as surely if not so quickly as whetted bronze.

He blew on the whistle again. Nothing happened.

They stumbled on, pausing betimes for breath. Each time the sounds of pursuit became louder. When the moon rose, Vakar straightened out their course towards the east, where, he hoped, the more rugged terrain would give them a better chance of escape.

Fual said: "Sir, why did you bring me on this terrible journey, where we spend all our time fleeing from one dire doom after another? You could have left me to serve your brother—"

"Shut up," said Vakar, gasping for breath.

He looked back down the valley they were now traversing and plainly saw the swarm of torches at the lower end. He raised the whistle to his lips, but Fual cried:

"Oh, pray don't blow that again! It only draws the dogs faster."

"They'll track us by smell in any case, and it's our last—"

Fual sank to his knees, weeping, and kissed Vakar's hand, but Vakar pushed him roughly back.

"I shall blow, and if it doesn't work, look to your sword. I'm too tired to run further, and we can at least take a few of these sons of sows with us."

Ignoring Fual's prayers, Vakar blew. The torches came closer and the barking became louder. Vakar was feeling his edge when a voice spoke in Euskerian:

"Who are you, and what do you wish?"

Vakar saw nobody, but replied: "We are two travelers whom the villagers of Sendeu seek to murder. We thought you might give us sanctuary."

"You do not look or speak like peasants. Could you do me a favor in return?"

"What favor?" said Vakar, with a lively memory of legends wherein people offered some petitioner anything he asked and lived to regret their impulsiveness.

"I wish help in getting back to my native land."

"We will do our best."

"Come then; but if this is a trap you shall be sorry."

There was a movement in the shrubbery on the hillside, and Vakar started towards the fugitive spot of pallor. His rest had given him strength to pull himself up the hillside. The three of them—Vakar, Fual, and their half-seen guide—crossed the crest of the ridge as the dogs and torches streamed past below. At the point where the fugitives turned off, the dogs halted and milled.

Vakar whispered: "Will they not follow our scent?"

"No, for I cast a spell upon them. But come, for these spells are short-lived."

An hour later, Vakar followed the satyr into a cave on a hillside, whose mouth was cunningly hidden by vegetation. The being rummaged in the darkness. Vakar saw the shower of sparks caused by striking flint against pyrites, and presently a rushlight glimmered.

"I do not use fire myself," said their rescuer, "but when my lovers used to come from the village, I found they liked to see what they were doing, so I laid in a store of these things."

Vakar looked. The satyr was a young female, naked, about five feet tall and quite human except for the horselike tail, snub nose, slanting eyes, and pointed ears. He asked:

"Have you a name?"

"Tiraafa."

"I am Vakar and he is Fual, my servant. What is this about human lovers, Tiraafa?" Vakar found the habits of the near-human species fascinating.

"With us," said Tiraafa, "one must have love, much more than among you cold and passionless humans. Since there are no others of my kind hereabouts, I encouraged the lustier young men of the village to visit me. Of course the love of a man is a limp and feeble thing compared to that of a satyr, but it was all I could do."

"Why are there no others of your kind?" said Fual. "I always understood satyrs dwelt in Atlantis."

"They do, but not of my tribe. I come from the Saturides, far to the north, having been seized by Foworian slavers. I was sold in Gadaira, but escaped and fled into the mountains. When I found a tribe of satyrs, they thought, because I was a stranger who spoke a dialect different from theirs, that I must be a spy sent against them by the human beings. They drove me off with sticks and stones—and here I am."

"You wish to return to the Satyr Isles?"

"Oh, yes! Could you help me?" She seized his wrist imploringly.

Fual, cheerful again, said: "Have no fear, Tiraafa. My lord can arrange anything."

"Maybe," grunted Vakar. "What ended your relations with Sendeu?"

"The maidens of the village complained to their fathers, who forbade their sons to visit me. No longer having the food they brought, I had to steal or persuade the children to bring me some, and the headman swore to kill me."

"We have had our troubles with Egon too," said Vakar. "A right friendly fellow. But as we seem safe for the moment, let us get some sleep and plan our next move in the morning."

"As you wish," said Tiraafa. "However, I have had no love for months, and expect as part of the price of your rescue—"

She began sliding her hands up his arms towards his neck in a way that reminded Vakar of Bili.

"Not me, little one," said Vakar. "I am a sick man. Begin with Fual, and in another day I may be able to help out. Fual, the lady wishes love; attend to it."

And Vakar, not waiting to see how Fual took this unusual command, curled up in his cloak and dropped off to sleep.

"As I see it," said Vakar as he shared Tiraafa's meager breakfast next morning, "we must all head north to Gadaira, where I can put Tiraafa on a ship for her native land while we proceed up the Baitis to Torrutseish. How far to Gadaira, Tiraafa?"

As satyrs seemed to have no notion of measurement, she was unable to answer his query. By questioning her closely about her erratic course from Gadaira to Sendeu, however, Vakar got the impression that the distance was somewhere between one and three hundred miles.

"Too far to walk," he said, "especially in a country where the peasantry sacrifice strangers to their gods. Whose horses are those I saw in the paddock last night?"

Tiraafa replied: "They belong to the village, which really means Egon, as he and his relatives control the village. They rear these creatures not to use themselves but to sell in Gadaira."

"Do they not plow with them?"

"What is plowing?"

It transpired that neither Tiraafa nor the Sendevians had ever seen a plow. Vakar said:

"If we could steal these horses, we should both provide ourselves with transportation and express our love for Headman Egon. They could not follow us, and we could sell those we did not need in Gadaira."

"Why are you going to Torrutseish?" asked Tiraafa.

"To seek the advice of the world's greatest magicians. Do you know which of them is the best?"

"Not much, but when I was captive in Gadaira I heard the name of Kurtevan. All of us satyrs are magicians of a sort, and such news gets around among the brotherhood."

Prince Vakar peered out of his hiding place. The twelve horses were pegged out in the meadow, and the youth who guarded them sat with his back to a tree, wrapped in his black Euskerian mantle, with his long, copper-headed spear across his legs. With this (probably the only metal weapon in the village) the horse-herd could stand off a prowling lion long enough for his yells to fetch help.

Vakar looked at the young man coldly, with neither hatred nor sympathy. He knew that many self-sufficient peasant communities looked upon city folk as legitimate prey, for their only contact with cities was when the latter sent tax-gathering parties among them. From the point of view of the villages, these were mere plundering expeditions for which they got nothing in return. But while he realized that the Sendevians' attack on him was not due to sheer malevolence, he would not on that account spare them if they got in his way.

Tiraafa peered around her tree and called softly: "Olik!"

The young man sprang up, gripping his spear, then laughed. "Tiraafa! According to my orders I ought to slay you."

"You would not do that! I loved you the best of all."

"Did you really?"

"Try me and see."

"By the gods, I will!"

Olik leaned his spear against his tree and started for Tiraafa with the lust-light in his eyes. His expression changed to amazement as Vakar leaped out of the bushes and ran full-tilt at him. Vakar saw his victim begin to turn and fill his lungs to shout just as Vakar's sword slid between his ribs up to the hilt.

Vakar, sheathing his blade, said: "Can either of you ride?"

Tiraafa and Fual, looking apprehensive, shook their heads.

"Well then, as it looks as though these beasts have never been ridden either, you both start from the same point."

Vakar walked out into the field, where the horses had laid back their ears and were tugging on their tethering ropes and rolling their eyes at the sight of strangers and the smell of blood. He selected the one who seemed the least disturbed, gentled it down, and began twisting its tethering rope into a bridle.

Several days later, riding bareback, they halted in sight of Gadaira. Vakar, looking toward the forest of masts and yards that could be seen over the low roofs, said:

"Fual, before we take our little sweetheart into the city, one of us must go ahead and buy her clothes, or the first slaver who sees her will seize her. And as you're a better bargainer than I, you are elected."

"Please, sir, then may I walk? I'm so stiff and sore from falling off this accursed animal that the thought of solid ground under my feet seems like a dream of heaven."

"Suit yourself. And while you're about it, inquire for a reliable sea captain sailing northward."

An hour later, Fual was back with a gray woolen dress and a black Euskerian cloak with a hood. The dress concealed Tiraafa's tail, and the hood her ears. Fual said:

"I learned that Captain Therlas sails for Kerys in three or four days with a cargo of cork and copper, and that he is said to be a man of his word." The little Aremorian hesitated, then burst out: "My lord, why don't you set me free? I'm as anxious to see my home again as she is, and I could keep an eye upon her until Therlas dropped her off on her wild islands."

"I didn't know you so wished to leave me," said Vakar. "Have I treated you badly?"

"No—at least not so badly as most masters—but there is nothing like freedom and one's home."

Vakar pondered. The appeal did touch him, as he was not unsympathetic for an aristocrat, and the ex-thief was at best an indifferent servant. On the other hand, Vakar was appalled by the prospect of finding a reliable new slave in this strange city, even though he did need someone with more thews and guts than his sensitive valet.

"I'll tell you," he said at last. "I won't free you now, because I badly need your help and I think Tiraafa can take care of herself. But when we win back to Lorsk with our mission accomplished, I'll not only free you but also provide you with the means of getting home."

Fual muttered a downcast "Thank you, sir," and turned his attention to other matters.

They found lodgings and sold eight of the twelve horses, keeping the four strongest for their own use. Vakar took a variety of trade goods in exchange for the animals: little ingots of silver stamped with the cartouche of King Asizhen of Tartessia; packets of rare spices from beyond Kheru and Thamuzeira in the Far East; and for small change the ordinary celt-shaped slugs and neck rings of copper. Fual, looking with undisguised hostility at the horses, suggested:

"At least, sir, you might buy a chariot so we could continue our journey in comfort . . ."

"No. Chariots are all right for cities, but we may be going where there are only foot tracks for roads."

When the time came, they escorted Tiraafa to the docks and saw her aboard ship with provisions for the journey. She kissed them fiercely, saying:

"I shall always remember you, for as human beings go you are quite fair lovers. I hope Captain Therlas will equal you in this regard."

On an impulse Vakar pressed a fistful of trade copper into Tiraafa's hands and helped her aboard. Fual wept and Vakar waved as the ship cast off, and then they turned away to the four horses hitched to one of the waterfront posts. Vakar vaulted on to his new saddle pad and clamped his knees on the barrel of the beast, which under his expert training had become quite manageable. Fual tried to imitate his master, but leaped too hard and fell off his mount into the mud on the other side, whereat Vakar roared. He was still laughing when he glanced out to sea, and the laugh died as if cut off by an ax.

"Fual," he said, "mount at once. Qasigan's galley is coming into the harbor."

A few seconds later, the four horses were headed away from the waterfront through the streets of Gadaira at a reckless gallop.

VIII

The Towers of Torrutseish

A HUNDRED AND SIXTY MILES UP THE BAITIS LAY mighty Torrutseish, the capital of the Tartessian Empire and the world's largest city, known by many names in different places and ages. In Vakar's time, it was so old that its origin was lost in the mists of myth.

In the days of Vakar Lorska, the king of Tartessia had extended his sway over most of the Euskerian nations: the Turdetanians, the Turdulians, and even the Phaiaxians who were not Euskerians at all. The city of Torrutseish, preëminent among all the cities of the world for its magic, stood on an island where the Baitis forked and rejoined itself again. Prince Vakar approached it up the river road, leading his two spare horses and followed by Fual (who kept his seat by gripping a fistful of his mount's mane.) To their left, the broad Baitis bore swarms of dugouts, rafts of inflated skins, and other fresh-water craft.

Vakar sighted the walls and towers of the metropolis as he came around a bend. The outer wall was circular, like that of Amferé but on a vaster scale. Like the lofty towers that rose behind it, it was built of red, white, and black stones arranged in bands and patterns to give a dazzling mosaic effect. The bright blue Euskerian sun flashed on the gilding of dome and spire and tourelle, and flags bearing the owl of Tartessia flapped lazily in the faint breeze.

Vakar thrilled at the sight of buildings of three or even four stories, though he would have enjoyed it more if he had not felt obliged to look back down the river every few minutes to see if the sinister black galley were rowing up behind him. For the Baitis was fully navigable thus far, and Vakar was sure that, with his supernatural methods of tracking, his enemy would soon be breasting the current in pursuit.

When he had passed the inspection of the guards at the city gate and had found quarters, Vakar asked where the house of Kurtevan the magician was to be found.

"You wish to see Kurtevan? In person?" said the innkeeper, his jaw sagging so that Vakar could see the fragments of the leek that he had been chewing.

"Why, yes. What is so peculiar about that?"

"Nothing, nothing, save that Kurtevan does not cultivate the custom of common men like us. He is the principal thaumaturge to King Asizhen."

Vakar raised his bushy eyebrows. "That is interesting, but I too am not without some small importance in my own land. Where can I find his house?"

The innkeeper told him, and as soon as he had washed and rested, Vakar set out with Fual in the direction indicated. They got lost amid the crooked streets of one of the older sections of the city and asked a potter, who sat in his stall slowly revolving his tournette:

"Could you tell us where to find the house of Kurtevan the magician?"

The man gave them an alarmed glance and began turning the tournette rapidly, so that the piece grew under his fingers like magic. Thinking that perhaps the fellow had not understood his broken Euskerian, Vakar laid a hand on his arm, saying:

"I asked you where to find the house of Kurtevan, friend. Do you not know, or did you not understand me?"

The man muttered: "I understood you, but not wishing you ill I forbore to answer, for prudent men do not disturb the great archimage without good cause."

"My cause is my own affair," said Vakar in some irritation. "Now will you answer a civil question or not?"

The Tartessian sighed and gave directions.

"Anyone would think," said Vakar as he set out in the direction indicated, "we were asking the way to the seven hells."

"Perhaps we are, sir," said Fual.

The house of Kurtevan turned out to be a tall tower of red stone in the midst of a courtyard surrounded by a wall. With the handle of his dagger, Vakar struck the copper gong that hung beside the gate. As the sound of the gong died away, the gate opened with a loud creak.

Vakar stepped in, took one look at the gate-keeper—and involuntarily stepped back, treading on Fual's toe.

"*Oi!*" said Fual. "What—"

Then he too caught sight of the gatekeeper, gasped, and turned to flee, but Vakar caught his clothing and dragged him inside. The gatekeeper pushed the gate shut and stood silently facing them. He was silent for the good reason that he had no head.

The gatekeeper was the headless body of a tall, swarthy man, dressed in a breech-clout only, whose neck stopped halfway up. Skin and a sparse growth of dark curly hair grew over the stump, except for a couple of obscene-looking irregular openings that presumably represented the thing's windpipe and gullet. A single eye stared out of its chest at the base of its neck. Its broad bare chest rose and fell slowly. A large curved bronze sword was thrust through its girdle.

Vakar looked blankly at this unusual ostiary, wondering how to communicate with one who lacked ears. Still, the thing must have heard the gong. Vakar cleared his throat uncertainly and spoke:

"My name is Vakar, and I should like to see Kurtevan."

The acephalus beckoned and led the way to the base of the tower. Here it unlocked the door with a large bronze key and opened it, motioning Vakar to enter.

Fual muttered: "Perhaps I should stay outside, sir. They seem all too willing to admit us to this suburb of hell . . ."

"Come along," snapped Vakar, nervously cracking his knuckle joints.

He stepped inside. The setting sun shot a golden shaft through the wall slit on the west side of the tower, almost horizontally across the room in which

Vakar found himself. As his eyes adapted to the gloom, he made out a lot of furniture gleaming with gold and precious stones, but the gleam was muted by quantities of dust and cobwebs.

Evidently, Vakar thought, headless servants did not make neat housekeepers.

He stood in a great circular room, which took in the whole of the first floor of the tower, except for a spiral stone staircase, which wound up to the floor above and down to some subterranean compartment below. There was nobody in the room; no sound save the frantic buzzing of a fly caught in one of the many spiderwebs. Overhead, a grid of heavy wooden beams crossed the stonework from one side to the other, supporting a floor of planks. Vakar tried in vain to see through the cracks in the planks.

"Let's try the next floor," he whispered.

Holding his scabbard, Vakar tiptoed over to the stair, followed by Fual wearing a stricken look. Up he went, though a stair to him was still a somewhat mysterious newfangled contrivance. Nothing barred his way as he came up the curving stair to the second floor. Here, however, he halted as his swift-darting glance caught the outlines of a man.

The man was sitting cross-legged on a low taboret with his eyes closed. He was a spare individual with the face of an aged hawk, and wrapped from head to foot in the typical black Euskerian mantle. The cloak was, however, made of some shiny fabric that Vakar had never seen. The man's hands lay limply in his lap. Before him stood a small tripod supporting a copper dish, in which burned a little heap of something. A thin, blue column of smoke arose steadily from the smolder. Vakar caught a whiff of a strange smell as he stalked towards the still figure.

Vakar froze as the man moved, though the movement was the slightest: a minute raising of his head and the opening of his eyes to slits. Vakar had an uncomfortable feeling that if the eyes opened all the way, the results might be unfortunate.

The man spoke in perfect Hesperian: "Hail, Prince Vakar Zhu of Lorsk; Vakar the son of Zhabutir."

"Greetings," said Vakar without wasting breath asking Kurtevan how he knew his name.

"You have come to me to seek that which the gods most fear."

"True."

"You are also fleeing from one Qasigan, a Gorgonian priest of Entigta—"

"A Gorgon?" said Vakar sharply.

"Yes; did you not know?"

"I guessed but was not sure."

"Very well, there shall be no charge for that bit of information. However, for the other matter, what are you prepared to pay for this powerful agency?"

Vakar, who had expected this question, named a figure in ounces of gold that amounted to about half the total value of his trade goods.

The old man's hooded eyes opened a tiny crack further. "That is ridiculous. Am I a village witch peddling spurious love philtres?"

Vakar raised his bid; and again, until he was offering all his wealth except barely enough to get him back to Lorsk.

Kurtevan smiled thinly. "I am merely playing with you, Vakar Zhu. I know the contents of that scrip down to the last packet of spice, and had you thrice that amount it would not suffice me. I am chief thaumaturge by appointment to King Asizhen and have no need to cultivate common magical practice."

Vakar stood silently, frowning and pulling his mustache. After a few seconds the wizard spoke again:

"Howsomever, if you cannot pay my price in gold and silver and spice, it is possible that you could recompense me in services. For I am in need of that which trade goods cannot buy."

"Yes?" said Vakar.

"As all men know, I am the leading wonder worker of Torrutseish and receive the king's exclusive custom in the field of thaumaturgy. That, however, is but half the practice of magic, the other half comprising the divinatory arts. Now the leading seer of the city, one Nichok, receives the king's patronage for oracles and prophecies and visions. I would add that art to my own practice."

Vakar nodded.

"I have composed a beautiful method of doing so, except that it requires the help of a strong man of more than common hardihood. Briefly, it is this: my rival Nichok lies most of the time in a trance while his soul goes forth to explore the world in space and time. If I could possess myself of his body while he is in one of these trances, I could seal it against the reëntry of his soul, and by threatening to destroy this body I could force Nichok's soul to divine for me as long as I wished."

"You wish me to steal this body for you?"

"Precisely."

"Why me?" said Vakar warily.

"Because the men of Torrutseish are so imbued with fear of us of the magical profession that none would dare let himself be involved in such a *coup-de-main*. Moreover, your slave has, I believe, some authentic knowledge of the theory and practice of larceny and could help you."

"Suppose that fear is well founded?"

"It is, to a degree. But this task, while admittedly dangerous, is by no means hopeless. Were I Nickok, I could give you the precise odds on your success. As it is, I can tell you that they are no worse than pursuing a wounded lion into its lair. As your friend Qasigan will not arrive in Torrutseish before tomorrow night, you have ample time."

Vakar stood silently until Kurtevan spoke again: "There is no likelihood of my reducing my demand, young man, so make up your mind. Either make this attempt or go elsewhere for means to thwart the Gorgons."

Mention of the Gorgons gave Vakar the extra push needed to make up his mind. If Qasigan were indeed a Gorgon, then Söl's story of the Gorgons' impending descent upon his homeland was true.

"I will try," he said. "What must we do?"

"First you must wait until dark and go to the tower

of Nichok. It is much like this one but smaller, and across the city—I will give you a map."

"How do I get in?"

"There is a secret entrance, which even Nichok does not know."

"How is that?"

"For the simple reason that I built his present tower and sold it to him when I erected this edifice fifty years ago. Now, when you have entered his tower by the secret entrance, you will find a trapdoor, and underneath the trapdoor a ladder leading down to the underground chamber where lies the body of Nichok. My arts tell me he is not lying completely unprotected; he has summoned a guardian from some other plane of existence, though its precise nature I cannot ascertain."

"Hmm. How shall I cope with this guardian? An armed man I can take a chance with, but some ten-armed demon from another universe ... What am I supposed to do when I cut at the creature and my sword goes through it like smoke?"

"Do not let that concern you. Things from other worlds and planes, if they would dwell in our world, must obey the laws thereof. Therefore if this guardian is sufficiently materialized on this dimension to harm you, by the same token it must be equally vulnerable to your attack."

"Well, if Nichok's soul is wandering about, how do you know it is not eavesdropping on us now?"

The wizard smiled. "Every dog is invincible on its home ground. For one thing, all openings in my tower are sealed with the juice of rue, garlic, asafetida, and other spirit-repellants. But come; it will be another hour before full darkness, and you must be hungry. Sup with me and then set out upon your task."

Kurtevan clapped his hands. The headless servitor appeared and set out two stools and a low table. At least *a* headless servant appeared; Vakar realized that without faces to go by, it was almost impossible to tell whether this were the same gatekeeper or not. He said:

"You have unusual servants, Master Kurtevan. Do you find them more obedient without heads? What *is* the creature?"

"A gift from the lord of Belem. Do you know Awoqqas?"

"I have heard sinister rumors of the land of Belem, that is all."

"King Awoqqas has found a method of reanimating a freshly decapitated corpse by constraining a certain type of spirit of the air to animate it. If the operation is performed carefully, so that the body is prevented from bleeding to death, the wound can be healed and a servant created who is more docile than any whole man. Its only disadvantage compared to a whole man, like yours, is that with that single eye in its chest it cannot look up or around. Awoqqas has a whole army of these izzuneg, as they are called in the language of Belem. If your travels should take you thither, I am sure you could persuade him to convert your slave to an izzuni."

"An interesting idea," said Vakar, "but I must take Fual's feelings into account. Being very sensitive, he might not like the loss of his head."

"Ahem. You see," continued Kurtevan, "there are three schools of thought regarding the location of the intelligence: that it resides in the head, or in the heart, or in the liver. Now Awoqqas appears to have proved the first-named correct. Lacking a brain, there is no likelihood that the memories and thought patterns that the acephalus had as a whole human being will be reanimated along with the rest of the organism, and perhaps interfere with the control of the body by the sylph . . ."

The thin old wizard became almost animated as he discussed magical theory. Vakar, despite Kurtevan's callous disregard for other human beings, became so absorbed that he almost forgot the peril ahead of him. Fual continued to quake. But when the food arrived, Vakar said:

"I trust you will not deem me unduly suspicious, but do you swear by your magical powers that this food contains nothing harmful—no drug or enchantment that might affect us at any time?"

Kurtevan smiled crookedly. "Old Ryn taught you

well. Of course even the most wholesome food can be harmful if eaten in abnormal quantities—"

"No quibbling, please. Do you swear?" For Vakar knew that if a magician swore falsely by his magical powers, these powers would at once leave him.

"I swear," said Kurtevan, and addressed himself to his plate. "Does this convince you?"

The tower of Nichok stood black against the stars. Although Kurtevan had said that it was smaller than his present keep, it loomed larger in the darkness. Vakar and Fual leaned against the wall surrounding the tower, listening. They had left their cloaks and satchel at Kurtevan's so as not to be encumbered more than was necessary.

Something moved around inside the wall, though the sound was not that of human footsteps. There was a curious shuffle and a scaly rattle about the sound, and something breathed with a hiss that was almost a whistle.

A light showed in the distance.

"The watch!" said Fual, convulsively gripping Vakar's arm.

"Well, don't twist my arm off. Remember what he told us."

In accordance with Kurtevan's instructions, both men put their backs to the wall and froze to immobility. The wizard had thrown a glamor over them so that, so long as they remained still, the watch would simply not notice them; they were for practical purposes invisible.

The watch—a group of eight citizens holding torches and with staves and zaghnals over their shoulders—tramped past. Vakar caught a muttered comment about the price of onions, and the group swung by, never looking towards Vakar and Fual. When the watch had passed out of sight, Vakar led Fual silently back to the place where they had been listening.

"Six paces from the gate," he breathed, "and two feet from the wall . . . . Fual, your feet are smaller than mine, more like those of a Euskerian. Put them one behind the other . . ."

Vakar marked the spot with his toe and began digging in the dirt with his fingers. When the ground proved too hard, he attacked it with the blade of his knife, going round and round in an increasing spiral from the spot where he had started, and also deeper and deeper.

Once the blade struck something. Vakar scrabbled eagerly, but it turned out to be a mere stone, not the bronze ring he sought.

On the other side of the wall, the peculiar footsteps came and went again.

Then the blade struck another obstacle. This time it was the ring, rough with corrosion. Vakar, wishing he had a shovel, cleared away the dirt around it; then grasped it with both hands and heaved. It stuck fast.

He cleared away more of the dirt from the stone slab in which the ring was set and motioned Fual to hook as many fingers as possible into the ring also. Both heaved, and with a loud scraping and grinding the ring rose. As the slab tilted up on one edge, dirt showered into the hole, about two feet square, that yawned beneath it. Vakar pulled the stone up until it stuck in a nearly vertical position.

"Come on," he whispered, lowering himself into the hole.

IX

Death By Fire

THEY HAD TO CRAWL THROUGH A MERE BURROW. Vakar's knees were sore and he was sure that the tunnel had taken them clear to the other side of Nichok's lot, when he rammed his head into the end of the tunnel.

He felt around overhead until he located the contours of the stone slab that topped this end of the

tunnel. Gathering his forces, he heaved. Inch by inch
the stone rose. A wan light wafted into the tunnel.

Vakar thrust his head up through the opening. A
single oil lamp feebly illumined a great round room
like that which comprised the ground floor of Kurtevan's tower. A massive timber door was bolted on the
inside.

Vakar climbed out, tiptoed over to the door, and listened. Although he thought he could hear those peculiar footsteps again, the door was too thick to be sure.
He began hunting for the trapdoor, which Kurtevan
had told him led to the underground chamber where
the rival wizard lay. It was not hard to find, for a
bronze ring like that of the first slab was stapled to its
upper surface. He bent and heaved upon the bronzen
ring. This slab came up easily, revealing a square hole
and the upper end of a ladder.

"Fual," he said, "get your sword ready ... What ails
you?"

The little man was kneeling with tears running down
his face. "Don't make me go down there, my lord! I
had rather die! I'll not go though you torture me!"

"Damned spineless coward!" hissed Vakar, and hit
Fual with the back of his hand, which merely made the
Aremorian weep harder. "I don't see how you could
have ever worked up the courage to steal anything
when you were a thief!"

In his nervous fury, Vakar could have killed the
valet, save that he feared making a lot of noise and
knew that he would need the fellow's help with Nichok's body later.

At this point, even Prince Vakar's grim resolution
nearly failed him. What if he went quietly away and returned home to say that he had failed in his search?
Perhaps he could find another magician. Or he need
not go home at all but could hire out as a mercenary
soldier in one of the mainland kingdoms, and to the
seven hells with Lorsk ...

Then he caught Fual's eye, and pride of caste stiff-
ened his sinews. It would never do to let a slave see
him quail before peril. He started down into the hole.

He descended rapidly, anxious to get the worst over.

The ladder led down into another chamber, smaller than that above and like it lit by a single lamp. This lamp stood on one end of a large bier of black marble, on which lay a pallet and on the pallet, supine, a man. The light of the lamp fell upon the man's upturned face and cast deep shadows across the hollows of his eyes and cheeks. The rest of his body, except for his sandaled feet, was wrapped in a black mantle.

The man lay quietly, only an occasional movement of his chest betraying the fact that he was alive. However, there should be something else in the room. In fact Vakar, though little given to fancies and premonitions, was sure there was something else. Something, he felt, was watching him. He could neither see it nor hear it, but the faint smell in the stagnant air was not simply that of an unventilated crypt.

Gripping his scabbard lest it clank, Vakar tiptoed toward the bier. He was about to mount the single step around the black block to look into Nichok's face when a noise caused him to start back.

Something stirred in the shadows on the far side of the bier. As Vakar watched, the thing unfolded and rose on many limbs until its stalked eyes looked across Nichok's body into those of Vakar Zhu.

It was an enormous crab.

The crab began to scuttle with horrifying speed around the bier. Before Vakar could move, it was coming at him from his right. As he leaped back, sidling around the bier in his turn to keep the obstacle between them, the crab swung round and with a sweep of a huge chela knocked the ladder down. It fell with a loud clatter. Sweating with terror, Vakar realized that this was no mere crab but an intelligent being.

The crab came at Vakar again, its claws rasping on the stone floor. Vakar dodged around the bier; the crab stopped and began circling the bier in the opposite direction. Vakar perforce reversed too.

How in the names of all the gods, he wondered, was he to get out of this? They could go on circling the stone block until one or the other collapsed from exhaustion, and he knew which that would be . . .

No, they would not circle indefinitely; the crab had

other ideas. Leg by leg it began climbing *over* the bier. Delicately it raised its feet so that its claws did not touch Nichok's body or the lamp, and stood swaying, balanced, its stalked eyes looking down into those of Vakar. The small forked antennae between the eye stalks quivered and the many pairs of mandibles opened and shut, emitting a froth of bubbles.

The thing started to topple towards Vakar, who whirled and snatched at the ladder in the forlorn hope of getting it back in position and bolting up it. He had it partly raised when he heard the sharp sound of the crab's eight claws striking the floor behind him, and then the ladder was snatched out of his grasp. As he turned, he heard the wood crunch under the grip of the great chelae, which could snip off his head as easily as he could pinch off the head of a daisy.

The crab flung the ladder across the room and scuttled towards Vakar, chelae spread and opened. Vakar, backing towards a corner, drew and cut at the monster as it came within reach, but the sharp bronze bounced back from the hard shell without even scratching it. When Kurtevan had spoken of the guardian demon's vulnerability, he had not mentioned the possibility of its having this loricated form.

Vakar felt the wall at his back. The chelae started to close in upon him.

In that last instant, before he was cut to bits like a paper-doll scissored by an angry child, a picture crossed Vakar's mind. It was of himself as a boy playing on one of the royal estates on the coast of Lorsk along the western margins of Poseidonis, in the Bay of Kort. He was talking to an old fisherman who held a vainly struggling crab from behind with one horny hand and said:

"Eh, lad, keep your thumb on the belly of him and your fingers on the back, and he can't reach around to nip ye . . ."

With that, Vakar knew what he had to do. As the chelae closed in he threw himself forward and down. He hit the floor beneath the crab's mandibles and rolled frantically under the creature's belly, which cleared the floor by about two feet. As the chelae closed on the empty air with a double snap, Vakar rose to his feet.

He was now behind the crab, which swivelled its eyestalks back towards him and began to turn to face him again. Vakar leaped to the creature's broad, hard-shelled back. With his free hand he seized one of the forked antennae, then pulled it back and held it like a rein, standing balanced with legs spread and knees bent on his unusual mount.

The crab circled, its chelae waving wildly and their great pincer-jaws snapping as it strove to reach back to grasp its foe, but the joints of its armor did not permit it that much flexibility.

Vakar swung his sword, with a silent prayer to the gods of Lorsk that his edge should prove true, and slashed at one of the eye stalks; then at the other. Blue blood bubbled as the blinded crab clattered sideways across the room—and blundered into the stone bier.

The impact threw Vakar off its back, breaking his grip on the antenna. He scrambled to his feet, ignoring the painful knock that he had received against the bier, and dodged away from the chelae. The crab set off in the opposite direction until it crashed into the wall. Then it crept slowly sideways, the hinder end of its shell scraping against the stone, until it reached the nearest corner. There it crouched, its chelae raised and spread defensively.

Moving quietly, Vakar picked up the sword he had dropped, sheathed it, and replaced the ladder. One of the rungs had been broken out of it when the crab seized it, and one of the uprights had been cracked by the pinch of the chelae. Vakar looked at it dubiously and then went to fetch the body of Nichok.

He heaved the man up over his shoulder, staggered to the ladder, and began to climb. An ominous crack-ing came from the weakened upright, and he could feel the thing begin to give and turn under his hand and feet. Wouldn't it be just fine if it broke and dumped him down again into the trance-chamber with the crab for company and no way out?

He heaved his way up. Just as the ladder seemed about to give completely, he heard Fual's voice:

"Hold, my lord! I'll pull him up."

Fual reached down and got hold of Nichok. With much grunting and heaving, they manhandled the body up through the hole. Vakar followed as quickly as he could. When he gained the surface above, he sat down with his feet dangling into the hole.

"Just a minute," he said.

He sat having a quiet case of the shakes while Fual whispered: "Let's hurry, sir; that thing outside is still prowling around ... When the crab came at you I was so sure you were a dead man I couldn't watch any longer; but when I looked around again you were putting up the ladder."

Vakar gave a last glance down into the hole. Though no sentimentalist, he felt a little sorry for the crab, crouching in darkness and waiting for the succor of a master who never came.

A few minutes later, they were outside Nichok's grounds, having issued forth by the same tunnel. They pushed down the hinged slab and held Nichok between them, one of his arms around each neck as if they were taking him home from a drunken party. As they staggered along, Vakar limping from his fall from the crab's back, they sang a lusty Lorskan drinking-song:

> With foam-bubbling beer and soul-warming wine,
> We drink to the deities who brought us these
> boons;
> Glory to the gods and well-being to war-
> riors ...

Kurtevan was bent over a heap of yellowed manuscripts, shuffling them back and forth and tracing out their lines of cryptic glyphs with a long fingernail, when Vakar and Fual staggered up the stairs into his living room with Nichok's body between them. They let the body slip to the ground, and Vakar said:

"Here you are."

Kurtevan raised his heavy lids a little. "Good."

Fual went over to Vakar's scrip and began checking its contents, under the contemptuous glance of the thaumaturge. He laid out the rings of gold and the ingots of silver, the copper torcs and celts, and the packets of spice in neat rows on a stool to facilitate counting. Vakar said:

"Well, sir magician, what is the thing the gods most fear?"

Kurtevan finished what he was reading, then rolled up the manuscripts and dropped them into a chest beside his taboret. He raised his head and said:

"The thing the gods most fear is the Ring of the Tritons."

"What is that?"

"A finger ring of curious gray metal, which is neither tin nor silver nor lead, and why the gods should fear it I cannot tell you. This ring is on the finger of the king of the Tritons, one Ximenon, whom you will find on the island of Menê in Lake Tritonis, in the land Tritonia, which lies south of the Thrinaxian Sea. Now you have all the information you need, pray leave me, for I have strenuous magical works to perform."

Vakar digested this speech with astonishment. "You mean—you do not have this thing here?"

"Of course not. Now go."

"I will be eternally cursed—of all the barefaced swindles—"

"That is enough, young man. I do not tolerate insolence, and I have not swindled you. If you remember our conversation, I did not make you any definite promise in return for your help in the matter of Nichok. You said you were seeking the object; very well, I have done what I could to help you by telling you where and what it is."

The fact that the wizard's statement was literally true did nothing to check Vakar's rising anger. He felt the blood rushing to his face as he shouted:

"Oh, is that so? You asked me how much I would pay for the thing itself, and if you—"

"Silence! Get out!"

"After I have taken my payment out of your hide—"

Vakar reached for his sword and took a stride towards Kurtevan. The wizard merely opened his eyes all the way and stared into those of Vakar.

"You," said the thaumaturge in a low voice, "are unable to move. You are rooted to the spot . . ."

To his horror, Vakar found that, as he advanced, he met more and more resistance, as if he were wading in cold honey. By exerting all his strength, he just barely made his next step and got his sword a few inches out of the scabbard. His eyes bulged and his muscles quivered with the strain. He was vaguely aware of Fual, crouched over their trade goods, gaping with an idiotic stare as if he, too, were ensorcelled. Meanwhile the wizard also seemed to strain.

"You are no spiritual weakling," grunted Kurtevan, "but you shall see that your will in no way compares with mine. Stand still while I make preparations for your disposal."

Kurtevan reached behind him and threw a powder into the brazier on the little tripod, which thereupon smoldered and smoked heavily. He picked a staff from the floor beside him and drew lines on the floor with it. Then he began an incantation in an arcane tongue.

Vakar strained like a dog on a leash. Sweat ran down his forehead as with a mighty effort he dragged his right foot a further inch along the floor and pulled his sword a finger's breadth more from the scabbard. Beyond that he could not go; he could not even turn his head or force his tongue to speak.

A shimmer appeared in the air over the diagram that Kurtevan had drawn. As the recondite syllables rolled on, the shimmer grew to a rosy brightness. A spindle-shaped mass of flame swayed and rippled in mid-air. Sometimes it looked vaguely manlike; again it reminded Vakar of a writhing reptile. He could feel its heat on his face and hands.

Kurtevan paused in his incantation to say: "A fire spirit makes an admirable means of disposing of garbage. It is unfortunate that you will not be able to appreciate the full effectiveness of the method—Ho, stay where you are!" he barked suddenly at the flame, raising his staff. "They are dangerous, like captive lions, and must be treated with firmness. You should have departed when I first commanded you, foolish boy. The responsibility is entirely yours."

Kurtevan began speaking to the flame again in an unknown tongue, evidently giving it orders for the disposal of Vakar and Fual. Vakar strained at his invisible bonds with the strength of a madman.

Then, just as Kurtevan was reaching the climax of his conjuration, Vakar saw a movement out of the corner of his eye. Something flew through the air and struck the wizard in the chest, to fall lightly to the floor.

Kurtevan stopped, his mouth open to show his blackened teeth. Then his head jerked back and forward in a tremendous sneeze.

As he opened his mouth for a second sneeze, the flame left its diagram and swooped upon the wizard. Vakar heard a single frightful scream as the body of the sorcerer disappeared in a mass of flame. Then the flame soared up and up until it licked the ceiling. It washed over the beams and the planks of the floor of the third storey, so that they began to blaze fiercely.

The main fire left the smoking body of Kurtevan, now nothing but a twisted black mass of char. The fire being drew itself up to the ceiling, oozed through the widening cracks between the blazing boards, and disappeared, leaving a roaring fire in its wake.

At the instant of Kurtevan's death scream, Vakar had found himself able to move again. A glance showed that Fual was sweeping their trade goods into the scrip. Vakar slammed his sword back into the scabbard, bounded forward even before the fire elemental had entirely disappeared, dug both arms into the open chest beside the burning taboret, and scooped up the mass of manuscripts piled therein. Some of them were beginning to burn at the edges and corners. Vakar held the papyrus in one arm and batted out the flames with the other as he turned for the exit.

He ran down the spiral stairs, Fual behind him. As they raced across the ground-floor chamber, a thunderous crackling above told them that the third-storey floor was giving way. Vakar could see the firelight through the cracks between the planks overhead. They rushed out.

In the yard, Vakar stumbled over the acephalus lying limp. Evidently, on Kurtevan's death, the spirit that animated it had fled. They burst through the gate and ran in the direction of their lodgings, just as people began to put their heads out to see what was up. Somebody banged a gong to turn out the neighborhood with buckets. Vakar doubled around several corners in case anybody should follow them, while behind him flame and sparks erupted out of the top of the tower of Kurtevan the magician.

Fual said: "Sir, these Euskerian wizards are not really gentlemen, or they would be served by proper human retinues and not by these acephali and crabs and such spooks. Why did you pause to gather up that stuff? Are you planning to become a magus yourself?"

"Not I. But I hated to see that arcane knowledge perish, and these sheets should fetch a pretty price among Kurtevan's colleagues, which will give us the means to reach Tritonia . . . Damnation, where are we?"

When Fual's sense of direction had straightened them out, Vakar continued: "I'm sorry about poor Nichok, but it's too late to drag him back to his dwelling now . . . What did you throw at Kurtevan?"

"Our rarest spice, sir. It's from the Farthest East, beyond fabled Thamuzeira. The merchant who sold it to us called it 'pepper'."

X

Lake Tritonis

A MONTH LATER, PRINCE VAKAR AND FUAL ARRIVED IN Huperea, the capital of Phaiaxia. They had followed a trade route that ran up the River Baitis, overland to the headwaters of the Anthemius, and down the latter stream to its issuance into the Thrinaxian Sea. They had had minor adventures: a narrow escape from a lion; another from a wild bull; another from a war party of Laistrugonian savages. At last they had entered Phaiaxia, a peaceful, smiling land where the language (unlike Euskerian) was closely related to Hesperian. After a few days of learning new inflectional endings, Vakar could make a stab at it.

Where the Anthemius widened out into the Thrinaxian Sea stood Huperea: a spacious city of well-built houses instead of the usual combination of stockaded castle surrounded by a huddle of huts. Vakar had no trouble getting through the gates and rode down a broad street flanked by houses, in front of which flowers grew in neat patterns around painted marble statues of gods and heroes. Feeling at peace with the world, Vakar sang as he rode:

In the red sunrise   *stood Vrir the Victorious,*
On a clutch of cadavers,   *splattered with scarlet,*
Declaiming defiance   *in tones triumphant . . .*

"Don't you have poetry in Kerys?" he asked Fual suddenly.

"Yes, my lord, but it's quite different from that of Lorsk. Rhymed triolets instead of this rhythmic alliterative verse with split lines. But I never went in for that sort of thing; I was too busy trying to steal the wherewithal for tomorrow's meal."

"That's your misfortune, for I find that verse provides one of the cheapest and most harmless of life's major pleasures. But here's somebody who can perhaps give us directions."

Vakar pulled up in front of a house where a stocky man sat naked on a bench and worked with adze and saw on a bed frame. He shouted:

"Ho there, my good man, where can I find lodgings for myself and my servant in Huperea?"

The man looked up and replied: "Strangers, if you seek a public inn like those of Torrutseish, know that there is none such here. Our custom is to lodge travellers among the citizens of the town, each in accordance with his rank. For three days you will be entertained without cost, except that you shall tell us freely of the land whence you come and of the world outside of Phaiaxia. After that you must be on your way, unless a pressing reason prevents."

"An interesting custom," said Vakar. "What is its purpose?"

"Thus we receive warning of dangers gathering against us and also learn of markets affording rich opportunities for our merchants. Now, if you will tell me your name and station, I will make arrangements."

The lack of servility in the man's manner suggested to Vakar that the fellow was no slave, as he had supposed, but a citizen of standing. Since his entertainment would be proportioned to his status, Vakar saw no reason to minimize the latter. He said:

"I am Vakar the son of Zhabutir, heir to the throne of Lorsk in Poseidonis."

The man wagged his full beard sagely. "I have heard of Poseidonis and Lorsk, though no Phaiaxian has ever travelled so far west. Stranger, it is proper that you should lodge with me."

The man picked up his cloak, threw it around him, fastened it with an ornate golden pin, and turned to call a servant to take the animals. Vakar was at first taken aback, wondering if the man disbelieved him. Then a horrid thought struck him. He said:

"May I ask who you are, sir?"

"Did you not know? I am Nausithion." As Vakar continued to look blank, the man added: "King of Phaiaxia."

Vakar felt his face reddening as he began to stammer apologies for his condescending tone, but King Nausithion said:

"Tush, tush, you are not the first to make such a mistake. We are a merchant kingdom and make no great parade of rank and precedence as do the Euskerians. And since I am the most skilled carpenter in Huperea, I prefer to make my own bed rather than to hire it done. But come in. You will wish warm baths and change of raiment, and tonight you shall tell your story to the leading lords of Phaiaxia. We believe that a man who can sing as I heard you do cannot be altogether evil."

Vakar found that he was enjoying himself among these hearty hedonists more than any time since the party at Queen Porfia's palace. He had cautiously watched his host's methods of eating and drinking so as not to commit any gaffes like those at Sederado. Here, for instance, it was customary and proper to convey one's meat to one's mouth on the point of one's dagger
. . .

The bard Damodox was singing, to the twang of his lyre, a lay about the lusts of the Phaiaxian gods: what happened to Aphradexa, the goddess of love and beauty, when her husband Hephastes learned of her tryst with the war-god. Vakar had been told that Damodox was the winner of last year's singing-contest, an event as important in Phaiaxia as athletic meets were in Lorsk. The paintings on the walls were the most vivid and realistic that Vakar had ever seen, and the repoussé patterns on the silver plates and beakers were of an incredible delicacy and perfection.

When the bar finished, Vakar said: "Master Damodox, you certainly have a fine voice. Mine cannot compare with it, even though at home I too am considered something of a singer."

The bard smiled. "I am sure that if you had spent as many years in practice as I, you would far surpass me. But such tricks are no credit to a lord like yourself, as they show he has been neglecting his proper business of war and statecraft."

"Are you sure your gods do not mind your speaking so frankly of their peccadilloes?"

"No, no, our gods are a jolly lot who relish a good joke. As a matter of fact, Aphradexa visited me only last night. She had a message for you from one of your western gods: Akima or some such name."

"Okma," said Vakar. "Say on."

"It is hard to remember exactly—you know dreams—but I think this Pusadian god was trying to warn you against a danger that has pursued you many miles, and that will soon catch up with you if you do not hasten."

"Oho! I will bear your warning in mind."

Vakar turned his attention back to his wine. Although he still felt that he had lost his heart to Ogugia, he thought that if he should ever have to leave Lorsk for good, and if Ogugia were forbidden to him because of the death of Thiegos, Phaiaxia would be the country for him. While they did not practice philosophy, they certainly lived well. He liked them and they seemed to like him, which for Vakar Zhu was a sufficiently unusual experience for him to treasure it. Could he get a dispensation from King Nausithion, marry some handsome Phaiaxian wench, and settle down here, and to the seven hells with windy Lorsk?

Then he thought of Porfia, and resolved not to commit himself irrevocably to anything until he had investigated his standing in that direction further.

He jerked out of his reverie with the realization that the king was speaking to him: "And whither are you bound after you leave here, my lord?"

"Tritonia. That lies south of here, does it not?"

"Southeast, rather. What is your purpose?"

If he had not been heated by the sweet wine of the banquet Vakar might have been more cautious, but as it was he told openly about his quest for the Ring of the Tritons.

The king and the other lords nodded, the former saying: "I have heard of that ring. It will take uncommon force, guile, or persuasiveness to get it away from King Ximenon."

"What," said Vakar, "is its precise nature? How does it differ from any other ring?"

A Phaiaxian lord said: "It is said to be a powerful specific against magic of all kinds and to have been cut by a coppersmith of Tartaros from a fallen star in the possession of the lord of Belem."

"Which," added Nausithion, "means it might as well be on the moon, for nobody leaves Belem alive. Tritonia is bad enough . . ."

"What is hazardous about Tritonia?" asked Vakar.

"The situation there is peculiar. There are two dominant peoples in Tritonia, the Amazons who live on the island of Kherronex in Lake Tritonis, and the Tritons who live on the island of Menê. The subject tribes live around the lake on the mainland. Now the Tritons and the Amazons are the men and women of what was once a single nation. In my father's time, they had a great war with the Atlanteans to the southwest of here, which so depleted their supply of fighting men that their king armed their women and defeated the Atlanteans. Then, however, the women, being the more numerous, conspired against the men, and rose against them in one night, stripping them of their arms and reducing them to subjugation.

"This condition endured for several years, with the women ruling and the men doing all the work, not only in field and meadow but in house and hearth as well. At last the men revolted and fled to the island of Menê, where they armed themselves and stood off the women. So now there is war between them, and when a stranger arrives in Tritonia both sides try to capture him—or her—to take to one island or the other. If the visitor is of the sex of that island, they enroll him in their army; if not, they amuse themselves carnally with the newcomer until the latter's powers are exhausted."

"A visit to Tritonia sounds strenuous," said Vakar. "If the men catch you, you are in for a lifetime of fighting, whereas if the women catch you—but what other nations lie near Phaiaxia?"

Nausithion began counting them off on his fingers: "To the east, along the shores of the Thrinaxian Sea, live the Laistrugonian savages who, alas, are not in the least charmed by our sweet songs. In fact their raids have so galled us that we have had to place ourselves under the protection of the king of Tartessia. South of the Laistrugonians lies Tritonia, the land of lakes, where men ride striped horses. East of Tritonia one comes to the Pelasgian Sea, which gives our merchants access to Kheru and Thamuzeira and other far-eastern lands.

"Southeast of Tritonia dwell many curious peoples: the Atarantians who curse the sun daily, instead of praying to it as do most folk, and who refuse to tell their names for fear a stranger should acquire magical power over them; the Garamantians who have no institution of marriage, but couple promiscuously at any time or place like beasts; and many others. Some paint themselves red all over; some dress their hair in outlandish fashion. Among some, at a wedding feast the bride entertains all the male guests in a manner that among most nations is reserved for the groom alone.

"South of Tritonia lies the dreaded land of Belem, and beyond that forbidding mountain-range the Desert of Gwedulia. There dwell only wild beasts and wilder men: the camel-riding Gwedulians who live by herding and robbery."

Vakar nodded understandingly, for of all kinds of men the nomadic herdsman, hardy, truculent, and predatory, was the most feared in his world. Nausithion continued:

"West of Belem, the Desert of Gwedulia sends north an arm called the Tamenruft, separating Belem from Gamphasantia. The Gamphasantians are said to be a peaceful folk with a high standard of ethics—so high in fact that it is unsafe to visit them, for normal mortals find their standards too lofty to adhere to for any length of time. North of them and west of us rises another mountain range, called Atlantis. West of Gamphasantia lies the free city of Kernê, whose merchants are so sharp that ours cannot compete with them, and south of Kernê is Tartaros with its black craftsmen."

Vakar asked: "What is south of the Desert of Gwedulia?"

"None knows; perhaps the traveller comes to the edge of the world-disk of which the philosophers tell and finds the stair leading down to the seven hells. But that is all we know; now tell us of Poseidonis."

Vakar had started an account of the glories of Lorsk (which with patriotic pride he unconsciously exaggerated) when a man came in and said: "My lord King, there are strangers outside who wish to speak to you."

Nausithion swallowed a mass of roast pork to make himself understood. "What sort of strangers?"

"Very odd strangers, sir. They drove up in a chariot. One is a giant who looks like a Laistrugonian but uglier; one is a pigmy with enormous ears . . ."

Vakar said: "Excuse me, King, but I feel unwell. May I withdraw for a moment?"

"Certainly . . . Ho, that is the way to the kitchen!"

Vakar plunged through the door and shouted: "Fual!"

"Yes, sir?" The Aremorian looked up from where he was eating.

"Qasigan has caught up with us. Get our gear and meet me in front, but don't go through the banquet hall."

"You mean to leave?" wailed Fual. "Oh, sir, these are the first people since Sederado who have shown us the respect due our rank—"

"Don't be a bigger fool than you can help. Where are the beasts?"

A few minutes later, Vakar led the four horses around the house to the front. Fual came after him. At the corner, Vakar paused to peer around in time to see the shaggy back of Nji the ape-man disappear into the king's mansion.

"Hold the horses," commanded Vakar.

He picked up a stone and walked towards the chariot hitched to the post in front of the king's residence. Several servants of the Phaiaxian lords clustered there, throwing knucklebones. Vakar strode around them, bent over the near wheel of the chariot, and with one blow of the stone knocked out the pin that held the wheel to the axle.

"Here, you help me!" he said, and such was his tone of assurance that two of the nearer gamblers got up and came over. "Grasp the edge of the chariot and lift."

The chariot was a heavy northern model with old-fashioned leather-tired solid wheels and a frame of elm and ash. The frame rose as the servants lifted. Vakar pulled off the wheel and rolled it ahead of him like a hoop to the corner of the house where Fual waited.

"Help me tie this on this horse," he said.

The servants stared after Vakar but showed no inclination to interfere. A laugh ran through the group as they evidently took the act for a practical joke and went back to their game.

"Now," said Vakar, "to Tritonia, and fast!"

Off they went. Not this time would he settle down in

fair Phaiaxia, forgetting his duty to his land and his dynasty.

"I can't tell whether it's a man or a woman," muttered Vakar, lying on his belly under a bush. "It looks more like a reptile with a man's shape."

He peered around the hill at the figure that sat the oddest horse that Vakar had ever seen: a creature entirely covered with black and white stripes. Behind him, up the draw, Fual held their own horses in a clump of acacias. They had ridden across Tritonia, where the people wore fringed buckskin kilts and goatskin cloaks with the hair dyed vermilion, to the shores of Lake Tritonis.

Vakar wriggled back out of sight of the immobile rider and told Fual: "The thing seems to be covered all over with scales, with a pair of enormous feathers sticking out of the top of its head. I'm sure King Nausithion didn't describe any race of reptile-men in his account of the peoples of Tritonia."

"He might have omitted to mention them," said Fual with a shudder. "I remember hearing the Tritons worshipped a snake-god named Drax. And who knows ...?"

Vakar said: "The only way to settle the question is to capture the thing. Luckily the shrubbery is dense. I'll circle around and come upon the creature from the far side while you creep out—"

"Me? No, my lord! The idea turns my bones to water—"

Vakar caught Fual's shirt in both fists and thrust an angry face into that of the Aremorian.

"You," he said, "shall do as you're told. When you've given me time to approach from the other side, you shall make some small noise to distract the thing's attention, and I'll do the rest. Be ready to rush in and help subdue it."

He was more than ordinarily exasperated by Fual, who still bore the marks of the beating Vakar had given him when Vakar learned that his servant had stolen one of Nausithion's silver plates in Huperea.

A quarter-hour later, Vakar crouched close by the

rider. He had laid aside his scabbard so as not to be encumbered in the kind of attack that he had in mind. Through a tiny gap in the leaves he saw that the scaly skin was a cleverly made armor of reptile hide, covering the entire rider except the face. The rider carried a long lance and a small round shield of hide.

Although Vakar waited and waited, no distracting sound came from the direction of the draw. The striped horse snorted and stamped, and Vakar feared that it smelled him.

At last he could wait no longer. He gathered his feet under him and sprang towards the sentry. The striped animal snorted again, rolling an eye towards Vakar, and shied away. Its rider turned too and began to swing the lance down to level.

Vakar left the ground in a long leap, caught the rider about the upper body as he struck it, and both tumbled to the turf on the far side in a tangle of thrashing limbs. Vakar, recovering first from the fall, slammed his fist into his victim's jaw. The slight body relaxed long enough for Vakar to roll it over and twist its arms behind its back.

"Fual!" he roared.

"Here, sir—"

"Where in the seven hells have you been?"

"I—I was just going to make the noise, my lord,—but it took me so long to work up my courage—"

"I'll deal with you later; meanwhile lively with that strap!"

Vakar indicated the wrists of the rider, which Fual bound. The rider began to struggle until Vakar belted it across the face with his fist.

"Now we'll see about its sex," he said.

The reptile-skin armor opened down one side and was kept closed by a series of thong ties. Vakar fumbled with the unfamiliar knots, then impatiently sawed the garment open with his dagger and pulled the front of it away from the wearer's chest. There was no questioning its femininity.

"Not bad for a warrior maiden," said Vakar, then spoke in Phaiaxian: "You! Do you understand me?"

"If you speak slowly," said the Amazon in a dialect of the same language.

"I wish to make contact with the Tritons, and you shall guide me to their camp."

"Then what will happen to me?"

"You may do as you like, once the Tritons are in sight. Come along."

With her hands still tied and Fual holding the striped horse, Vakar boosted the Amazon back on to her mount. She sat glowering at him with her torso bare to the waist. Vakar handed the shield and lance to Fual, put his own baldric back on, mounted, and drew his sword.

"Which way?" he asked, grasping the Amazon's bridle.

The Amazon jerked her head westward, so Vakar set off along the trail in that direction. After they had ridden for some time he turned his head to ask:

"What do you call these horses with the giddy color-scheme?"

She glared silently until he hefted his sword in a meaningful manner, then sullenly answered: "Zebras."

"And what is that shield made of? The hide of some great beast?"

"A rhinoceros. A beast with a horn on its nose."

"Oh. I saw one of those on my ride thither, like a giant pig. And what do those feathers come from?"

"A bird called an ostrich, found in the Desert of Gwedulia."

"A bird with such feathers must overshadow the earth with its wings like a thundercloud when it flies."

"Ha, it does not fly at all. It runs like a horse and stands as tall as you and your mount together."

"How about your armor?"

"That is from the great serpents found in the swamps around Lake Tritonis."

"Truly Tritonia must be a land of many strange beasts. Yesterday I saw three beasts like our Pusadian mammoth, but hairless— *Hé!*"

Everything happened at once. They had come around a hill to see a group of Amazons trotting towards them along a side road leading up from the lake, which showed blue through notches in the dusty olive-green landscape. The captive Amazon leaned forwards and dug her heels into the zebra's ribs. The animal bounded, tearing the bridle out of Vakar's grasp. The Amazon shrieked something and galloped towards her fellows.

Vakar slashed at her as she went by him. Although he struck to kill, he struck too late; the blade whistled through empty air.

He leaned forward in his turn and galloped. As the Amazons came up to the main road, Vakar and Fual and the spare horses thundered past, going in the same direction as before. A glance showed Vakar that his ex-captive, hampered by her bound arms, had fallen off her zebra. Vakar hoped that she had broken her neck.

Vakar's animals had been traveling all day and so were too tired to keep ahead of their fresh pursuers. Little by little the Amazons gained. Vakar thanked the gods of Lorsk that none of them carried bows; no doubt the scrubby trees of this dry country did not provide good wood for bow staves.

Still, the long slender lances came closer through the clouds of dust. A determined thrust would get through Vakar's leather jack, and even if it did not they would kill Fual and take the spare mounts and the baggage. There were five of them, too many for Vakar to wheel and charge into the midst of them.

A few more paces and they would be up . . .

The pursuers reined in with high feminine cries. Ahead of them appeared a score of riders clad in similar snakeskin armor, with crests of zebra tail instead of ostrich plumes. The Amazons galloped off. Vakar was tempted to do likewise, but reason told him that the panting horses would not get very far. Besides, these were probably the Tritons whom he wished to reach.

As they came up he called: "The gods be with you!"

They surrounded him, long lances levelled, and one said: "Who are you?"

"Vakar of Lorsk, on my way to visit your king."

"Indeed? Our king does not admit every passing

vagabond to his intimacy. You shall enter our service at the bottom and work your way up, if you have the guts. Seize him, men."

XI

The Tritonian Ring

THEY TOOK AWAY VAKAR'S SWORD AND KNIFE BUT missed the poisoned dagger in his shirt. They tied his and Fual's hands, while one rummaged through Vakar's scrip and exclaimed with delight over the wealth therein.

"Come along," said the leader.

Vakar rode slowly in the midst of them, with spear points poised to prod him should he make a break.

"Am I a dog?" he growled. "I am a prince in my own country, and if you do not treat me as such it will be the worse for you."

The leader leaned over and slapped Vakar's face with his gauntleted hand.

"Shut up," he said. "What you may be in another country means nothing to us."

Vakar's face became suffused with blood and he gritted his teeth. He rode silently fuming until they came to the shores of the lake, where a permanent fortified camp was set up. On the lakeward side of the camp, a jetty had been built out into the water, and to this was secured a big shallow-draft galley-barge.

The leader of the Tritons placed his hand against Vakar's shoulder and gave a sharp push. Vakar fell off his horse into the dirt, giving his shoulder a painful bruise. Fual followed his master into the muck, and the Tritons laughed loudly.

While Vakar was struggling into a sitting position, a kick in the ribs knocked him over again, sick and dizzy with pain.

"Get up, lazybones!" said the officer. "And get aboard."

Vakar hobbled down the slope to the barge, while the Tritons made off with his horses and property. He and Fual were prodded aboard, and the boat was cast off and rowed out into the lake. Vakar huddled in the bow, too despondent to pay heed to his surroundings until Fual beside him exclaimed:

"Sir! Prince Vakar! Look at that!"

Something was floating beside the barge: a thing like a great rough-barked log, except that logs do not keep up with galleys by swimming with an undulant motion. Vakar gulped and said to the nearest Triton:

"What is that? One of your great serpents?"

"That is a crocodile," said the man. "The serpents keep to the swamps. The abundance of crocodiles accounts for the fact that although we live on the water, no Triton can swim, for if you fell overboard, that fellow yonder would have you before you could yell for a rope. So think not to escape from Menê by swimming."

Another Triton said: "It would be fun to lower him by a rope and then snatch him out when the crocodile snapped at him."

"Amusing, but it would probably cost us a recruit. Do you not value unlimited commerce with women more highly?"

Vakar mulled over this exchange. The last remark no doubt referred to the Tritons' hopes of winning their war and reducing the Amazons to the status of housewives whence they had risen. It gave him an idea of how to approach King Ximenon. After all, he had helped to negotiate the treaty with Zhysk last year. If he was not overly likeable, his dour reserve gave some folk a trust in his impartiality that they might not otherwise have.

When an hour later they tied up at a similar pier on the island of Menê, the Tritons hustled Vakar and Fual ashore. A small fortified city, also called Menê, stood tangent to the shorefront. The Tritons conducted Vakar to a stockade, thrust him inside, removed his bonds. and left him. Fual they took elsewhere.

Vakar stretched his cramped arms and looked

around. There were about a score of men of various
tribes and races, from a stout ebony-skinned fellow
from Blackland to a towering fair-haired Atlantean.
Most wore ragged clothing and straggly beards.

"Good day," said Vakar.

The men looked at him and at each other and began
to sidle towards him. Soon they were all around him,
grinning. One of them professed much interest in his
clothing, pinching it and saying:

"A gentleman, eh?"

Another gave Vakar a sharp push, which made him
stagger against another, who pushed him back. Prince
Vakar had never been hazed in his life, so this treatment bewildered and infuriated him. At the next push
he shouted: "I'll show you swine!" and hit the pusher
in the face.

He never had a chance to see how effective his blow
had been, because they all jumped on him at once.
They caught his arms, and blows rained upon him . . .

Vakar came to an indefinite time later, lying in a
corner of the stockade. He tried to move and groaned.
His body seemed to be one vast bruise. He inched up
into a sitting position and found that he was nursing a
swollen nose, a split lip, a pair of black eyes, and a few
loose teeth. They must have stamped on him.

He peered through swollen lids at the others, who
huddled on the far side of the enclosure around some
game of chance. For the time being they ignored him.
He chewed his bruised lips with hatred. If he had
thought that he could get away with it he would have
planned to wait until they were all asleep and then to
murder the whole lot with his poisoned dagger. As it
was, he could only huddle miserably and wait for his
hurts to heal. He thought of using the dagger on himself; what had he to look forward to save a life of
deepening misery and degradation?

The sun was low when the gate of the stockade
opened and a man stepped in with two buckets, one
full of water and the other of a repellant-looking barley
porridge. The men crowded around the buckets,
scooping up water and mush with their hands. A cou-

ple of fights broke out. Vakar, though hungry, felt that he had no stomach for such rugged competition in his present state. The turmoil around the buckets subsided as the men stilled their most acute pangs of hunger.

"Here, stranger," said a voice, and Vakar looked up from his broodings to see the black standing over him with an outstretched fist.

Vakar held out his cupped hands and received a gob of mush. The Negro said:

"You did not look as though you could get any for yourself. Next time the boys want a little fun with you, do not be a fool."

Vakar said: "Thank you," and fell to eating.

The following morning the same man came in, this time with an apronful of pieces of stale bread. Vakar hobbled over and snatched up a piece that rolled to his feet out of the scrimmage. He turned back towards his solitary place to eat it when a long arm came over his shoulder and tore the bread from his grasp.

He whirled. The tall blond Atlantean who had taken his bread was already turning away and beginning to eat it, confident in his superior size. He was the biggest man in the enclosure, and Vakar had inferred that he was the unofficial leader.

Vakar saw red. His hand darted inside his shirt and came out with the dagger. A second later he had buried the blade in the Atlantean's broad back. The Atlantean gave a strangled noise, jerked away, and collapsed.

The rest of the men chattered excitedly in a dozen languages. They looked at Vakar, standing over the dead man with the dripping dagger, with more respect than they had shown before. One said:

"Quick, hide that thing! They will be here any minute!"

It sounded like good advice. Vakar wiped the dagger on the Atlantean's leather kilt, took off the harness under his shirt, sheathed the blade, dug a hole in the dirt with his fingers, buried the weapon, and stamped the earth into place over it.

He had hardly done so when a pair of Tritons entered. When they saw the corpse one of them shouted:

"What happened? Who did this? You there, speak!"

The man addressed said: "I do not know. I was relieving myself with my back to the rest, and heard a scuffle, and when I looked around he was dead."

The Triton asked the same questions of the others, but got similar answers: "I was throwing knuckle-bones and was not watching . . . ." "I was taking a snooze . . . ."

"Line up," said the Triton and passed down the line searching the men's scanty clothing. He finally said: "We could torture you, but you would tell so many lies it would not be worth while. Off you go to drill. Lively, now. Ho, you!"

Vakar saw that the Triton was addressing him.

"You looked battered. Have they roughed you up?"

Vakar, who had been limping towards the gate, said: "I fell."

"Well, you need not drill today."

"I am Prince Vakar of Lorsk, and I wish to speak to your king."

"Shut up before I change my mind about the drill," said the Triton, following the recruits out.

Vakar found an uncontaminated spot and sat down wearily. After a while, a couple of slaves came in and dragged out the Atlantean. The day wore on until Vakar became so restless with boredom that he wished that he had gone to drill despite his hurts.

In the afternoon, the men came in again to loaf, gamble, or chatter until the evening meal. Vakar wondered how some of them seemed able to do nothing indefinitely without going mad.

The next day he felt better and went to drill. He found that the men were being taught the rudiments of marching and handling a spear. As an experienced rider and swordsman, he was told off to supervise some of the others. He asked the drillmaster to be allowed to see the king, and was told:

"One more of those silly requests, young man, and you shall be beaten. Now shut up and get back to work."

After about the tenth day, Vakar lost track of the time he spent in the stockade. He learned that life among these unwilling soldiers was on a lower level than he had ever known to exist; no self-respecting savage would live like that. Dirt was ubiquitous and perversations were rampant. The only kindly gesture he ever saw was from the Black on the first day. When he had murdered the Atlantean, the men had protected him not because they liked him, but because they hated him less than they did the Tritons. For their own protection they recognized one iron law: death to tattletales. It was lucky for Vakar that he had not complained about his hazing.

For the rest he found little among them but stupidity and mutual hatred. They seemed for a while to have been willing to take him as their leader, since he had killed the old, but when he did nothing to confirm his title they turned to a swarthy, thick-thewed Atarantian who had gouged out a man's eye in one of the daily fights.

So long as Vakar wore his dagger, nobody molested him. When he had somewhat recovered from the despair induced by his beating, he engaged some of his fellow-inmates in conversation, picking up what information he could about the peoples and customs of the surrounding regions and a few words of their languages. In line with the scheme that he was concocting, he asked what the Tritons deemed their most sacred oath.

"They swear by the horns of Aumon," a small Pharusian told him. "That is some sheep-headed fertility god of theirs. While they break all other oaths, that one holds them. Though why any right-minded people should choose such a stupid and timid beast . . ."

Before a month had elapsed, a day came when the Tritons announced that as the men were now well enough trained, they would be moved elsewhere. But instead of sending Vakar off with the rest, one of them told him:

"You shall see the king after all. Step lively, and bear yourself respectfully in his presence."

"What am I supposed to do? Kiss his butt, or bang my head on the floor?"

"No insolence! You shall kneel until he tells you to rise, that is all."

Vakar was conducted back to the waterfront of the city of Menê and aboard a large red galley. On the poop, in a chair of pretence, sat the man whom he had come to see: King Ximenon, big, stout, clean-shaven, in bright shimmering robes, with a golden wreath on his curly graying hair. Beside him stood a man in gilded snakeskin armor, and a pet cheetah lay purring at the king's feet. On the middle finger of his left hand, Vakar saw, he wore a broad plain ring of dull-gray metal.

The Ring of the Tritons.

"Well?" said the king.

Vakar gathered his forces. "Have they told you who I am, King?"

"Something about your being a prince in some far-western land, but that means nothing to us. We cannot prove you are not lying. Get to your business, or by the fangs of Drax it will go hard with you."

Vakar suppressed an urge to make pointed remarks about his unroyal reception in Tritonia. Back in Lorsk, his sharp tongue was always getting him into trouble, but now that it was a matter of life and death, he found that he could control it. He said:

"All I wish to suggest is that I may be able to end your war with the Amazons."

The king's porcine eyes glittered with interest. "So? Some new weapon or stratagem? I listen."

"Not exactly, sir, but I think I could negotiate a treaty of peace with them."

The king leaned forward with an impatient motion. "Peace? On what terms? Have you reason to think these doxies are ready to surrender?"

"Not at all."

"Then are you proposing that *we* give up? I will have you flayed—"

"No, sir. I had in mind a half-and-half arrangement, whereby each should respect the rights of the other. It might not give you all you would like, but at least thereafter you could strive with them as men and women should strive, on a well-padded bed . . ."

Vakar gave King Ximenon another quarter-hour of argument, with an eloquence that he had not known he possessed. He depicted the beauties of cohabitation until the king, squirming with concupiscence, said:

"A splendid idea! We should have tried it sooner, but after the bloodshed and bitterness between us, no one on either side would make the first move. As an outsider you are in a position of advantage. Queen Aramnê is a fine-looking woman; could you arrange for me to wed her as part of the peace settlement?"

"I can try."

"If you can do that along with the rest, you can practically name your own reward."

"I have already chosen it, my lord."

"Huh? What then?"

"The Tritonian Ring."

"What? Are you mad?" shouted the king, looking at the dull circlet on his finger. "I will have you——"

At that instance the man who stood beside the king's chair leaned over and spoke in the king's ear. They muttered back and forth, and the king said to Vakar:

"Your price is impossible. We will instead give you all the gold you can carry."

"No, sir."

The king roared and threatened and haggled, and still Vakar held out. Finally Ximenon said:

"If you had not caught us at a time when prolonged continence has driven us nearly mad ... But so be it. If you can put this treaty through, you shall have the ring."

"Do you swear by the horns of Aumon?"

The king looked startled. "You have been inquiring into our customs, I see. Very well. I swear by the holy horns of Aumon that if you negotiate this treaty with the Amazons successfully, without impairing our masculine rights to equal treatment, and get me Queen Aramnê to wife, I will give you the Ring of the Tritons. You are a witness, Sphaxas," he said to the man beside him, and again to Vakar: "Does that satisfy you? Good. How soon can you set forth for Kherronex?"

XII

The Horns of Aumon

QUEEN ARAMNÊ WAS INDEED AN IMPRESSIVE-LOOKING woman, as tall as Vakar, with a broad-shouldered, mannish figure clad in a loose short tunic that left one small breast bare. She sat in a chair of pretence on her galley-barge, the torchlight gleaming on the pearls in her diadem, and rested her chin on one capable fist. Vakar guessed her age as the middle thirties. She said:

"Your words are persuasive, Prince Vakar. In fact, a party among us has been urging that we take the initiative in such negotiations. However, before I make my decision, we will undertake a divination to aid us. Zoutha, proceed!"

There was a burst of activity among the attendant Amazons. Some set up a small stand with a copper bowl on it while others dragged in a naked man whom they forced to his knees in front of the bowl. There was nothing to indicate what sort of man he was, and Vakar thought it injudicious to ask.

An elderly woman, who seemed to be high priestess or head sibyl, prayed, and then the man's head was forced down while Zoutha, the old woman, cut his throat so that his blood poured into the bowl. When the man's throat stopped gushing, the Amazons threw the limp body over the side, where the crocodiles soon carried it off.

Zoutha stared into the bowl a long time. She dipped a finger into the blood and tasted it, and said:

"Queen, a thing will almost come to pass."

"Is that all?" said Aramnê.

"That is all."

The queen said to Vakar: "I have almost decided to

accede to your proposal—with a few minor reservations. However, words are not enough."

"Yes?" Vakar wondered what was in store for him this time.

"Before I commit my people to this course, I should like a sample of the benefits offered by King Ximenon."

Vakar's heavy eyebrows rose. "You mean, madam . . ."

"Exactly. You shall attend me tonight." A faint smile touched the queen's frosty face. "I, too, have lost time to make up for."

At least, thought Vakar, this new test promised to be one that he was competent to surmount, even though he had never contemplated it as a method of earning a living.

The sun was well up the next morning when Vakar confronted a wan and peaked reflection of himself in Queen Aramnê's silver mirror as he fumbled for his razor. Behind him, the queen stretched like a lazy lioness where she lay and said:

"Vakar, if some unforeseen accident should remove King Ximenon, would you be interested in—ah—"

"You honor me beyond my wildest dreams, but I fear that duty calls me back to my homeland," he replied, conscious that accidents that happened to his predecessors might some day happen to him also. "By the way, do you Amazons eat breakfast? I could devour one of those beasts you call a hippopotamus whole, I think."

Aramnê sighed. "Men! Before they have their pleasure they will promise anything, but immediately afterwards they rush off, full of plans and bustle, with less thought for their late partner than for their favorite hound or hawk."

For the next few days, Vakar shuttled back and forth between Menê and Kherronex while King Ximenon and Queen Aramnê bargained over the final terms of the treaty: what rights each sex should have in the reunited Tritonian state, the marriage contract between the king and the queen, and other details.

At last all was settled. The royal galleys of the two sovereigns should meet in the lake midway between the islands. To show mutual trust, Queen Aramnê should come aboard the king's galley for the signing of the contract; then the king should board hers for the wedding ceremony and the feast to follow.

The ships met. A dinghy brought the queen across the short stretch of the glassy lake between them. The red ball of the sun was just touching the smooth blue horizon when Aramnê, followed by a small guard of Amazons, clambered up the side of the king's galley.

Sphaxas, Ximenon's minister, spread a big sheet of brown papyrus on a table on the deck and read the terms. The king and queen swore by Aumon and Drax and all the other gods of Tritonia to abide by the terms of the treaty and called down an endless concatenation of dooms and disasters upon their own heads should they fail. Finally (as neither could write) they impressed their seals upon the papyrus and exchanged a kiss as a pledge of amity. Then they turned, the tall woman and the grossly massive man, towards the companionway, laughing at some private joke. Sphaxas followed. Before they put foot over the side, the queen turned her head back and said:

"You shall come too, Prince Vakar. What would the celebration be without the man who did the most to bring it about?"

Vakar followed, grinning. Impatient as he was to get his ring and begone, he saw no harm in one good binge. The gods knew that he had suffered enough in that stinking pen, living on stale bread and barley porridge.

On the queen's ship, a priest of Aumon performed the marriage ceremony. The king cut the throat of a white lamb and let the blood trickle on the altar. He dipped a finger in the blood and marked a symbol on the queen's forehead, and she did likewise to him. All sang a paean to the gods of Tritonia, after which there was much familiar back-slapping and lewd jests. Vakar, feeling thoroughly pleased with himself, said:

"And now, King, how about my ring?"

King Ximenon grinned broadly and pulled the ring off his finger. "Here," he said dropping it into Vakar's palm.

"And now," continued the king, "there is one other small matter we must attend to before proceeding with the feast. Seize him!"

Before Vakar knew what was happening, muscular hands gripped his arms. His mouth fell open in bewilderment as the king stepped forward and wrenched the ring out of his hand.

"I will borrow this," said the king, slipping it back upon his finger. "Strip him for sacrifice."

"Ho!" said Vakar. "Are you mad? What are you doing?"

Ximenon replied: "We are about to sacrifice you to Drax."

"But why, in the name of Lyr's barnacles?"

"For two reasons: First, old Drax has not had much attention from us lately. Curiously, since I came into possession of the ring, not one god has visited me in slumber. Secondly, I have sworn by the horns of Aumon to give you the ring. But I have not sworn to respect your life and liberty afterwards, and I cannot let so valuable a talisman leave the kingdom."

"Well, take the damned thing!" cried Vakar, sweating, as the guards peeled off the gaudy Tritonian raiment that had been lent him for the occasion.

"No, for your giving it to me under duress would not be a true legal gift. On the other hand, when you die, having no legal heirs in Tritonia, your property falls to the throne. Therefore the only way I can legally fulfill my oath and retain the ring at the same time is to kill you."

"Queen Aramnê!" shouted Vakar. "Can you do nothing about this?"

The queen smiled frostily. "It is your misfortune, but I fully agree with my consort. We planned this stroke just now on the king's barge, while you were gauping at the flute girls. And why should you complain? Better men than you have died upon our altars to insure our land's fertility."

"Strumpet!" screamed Vakar, straining in the grip of the guards. "Was my nocturnal performance then insufficient, that you turn me over to this treacherous hyena?"

He went on to shout intimate details of an imaginary liaison with the queen on Kherronex. At least, he thought, he might stir up jealous dissention between his two murderers, and escape in the turmoil or at any rate spoil their pleasure.

The king put on a sardonic smile, saying: "If you had been wise you would have kept your mouth shut and gained a quick death. Now, for slandering the queen, you must receive additional punishment. Flog him."

"How many strokes, my lord?" said a voice behind Vakar.

"Until I tell you to stop."

The first stars were coming out as Vakar's wrists were bound and hoisted above his head, so that he half-dangled with only his toes on the deck. He had sometimes wondered what he would do if flogged and had firmly resolved not to give his tormentors the satisfaction of seeing him weep or hearing him scream.

But when the whip whistled behind him and struck across his bare back, sending a white-hot sheet of pain shooting through his torso, he found it much harder to bear than he had ever imagined. The first blow he took in silence, and the second, but the third brought a grunt out of him, and the fourth a yell. By the tenth he was screaming like all the others, and felt warm blood trickling down his back.

Swish—crack! Swish—crack! He jerked and screeched with each blow, though hating himself for doing so. The pain filled his whole universe. He would do anything—anything—

Then a vestige of his natural craft asserted itself. With a terrible effort he stopped screaming and relaxed, letting his legs bend, his head loll, and his eyes close.

After a few more lashes came a pause. A voice said: "The wretch has swooned. What now, sir?"

"Wake him up," said the king.

The rope that held Vakar's wrists was let run so that he fell at full length on the blood-spattered deck. He continued to play dead, even when a heavy boot slammed into his ribs and when a gout of cold water splashed over his head.

The queen said: "Let us waste no more time on him; I am hungry. Sacrifice him now."

"Very well," came the voice of the king. "Drag him over to the altar. You shall do the honors, Spaxas."

Vakar felt his wrists being untied. He was dragged across the deck to the small altar on which the lamb had been sacrificed for the wedding. Watching through slitted lids, Vakar saw the minister draw the broad knife and try the edge with his thumb, while the king stood nearby, leaning back against the rail.

Vakar relaxed as completely as possible, so that the Tritons had more trouble dragging him than they otherwise would have. When they got him to the altar they asked another of their number to help them hoist him across it, for by Tritonian standards Vakar was a big man.

Then came the moment when the grips on his arms were relaxed, while the Tritons braced their feet and shifted their hands to lift him. In that second, Vakar came to life with the suddenness of a levinbolt.

With a mighty twist and jerk, he broke the loose grips upon his arms, got his feet under him, and dealt the nearest Triton a punch in the belly that doubled the man up in a spasm of gasps and coughs. There was a shout from those watching:

"Watch out!" "Seize him!" "He is—"

Hands reached out from all sides, but before they could fasten on to his naked hide, slippery with sweat and blood, Vakar burst through them. He brushed past Sphaxas, standing open-mouthed with the sacrificial knife in his hand, and as he passed dealt the minister a buffet below the ear that stretched his length upon the deck.

Now one man stood between Vakar and the rail: King Ximenon, three paces away. Vakar strained forward, leaning as if he were starting a hundred-yard sprint, and smote the deck, with the balls of his feet while the hands of the closing Tritons snatched at his bloody back. At the first break, Ximenon had reached for the silver-shafted palstave thrust through his girdle, and as Vakar bounded forward, the bronze hatchet head whipped up and back for a skull-shattering blow.

Vakar left the deck in a diving leap and, as the palstave started down, struck the upper part of the king's body head-first with outstretched arms. The stubble on the king's chin rasped his ear as he caught the king around the neck, and his momentum bore the king back against the crotch-high rail. Down and back went the king's torso and up flew his feet. In deadly embrace, the two men tumbled over the rail into the dark water below.

The Lorskan let go as soon as they struck the water. With his eyes open under water, he saw the cloud of bubbles that represented King Ximenon, the weedy bottom of the queen's ship beyond, and the king's tomahawk gyrating down into the blackness beneath. As his head broke the water, he was aware of a strangled shout from the floundering king through the bedlam that had broken out upon the deck a few feet over his head.

Vakar took a deep breath, dove, and seized a sandalled foot that lashed out from the swirl of robes. He pulled it downward. The king came with it, eyes popping and mouth emitting bubbles. Vakar remembered that Tritons could not swim. Even if Ximenon were an exception, the fact that he was fully clothed and weighted with gold and jewels, while Vakar was nude, gave the latter an advantage. As the king started to rise towards the surface, arms and legs jerking wildly, Vakar pulled him under again.

Then Vakar felt a movement of the water behind him: the fluid pushed sharply at him as if displaced by the passage of a large body. A glance over his shoulder saw an immense crocodile, a forty-footer, bearing down upon them from the murk.

Vakar let go the king to use his arms for swimming just as the crocodile arrived with a tigerish rush. The great jaws gaped and clomped on the still struggling king. A hide of horny leather brushed past Vakar, tumbling him over in the water and lacerating him with its projections. He had a brief impression of the great serrated tail undulating lazily as it propelled the monster past him.

Vakar came to the surface again. As he shook the water out of his eyes and ears, he perceived that he was now somewhat further from the galley, on which people rushed about madly, some yelling for bows, some for spears, and some for oars.

A bowshot away lay the king's galley. Vakar struck out for it, simultaneously trying to think up some specious story.

He swam as he had never swum before, ears straining to hear the first splash of the oars of the queen's galley behind him. He was over halfway to the king's ship when he heard it. At the same time an arrow plunked into the water nearby.

He plowed on. Another arrow came closer. The king's ship was near now; a row of expectant faces lined the rail. Someone called:

"What in Drax's name goes on over there?"

"A rope!" yelled Vakar.

The oars of the king's ship moved too, gently so as not to run Vakar down. A rope slapped across his tortured back. He grabbed it but was too exhausted to climb. At last they dropped a bight for him to wriggle into and hauled him up. He gasped:

"They slew the king! It was all a plot to get him into their hands. They cut the throats of the king and Sphaxas and all the other Tritons and would have cut mine had I not dived over the side."

Exclamations of horror and amazement burst from the Tritons crowding round. An officer of the galley said:

"How do we know you are not lying?"

"Look at my back! Does that look like a fake?"

The captain of the galley roared: "I knew there was some such trick in the offing! Bend the oars; we will sink them before they slip away in the darkness! Stroke! Stroke!"

The galley moved with increasing speed in a path that curved towards the other ship. As the king's barge bore down, the oars of the queen's ship, which had been idle for some minutes, began to move again. But the king's ship was going too fast for the other to dodge. As the former neared its target, a chorus of screams burst from the queen's barge. In the dusk, Vakar could see the Amazons running about, waving arms, and shrieking at the approaching ship.

Crash!

The ram of the king's ship crunched through the side of the other as if it had been papyrus. With a terrible clatter and roar of breaking timbers and a thin screaming of women, the queen's barge broke up into a floating tangle of boards, ropes, oars, gilded ornaments, bright hangings, and thrashing human limbs. The king's ship plowed through the mass and out the other side, ropes trailing from her ram.

As the king's galley turned and headed back towards Menê, Vakar caught sight of a couple of moving objects on the dark surface of Lake Tritonis: crocodiles swimming towards the wreck. He felt a little badly about having caused the deaths of all those Amazons of lesser degree, who might not have had anything to do with the attempt to murder him. Vakar disliked killing women on grounds of waste not, want not. But then, he consoled himself, they were probably all as perfidious as their queen. And what else could he have done?

Though his experience had been exhausting, Vakar Zhu turned his mind immediately to his next step. The Tritonian Ring was gone for good in the belly of a crocodile, but the thing from which it had been cut, the "fallen star" (whatever that was) lay to the south in the realm of Belem. And if one ring had been made from it, another could be.

He must persuade the Tritons to give him back his property and be on his way—quickly, before somebody suggested that the death of King Ximenon had been his fault and they dealt with him accordingly.

Drax said: "The wretch has departed from amongst the Tritonians and is now riding south, with his man-servant, towards Belem. While I cannot foresee events to happen in the neighborhood of Niowat, for reasons you know, I fear that his journey concerns the Ta-hakh."

The gods all shuddered. Entigta gurgled: "Somebody must warn King Awoqqas and set him against this man, or it will be too late." The squid-god spoke to Immut, the god of death of Belem. "Cousin, will you see to the matter?"

Drax glared round the circle and hissed: "I think there has been too much warning—to the wrong party." He looked hard at the Pusadian gods. "Are you sure none of you has been dropping a quiet word here and there to forewarn this Vakar of the doom intended for him?"

Lyr and Okma and the rest looked innocent, and Vakar Lorska cantered across the parklands south of Lake Tritonis.

They crossed wide grassy plains, seeing immense herds of gazelles, antelopes, buffalo, ostriches, zebras, elephants, and other game. They skirted Lake Tashorin, where crocodiles lay in wait in the shallows and herds of hippopotami bellowed and splashed, and finally rode up the dark defiles that led into the rocky range of Belem.

For several days after the Tritons had released him, Vakar had been in his gloomiest mood, seldom speaking save to snarl at Fual, and brooding on his own insufficiencies. Besides the tenderness of his healing back, there was the feeling of defilement and degradation at having been flogged like a mere slave.

Then as the scenery became more somber, Vakar cheered up. He said: "We were lucky to get away from that treacherous crew so easily. You know, Fual, it occurs to me that it must hurt you to be flogged just as much as it does me!"

"And why shouldn't it, my lord?"

"No reason; I've simply never considered the matter. You must hate me for the times I've beaten you. Do you? Be honest."

"No-no, sir. Save when you lose your lordly temper,

you're not a hard master to serve. Most slaves get far more beatings than I."

"Well, I apologize for any beatings I've given you in excess of your deserts." Then Vakar amused himself by singing an old Lorskan lay, *The Death of Zormé:*

Heaped up in hills   lay Bruthonian bodies
When a hailstorm of hits   felled the far-famed one . . .

"There goes another!" He pointed to where a goatherd bounded barefoot from rock to rock, his vermilion-dyed goatskin cloak flapping, until he disappeared. "Why should they all run from us as from a pair of fiends? We're not such fearsome fellows."

"I can't imagine," said Fual, "but I wish you'd never brought me to these dreadful lands of violence and sorcery. Ah, could I but see the gray towers of Kerys and the silver beaches of Aremoria once again before I die!"

The valet wept great tears. Vakar, with a snort of impatience said:

"Do you think I revel in sleeping on the ground and dodging death from wild beasts and wilder men? I'd rather settle down in some civilized city to the study of literature and philosophy, but I don't complain at every step. Having put our hands to the plow we must finish the furrow." He paused. "However, in view of Belem's unsavory reputation, you'd better get out my shield."

With the bronze buckler slung against his back, Vakar felt better, though the sparse inhabitants of this barren land continued to flee from the sight of him.

"Why no houses?" he said. "I never heard the Belemians lived in the open like wild beasts."

Fual shrugged, but when Vakar began another song, the Aremorian pointed and said: "Isn't that a house, sir?"

Vakar guided his horse in the direction indicated. The structure was a round hut of stones, roughly chinked with mud, which blended into the stony landscape. It had once possessed a roof of wood and thatch, but this had been burned off.

Vakar dismounted and kicked a skull that lay near

the threshold of the hut, saying: "That was a child. There must have been war hereabouts. Since we can't get to Niowat tonight, this place will do."

As Fual set up the cooking pot he said: "We haven't seen any of Awoqqas's headless servants, my lord. Let's hope we never do." He struck sparks from his flint and pyrites to start the fire. "Material dangers we've surmounted, but this is the home of the blackest magic in the world."

All was peaceful as they ate their frugal meal, watching the long shadows climb up those cliff faces that were still illuminated. A hyena gave its gruesome laugh somewhere in the hills. Vakar said:

"Look at the horses."

The four animals were tugging at their tethers, rolling their eyes, and swinging their ears this way and that. Both men peered about and up and down, and Vakar's uneasy gaze caught a movement among the rocks. There was a shrill yell and—

"Great gods!" yelped Fual. "Look at them!"

Scores of men popped into view and rushed down the steep slopes, bounding from rock to rock and screeching. Some wore goat skins, some were naked, and all were hairy and filthy. They carried clubs, stones, and boomerangs, and as they came closer the stones and throw-sticks began to whizz through the air.

"To horse!" cried Vakar, vaulting on to his own animal.

A stone clanged against the shield at Vakar's back as Fual scrambled on to his own mount with his usual awkwardness. A thump behind Vakar and a neigh told him that another missile had struck one of the horses. With a quick glance to see that his cavalcade was in order, Vakar set off at a canter along the winding track to the south, hoping that his beast would not stumble in the twilight.

"Now," said Fual mournfully, "we have lost not only that good meal I was preparing for you, my lord, but also our only cooking pot."

Vakar shrugged. "You can steal another."

"Why did they attack us?"

"I don't know; maybe they're cannibals. They kept

yelling a word like *'Ullimen, ullimen'* which as I remember means 'lords' or 'gentlemen.' But if they considered us aristocrats, why should they mob us? This part of the world must be stark mad."

Vakar led the way southward until darkness forced them to halt again. They snatched a cold meal and an uneasy sleep, watching alternately as usual, and took off before dawn.

The mountains became ever steeper and rockier and grimmer-looking. The morning was well advanced when they entered a prodigiously long, deep, and narrow defile, which wound south and up into the very heart of the Belemian Mountains. They rode on and on, winding between the rough steep skirts of the slopes on either side, the rocks sometimes brushing against their legs, the hoof-falls echoing loudly. After a long ride, they pulled up for a breather.

"This seems to go on forev— What's that?" said Vakar, whose ears had picked up the echo of the sound of many men moving. "Are some more of our unwashed friends coming to greet us?"

He set his horse in motion at a walk, peering ahead. The sounds grew louder. After an interminable time, the source of the sounds came in sight, and both Vakar and Fual gave an involuntary cry of astonishment and horror.

The noise came from a group of twenty-odd izzuneg—the headless zombies that served Lord Awoqqas. These were dog-trotting three abreast down the road, carrying copper-headed spears. Behind them a pair of men rode small horses, like sheep dogs herding their flock. These men shouted and pointed at the travellers, and the izzuneg broke into a run, their spears raised and their single pectoral eyes staring blankly ahead.

XIII

The Kingdom of the Headless

VAKAR WHEELED HIS HORSE AND STARTED BACK DOWN
the defile. As he turned, he saw that Fual had already
done so and was going at a reckless gallop, though the
little Aremorian was usually afraid of anything faster
than an easy canter. Vakar could hear the slap of the
bare feet of the izzuneg on the trail behind him. A
glance back showed that he was gaining on the pursuers, and after a few more bends in the defile they
were out of sight. Vakar kept on at an easier pace as
Fual called back:

"Do they wish to kill us too, sir?"

"I know not. How can you judge the expression on a
man's face when he has no face? But that charge
looked hostile. It seems we are not welcome in Belem."

"What shall we do now, sir? Try to find another
road to Niowat?"

"I'm cursed if I know. If somebody in this accursed
land would only stand still long enough to talk to
him . . ."

They rode on until Vakar began to look for the
lower end of the defile. And then—

They came around a bend in the road and almost
ran headlong into another group of izzuneg with a
single mounted man behind them. Again the horseman
pointed and shouted, and the headless ones rushed.

Vakar and Fual whirled again and galloped up the
trail down which they had just come. Behind him
Vakar heard Fual's wail:

"We're lost! We're caught between two armies!"

"Not yet lost," grunted Vakar. "Keep your eye
peeled for a place to climb."

He remembered Kurtevan's remark that the izzuneg

could not look around or up, and the sides of the defile, while steep, were not unscalable. After several minutes of hard riding, he sighted a suitable place. With a warning cry to Fual, he thrust down upon his horse's back with his hands and threw himself into a crouch, his feet on the saddle pad. Then, before he could lose his balance, he leaped up and to the side.

He landed on a ledge six feet above the roadway, skinned a knee, and then went bounding and scrambling up the hillside, sending down a small landslide of rocks and pebbles. Fual panted and clawed after him. Below them the horses trotted a few paces further, then stopped to eat the scanty herbage.

"Hurry up there," gritted Vakar. "And no noise!"

They clambered on up but had not yet reached the top of the slope when Vakar heard the sound of the approaching enemy. The horses snorted and ran off to southward, but in a few minutes were back again. Vakar said:

"Flatten out on this ledge and keep still."

The horses snorted and whinnied as the two groups of izzuneg converged. The animals collected in a solid group, rolling their eyes and showing their teeth. The headless ones trotted from either hand and met right below Vakar, milling witlessly and accidentally pricking each other with their pikes. As they brushed against the horses, these lashed out with teeth and hooves. One headless one was hurled flat and lay still.

The horsemen shouted back and forth over the neck-stumps of their strange force, carrying on a conversation in which Vakar could sense astonishment and frustration. Finally one of them dismounted, gave his bridle to an izzuni to hold, and pushed through the crowd toward the horses. He reached for the bridle of Vakar's own horse.

Watching from his ledge, Vakar felt red rage rise within him. It was bad enough to be attacked and chased by everybody whom one saw in this wretched country; to be stranded afoot and destitute would be worse. And the disparity in numbers would not much matter if he made use of his altitude . . .

"Come on," he muttered and rose to his feet. He

seized the nearest stone of convenient size and sent it crashing down the slope; then another and another. Fual joined him.

The rocks bounded and plowed into the milling mass below. Some struck other rocks and started them too rolling down. Horses screamed; the three men with heads yelled and pointed to where Vakar and Fual, working like demons, were hurling every stone within reach. The bigger stones plunged in among the izzuneg, who did nothing to avoid them, with a sound of snapping spear shafts and breaking bones. Several of the creatures were down. The man who had tried to take Vakar's horses in tow started to push his way back out of the crowd towards his own horse.

Vakar found a precariously perched boulder as tall as himself. He called to Fual, and both put their shoulders against it and heaved. It gave a little with a deep grinding sound, then rolled down the hill after the others. The ground shook with the vibration of its passage, and as it went it started more stones rolling until the entire hillside below Vakar and Fual came loose with a thunderous roar and slid down upon the enemy. Vakar was reminded of a pailful of gravel being poured upon a disturbed anthill.

When the slide stopped, the mass of izzuneg was nearly buried along with the officer who had dismounted. Limbs and spears stuck up here and there among the rocks, and all four of Vakar's horses were more or less buried. At the north end of the slide, the izzuni to whom the dead officer had given his reins still stood holding the horse, while at the other end, the remaining two mounted men still sat their horses.

As Vakar started down the hill, these two leaped off their animals and began climbing up towards him.

"Come on, Fual, your sword!" said Vakar, unslinging his buckler.

He leaped down upon the first of the two. The man bore a small shield of hide and brandished a copper battle adze, while his fellow swarmed up behind him with a stone-headed casse-tête.

As the man with the adze swung his awkward weapon, Vakar slammed his shield into his face. The adze clanked against the thin bronze, and Vakar made a low deep thrust with his sword under both shields. The blade ripped into the man's belly, and he screamed and fell backwards in a tangle of his own guts.

Vakar started for the other, the one with the club, but a stone thrown by Fual flew past his head and struck the man in the chest. The man turned and bounded down the slope that he had just climbed. At the bottom he took off in a great leap that landed him on the back of his pony, and seconds later he streaked out of sight up the gorge to southward.

While the sound of his hooves still drummed in his ears, the Lorskan turned towards the remaining izzuni. The creature had not moved, and did not move even when Vakar climbed over the landslide and faced it. The single eye looked calmly out of its chest as Vakar approached.

"Can you hear me?" said Vakar to the thing in his rudimentary Belemian. Nothing happened.

"Let go that bridle." Still no action.

"Well then, don't!" cried Vakar, and drove his bloody sword into the creature's chest.

The body swayed and collapsed. Vakar snatched at the bridle and caught the horse before it had time to shy away. He tethered it and went back to the rock slide.

Three of his horses were dead and the remaining one had a broken leg. Vakar cut its throat and then chased the remaining horse, the one belonging to the officer he had killed, until he had backed it up against the rock slide and caught its reins. With both animals secured, he went back to the slide. A few of the projecting members of the izzuneg still twitched, but none seemed dangerous. The corpses of the whole men, he noted, were well-dressed in turbans and knee-length tunics of fine wool, with elaborate girdles of woven leather set with semi-precious stones. They also had golden rings in their ears and on their fingers (which Fual promptly took) and were evidently men of substance by the standards of these mountains.

Vakar and Fual sweated for an hour moving the

rocks that had half buried their horses so that they could get at their belongings. With his sword, Vakar cut a haunch off one of the dead horses for food, and by main force they pulled and pushed the live horse at the north end of the slide over the rocks to the south end. Fual said:

"My lord, aren't you going to give up this mad enterprise *now?*"

"And have Kuros taunt me for cowardice? Never! Get on your nag and we'll go on to Niowat."

Vakar did not like his new mount, for it was smaller and, being unused to him and his style of riding, skittish and recalcitrant.

"All the same," grumbled Fual, "there's a word for a man who attacks a hostile kingdom single-handed, and it isn't 'brave'."

Vakar grinned. Though tired, he was proud of having come through one more trial. He said:

"That's all right; some of the greatest heroes have been mad too. As in *The Madness of Vrir:*

Foaming with fury   *he hurled the hatchet*
At his helpless helpmeet,   *whose brains bespattered*
The wattled walls;   *a dreadful deed . . .*

Fual shuddered but said no more.

Next day, a man rode out of the mountains ahead of them and held up an empty hand in a gesture of peace. Vakar let him approach but kept his hand near his hilt. The man spoke a little Tritonian and Vakar a few words of Belemian, so that with effort enough they managed to make themselves mutually understood. The man said:

"I am Lord Shagarnin, and I have been sent by King Awoqqas to welcome you to our land and guide you to Niowat."

"That is kind of Awoqqas," said Vakar. "Were those his servants who gave us such a boisterous reception yesterday?"

"Yes, but that was an error. The gods had warned Awoqqas that a certain Vakar Lorska was approaching from Tritonia, and that the interests of gods and men required that he be destroyed. You are not he, are you?"

"No, I am Thiegos of Sederado," said Vakar, giving the first name that popped into his head.

"That is what the king thought when report was brought to him of what a mighty magician you are, for the gods had specifically described Vakar as an ordinary man of no fearsome powers. So when the lone survivor of this unfortunate attack told how you flew straight up in the air on bat's wings and hurled a mountain upon your attackers by your spells, he thought there must be some mistake. He hopes you will pardon his fault and accept his hospitality."

"I shall be glad to do so," said Vakar.

He understood what had happened: The surviving officer had galloped back to Niowat and, to avoid blame for the disaster, had told a highly colored tale of the battle. Vakar was not sure that Shagarnin or the king would be taken in by his denial of his identity; this looked like an effort to lure him to destruction. Having failed to kill him by brute force, they would now try guile. His previous narrow escapes had made Vakar suspicious almost to the point of mania. He said:

"This is the most remarkable land I have seen in my travels. For example, the day before yesterday we were also attacked, but by savages with heads."

"That is unfortunate," said Shagarnin, eyes opening in something like fear. "It must have been some of our commoners. The disorderly beasts attack the better sort of people whenever they catch one or two alone, so that it is unsafe to travel away from Niowat without an escort. We shall have to send a detachment to wipe out this band."

"Why do your commoners attack you?"

"Because the fools do not wish King Awoqqas to make izzuneg of them. As if such filth had rights!" Shagarnin spat.

"Does he plan to make your whole commonality into these—izzuneg?" asked Vakar, keeping the astonishment out of his voice.

"Yes; it is his great plan. For our king is the world's

greatest magician and has learned that izzuneg make ideal subjects: docile, tireless, fearless, orderly, with no subversive thoughts of their own. He has even found it possible to breed them, though the children have heads like normal folk. Come back in a few years and you shall see an ideal kingdom: The *ullimen,* that is to say us, ruling a completely headless subject population, and everybody orderly and happy."

"It is an astounding idea," said Vakar.

"I am glad you think so. Meanwhile, we have trouble rounding up our subjects for decapitation. As if heads did the rabble any good! And since the making of an izzuni requires a mighty spell, this great design cannot be accomplished all at once. Our poor king labors day and night, so that we who love him fear for his health."

Vakar nodded sympathetically. "The rabble never know what is good for them, do they? I think I understand, however, why that mob attacked us."

"I am glad. But, Lord Thiegos, what is your purpose here?"

"I travel for pleasure."

Shagarnin looked at Vakar curiously. "I cannot imagine traveling for pleasure; but perhaps in your country things are different."

Vakar shrugged. "I understand Awoqqas owns a fallen star?"

"The Tahakh. Yes, he does, but you will have to ask him about it."

As they neared Niowat, Vakar saw more of the round stone huts but few people. Those whom he did see darted into huts or behind rocks with the speed of a lizard fleeing into a crack in the wall. Once he saw a little group of filthy faces peering around a hut with an expression of such concentrated hatred as to make him shudder. As they rode higher up the road, they passed substantial stone houses, which Vakar took for those of the aristocracy.

"Here is the palace," said Shagarnin.

Vakar did not at first see what the Belemian meant. Then he observed a hole in the side of a craggy hill, which dominated Niowat. A bridge of logs with a straw paving crossed a deep ditch in front of this opening. Several izzuneg stood about the entrance with spears.

As the party trotted over the bridge, the hooves of the horses sounded like muffled drums. They dismounted, and an izzuni led the horses away. Shagarnin parleyed with a whole man inside the entrance to the tunnel, then said: "Come."

He led them through a maze of tunnels. Vakar whistled: If the palace was a rabbit-warren of holes dug out of the inside of the hill, Awoqqas had spared no trouble to make it a handsome warren. The walls were plastered and painted with geometrical patterns outlined with nails of gold and silver; no representations of living beings as in Ogugia and Phaiaxia. Every few feet, a yellow oil flame danced on top of a great copper torchère. Vakar passed an izzuni lugging a copper kettle along the corridor and pouring oil into the lamps as he went. Vakar tried to remember the turns and cross-tunnels but soon gave up, saying in Lorskan to Fual:

"I hope we shan't have to leave in a hurry, because we should never get out without a guide."

After much winding and waiting and passing of passwords and pushing through massive doors ornamented with gold and precious stones, Shagarnin led them into a room where several izzuneg stood guard. The nobleman said:

"Take off your weapons and hand them to this izzuni."

As this was a standard regulation for visitors to royalty, Vakar complied. Another izzuni opened a door on the far side and Shagarnin said:

"The king! Prostrate yourselves in adoration."

Coming from Lorsk with its free-and-easy manners, Vakar did not like prostrating himself for any mortal and would have even been choosy about which gods he so honored. Not wishing, however, to become an izzuni over a matter of protocol, he did as he was bid until a squeaky voice said:

"Rise. Shagarnin, show our visitor's slave to the chamber they will occupy, so that he shall prepare it for his master. You—what did you say your name was?"

"Thiegos of Sederado," replied Vakar.

"Fiegos, remain where you are and be quiet, for I am about to perform a divination."

Vakar looked around. The man speaking to him sat on a throne cut in the stone of the side of the chamber, six steps above the floor level. He wore many-colored robes of that shimmery stuff called silk, which Kurtevan had also worn, and which Vakar had been told came from the land of Sericana beyond the sunrise. Awoqqas was a slim, yellow-skinned, balding man with deep lines in his careworn face—commonplace-looking enough except for his size. He was, Vakar judged, less than five feet tall.

In a flash of insight, Vakar realized why Awoqqas sat upon a throne six feet up and why he was beheading the entire commonality of his kingdom. He could not bear to be smaller than his subjects and was therefore employing this drastic method of reducing their stature, so that they should no longer look down upon him in any sense of the phrase.

Not wishing to give Awoqqas any unwholesome ideas, Vakar deliberately slouched to subtract a couple of inches from his own stature.

Awoqqas was staring at a cleared space on the stone floor in front of his throne. On the edges of this space, two small oil lamps with copper reflectors burned. As Vakar watched, an izzuni came in and extinguished the torchères, leaving the chamber illuminated only by the two little lamps on the floor.

The space lit by the lamps, Vakar saw, was marked with a large and complex pentacle. Awoqqas extended his arms towards it, fingers pointing, and muttered a spell in a language that the Lorskan did not know. Gradually the pentacle faded from sight as a phantasm appeared on the illuminated space. The phantasm was a reproduction in miniature of a stretch of sandy desert, across which flowed a mass of riders. These riders bestrode tall humped animals, which Vakar recognized from descriptions as camels. Like the rest of the scene, they were in miniature, man and camel together standing no more than a span in height. The men wore shroudlike black cloths, which were fastened to their heads by head bands and fell away in folds to cover most of their bodies, and the lower parts of their faces were concealed by veils. They carried long spears. Their number seemed endless; as some passed out of sight on one side of the phantasm, others came into view on the other.

King Awoqqas spoke a word, and the phantasm vanished. As the izzuni came in again and relit the torchères, the king said:

"You have seen the army of the Gwedulians marching westward along the southerly borders of my land. I thought they might turn north to attack us; but they are continuing west. I suspect they mean to cross the Tamenruft to assail Gamphasantia."

Vakar said: "Do you mean to warn the Gamphasantians, King?"

"Nay. I have nothing to do with them; I do not wish to antagonize the Gwedulians; and it would do no good, for the Gamphasants pay no heed to outside advice."

"Are they a civilized people?"

"One might say so; they have a capital city and raise their food by farming. In other respects they are very odd. But tell me what you are doing here, Master Fiegos?"

"I am travelling for pleasure, to see places far and strange before settling down. For instance, I have heard of the—ah—unusual customs of Belem, and of your talisman, the Tahakh, and should like to see these marvels with my own eyes."

Awoqqas nodded. "It is proper that the barbarous and disorderly outer lands should send men to learn our superior ways. Perhaps some day they will all be as orderly as we. You have seen the izzuneg, and tomorrow I will have you shown the fallen star. There is a fascinating story of how it got into my possession after it originally fell in Tartaros. But—you are something of a magician yourself, are you not?"

Vakar made a modest gesture. "Not compared to you, my lord King."

Awoqqas nodded with the ghost of a smile. "That is the spirit I like. Most travellers are insufferable braggarts and disorderly to boot. But I cannot continue this audience, because I must be about my great work."

"Making more izzuneg?"

"Precisely. It is the greatest feat of thaumaturgy in the history of magic. By it, I not only reduce my subjects to order; I please Immut, the god of death and the greatest of all the gods. Now, you may watch me eat as a mark of special favor." The king clapped his hands.

"Is this the usual time of dining in Belem?" asked Vakar.

"*My* usual time is whenever I hunger. As I remain underground nearly all the time, the revolutions of the heavenly bodies mean little to me save as their astrological aspects affect my magical operations." As an izzuni came in with a tray of food and drink, the king added: "Shall I have you served also?"

"Pray excuse me. My stomach has been upset, and I am fasting to let it settle." Vakar's real reason for declining the offer was fear of poison.

The king ate for a few minutes, then said: "Perhaps you would like livelier entertainment," and to the izzuneg: "Send in Rezzâra and a musician."

As the headless servant went out, Vakar asked: "How do you control those beings? How can they hear you without ears?"

"They do not hear with material ears. When you speak to one, your thoughts are perceived directly by the sylph animating it. The sylph will, however, obey only me or one whom I have expressly delegated to command it; otherwise a fearful disorder would ensue. Ah, here is our most accomplished dancer. Dance for the visitor, Rezzâra!"

Two people had come in: a small Belemian with a tootle-pipe and a woman. The latter was young and voluptuously formed—a fact that was patent at once, for she wore nothing but an assortment of rings, beads suspended from ears, neck, and waist. This bracelets, anklets, and pendants of jewels and amber gaudery clattered and clicked as she moved.

The little man sat cross-legged on the floor and began playing a wailing tune, which reminded Vakar of the music that Qasigan had played in Sederado when he had brought the serpent to life. Vakar braced himself for some such marvel, but all that happened was that Rezzâra went into a sensuous dance. She sank to her knees before him, leaning back and looking up through half-closed lids, her arms writhing like serpents. Had he been alone with her . . .

As it was, he had to sit with the blood pounding in his ears while Rezzâra strove by all the arts known to the dancing girl to stimulate him to madness. She had a trick of making her breasts jiggle while all the rest of her remained immobile. He could feel his face flushing and was not displeased when Rezzâra finished her act with a prostration in front of Awoqqas and ran out, her ornaments jingling. Her accompanist followed.

"A splendid performance," said Vakar sincerely.

"Yes, she, too, is among the wonders of Belem. Now I must return to my labors. You shall hear when it is convenient for you to be shown the Tahakh."

"Thank you, sir," said Vakar, making his bellyflop.

An izzuni at the door handed Vakar back his sword and guided him through the maze of tunnels to a chamber lined with gay-colored cloths, which concealed the cold rough rock behind them. There was a substantial bed with a kind of canopy over it, a couple of stools, and a niche in the wall in which stood an ivory carving of an ugly Belemian god. Fual, who had been sitting on one of the stools, rose and indicated a tray of food and a jug of wine.

"Now where," said Vakar, "did you get those?"

"I stole them from the king's kitchen while the chief cook's back was turned. As the under-cooks are all headless, they presented no problem. Let me pour you some of this wine. Sour stuff, but better than water."

Vakar sat down upon the edge of the bed saying: "I could use a little, after my interview with the wizard-king."

"How did it go, sir?" said Fual, handing his master a brimming silver cup.

"I thought I'd seen everything, but—"

A knock interrupted. Vakar called: "Come in!"

The golden rivets of the door glittered as it swung inward to reveal Rezzâra the dancer, who said: "Send your servant away, my lord Thiegos. I would speak to you alone."

XIV

The Naked Puritans

FUAL LOOKED ALARMED, BUT VAKAR HITCHED HIS sword around and said: "Go on, Fual. What is it, Rezzâra?"

Fual went out. Vakar tensed himself but reflected that at least he need not worry about her whisking a dagger from her clothing. Any weapon that could be concealed in her costume would be too small for anything but cleaning finger nails.

She waited until the door closed, then said: "Lord, when do you plan to go?"

"I had not planned. Why?"

"Take me with you! I can stay here no longer."

"Huh? What is this?" Vakar's suspicions were at once alert.

"I hate King Awoqqas and I love you."

"*What?* By Tandyla's third eye, this is sudden!"

She blinked her large dark eyes at him. "I cannot endure that fiend, with his fanatical notions of order, and I burned with passion for you from the moment I saw you. Oh, take me! You shall never regret it!"

"An interesting idea," said Vakar dryly, sipping his wine, "but how should I carry it out?"

"You are a man. You can overcome obstacles. What are you really here for?"

"To see the sights."

"I do not believe that. You wish to steal the Ta-hakh."

"The Tahakh is certainly valuable. Would you like some wine?"

"No! All I wish is for you to crush me in your strong arms and cover my eager body with your burning kisses." She writhed at him.

"You are nothing if not explicit, Rezzâra. But—"

"Do you seek the Tahakh? Do you?" She grasped his wrist in both her hands and shook him.

"I have come a long way to see it."

"If I show it to you, to do with as you wish, will you take me?"

"If I can," he said, stroking his mustache.

She stepped over to the niche in the wall and lifted out the ugly ivory image. Behind it Vakar glimpsed something dark.

"There," she said. "Take it yourself, but be careful not to get it near me. Its touch is said to make women barren."

"Hm." Vakar advanced cautiously and looked into the niche. There lay what looked like a stone: about the size of two fists, a dark brown that was almost black, and rough and pitted on its irregular surface.

He extended a finger. When nothing happened, he continued to advance his finger until it touched the stone. It felt colder than he would have expected. He grasped it and lifted it out with a grunt of surprise. It must weigh well over ten pounds.

He turned the thing over and found a place where tools had worked upon it; evidently to saw or chisel off the small piece from which the smith of Tartaros had made the Ring of the Tritons. He gazed at it in wonder. So this was what a star looked like up close? He would have expected something bigger. He asked:

"Are you sure this is the Tahakh?"

"Quite sure."

"Why does Awoqqas leave it in such an accessible place? One would think to find it in an underground chamber guarded by an army of izzuneg and a couple of dragons."

"He is a man of strange quirks. Perhaps he thought if it were left practically in the open nobody would notice it. But let us talk of other matters, my lord."

She lay back on the bed, stretching luxuriously. "You will soon realize you have never known what joy life can hold. Come kiss me!"

She held up her arms. Well, thought Vakar, why not? Life did not go on forever, and in this career of adventure into which he had been pitched it was likely to be even shorter than otherwise. He laid down the Tahakh, lifted his sword belt off over his head and laid baldric and scabbard beside the fallen star, and picked up the silver wine cup for one more swallow.

He stood by the bed, holding the cup in his hand and looking down at Rezzâra's sleek, olive-skinned form, from which the jewels winked up, adorning without concealing. He realized that these ornaments represented enough of an asset to take a traveller a long way . . .

And then the wine-cup dropped from Vakar's limp fingers as a horrifying change took place before his eyes. The girl's head faded from view, leaving her nothing but a female izzuni.

"Rezzâra!" he called sharply.

A faint voice—Rezzâra's, but barely audible, sounding inside his skull, replied: "Come, my love, let us take our fill of passion . . . I burn for you . . ."

He leaned over and passed his hand through the air where her head had been. It met no resistance. He could not quite force himself to touch the downy neck stump. Again that tiny voice sounded in his head, like the cry of a distant bird flying off into the sunset:

"So—you know? Do not blame me, stranger, for I am but a wandering sylph, constrained by Awoqqas's will. He cast a glamor upon this body to beguile you. If you wish, you may still . . ."

The suggestion was never completed, for a sound over Vakar's head caused him to look up and then to jerk frantically back as a great net detached itself from the canopy. It fell down upon the bed and was drawn tight over Rezzâra's body. One of the ropes brushed Vakar's hair as he leaped, and at that instant the door flew open.

In rushed a squad of izzuneg, unarmed, with hands

outspread to clutch, and behind them came the little king.

Vakar stooped for his sword. His right hand snatched up the scabbard while his left touched the Tahakh. He rose, whirling to face the intruders with both objects, and hardly knowing what he did he hurled the heavy stone over the izzuneg at Awoqqas, then drew his sword just as the izzuneg reached him. There was no time for thrusting. Sidestepping, he struck right and left, slicing open torsos and reaching arms. The izzuneg, spraying blood, came on anyway. Hands clamped upon his arms . . .

The grip of the hands relaxed. All the izzuneg, with a faint exhalation of breath, slumped to the floor in a tangle of bare brown bodies. Looking across the shambles, Vakar saw the king lying near the door with his head staved in. And in his mind the thin voice of the sylph that had animated Rezzâra sounded:

"The spell is broken and we are all free . . . Thank you, stranger, and farewell . . ."

Vakar stood staring stupidly, his mind wandering, until Fual burst in, crying: "What's happened, my lord? I was in the kitchens, where this king ordered me to go, when all the headless ones fell dead! Isn't that the king, dead too? And who's that on the bed? Have you cut off her head? I should not have thought that of you, sir . . ."

"She never had any, poor thing," said Vakar slowly. "She was an izzuni like the others, but Awoqqas put a spell upon her to make her look like a whole woman. Thinking me a great wizard, he sent me into the room containing the Tahakh with the intention that I should touch it and lose my magical powers. Then Rezzâra should lure me on to the bed. The door has a spy hole, and the king meant to watch me through it and drop the net over us both, as in that myth about the goddess Aphradexa that fellow sang of in Huperea. Then Awoqqas would rush in to secure me, no doubt to turn us into izzuneg. But I'm no wizard, and the wine showed me Rezzâra's true shape."

Fual's teeth chattered. "What now, sir?"

"Collect our stuff and get out."

Fual leaned over the body of Rezzâra, cut the ropes of the net with his dagger, and started stripping the carcass of its ornaments. The bodies began to stink of decay with unnatural rapidity. He said over his shoulder:

"My lord, whither now?"

"Since the smiths of Tartaros seem to know how to make things of this star-stuff, I thought we should go there."

"To Blackland? But they *eat* people!" wailed the Aremorian.

"Not all of them, and we're too lean to be appetizing. Roll the Tahakh up in our blanket."

A few minutes later, they were walking the corridors, Vakar prowling in the lead with buckler before him and sword out, Fual clumping behind. Here and there they passed the sprawled corpse of an izzuni. Once a whole man brushed past them and ran down the corridor, his sandals slapping. Vakar gazed after him, then whirled as another charged around a corner.

"Halt there!" cried Vakar, stepping in front of the man. He recognized the fellow as his acquaintance Shagarnin, who had guided them to Niowat. The Belemian tried to dodge past, but Vakar held his arms out. "How do you get out of here?"

The man breathed heavily and his face was distorted with fear. "Izzuneg all dead," he gasped. "The commoners are up in disorder and are tearing all the *ulli-men* to bits! Let me go—they will kill me—they will kill me—"

"Stand still!" shouted Vakar. "Tell me how to get out of here or I will rob the commoners of that pleasure!"

"Go the way I just came—turn right, then left, then go straight . . ."

"Where are our horses?"

"Paddock off to the right as you come out the entrance, but the rabble will be there. Let me go . . ."

"Why not come with us? You would have some chance to save your worthless life."

"No—I am afraid—they will kill me—" Shagarnin

ducked under Vakar's arm and raced down the corridor as his predecessor had done.

"Hurry," said Vakar, setting a pace that Fual with his burdens could scarcely follow.

As they neared the entrance to the tunnel-palace, Vakar became conscious of a buzzing sound as of an overturned beehive. When the tunnel entrance came in sight, he was struck by the red glow around it. It would, he reflected, be just about sunset.

But the glow was not sunset, though the sun had already set behind the peaks. The redness was the light of the fires that were burning the houses of all the *ullimen* of Belem. Here and there in the city below the palace lay little groups of bodies of both sexes and all ages, stripped and mutilated, while a crowd of several hundred commoners danced shrieking around the burning houses. In one place, Vakar saw a group gathered about an aristocrat whom they had tied to a tree and were skinning alive; another group was torturing a young girl with fire. The stench of rotting izzuneg combined noisomely with that of burning human flesh.

"Let's go quickly," said Vakar, and led the way to the paddock, where lay another clump of dead izzuneg.

An outburst of yells from the mob below caused Fual to look back: "They've seen us, sir! They're coming this way!"

"Well, help me catch these damned animals!" snarled Vakar.

Presently they had rounded up three of the least skittish, bridled them (the Belemians rode bareback) and lashed their load to one. The screams of the approaching mob grew louder.

"Our only chance is to go through them at full speed," said Vakar. "Ready?"

He slapped his horse's rump with the flat of his sword, and the animal started as if bitten and bounded out of the paddock. The commoners were swarming all around the entrance to the palace; some were pushing into the tunnels, while a group of others was coming towards the paddock. The yells redoubled in volume. A stone struck Vakar's shield with a clank and another glanced off his helmet.

The horse tried to leap over the side of the path, but Vakar hauled it back with brutal jerk, knowing that if they tried to gallop down the steep hillside they would surely be unhorsed. He forced the animal right at the screeching savages, who tumbled out of the way as he leaned forward, howling like a demon himself and cutting right and left. He looked one of them in the face: a face covered with dirt and matted hair, out of which a pair of bloodshot eyes glared insanely. He struck at it and felt the blade bite into the skull; felt his horse stumble on the body and jerked the reins to bring the beast's head up . . .

They pounded across the echoing bridge and down the main street of Niowat, skimming through the scattered crowds, and then they were out of town. Behind them the yells of the commoners died away, and the flames of the burning houses vanished around the bends in the road.

Vakar said to Fual: "I've never been for pampering the commoners, but neither is there any sense to oppressing them to madness. Cutting off all their heads, forsooth! No wonder they wished to flay Awoqqas and his nobles. The only sad thing is that they will in their stupid fury have destroyed all the amenities of civilized life in Belem, so that there will remain nothing but wretched savages, unable to rise from their own filth . . ."

They were riding towards Lake Kokutos, the chief body of water in Gamphasantia. They had retraced part of their route from Tritonia to Belem and then turned off westward at Lake Tashorin, skirting around the northern end of the Tamenruft. The tropical midsummer sun glared down cruelly upon them from a cloudless sky.

Fual said: "Let's hope these next people won't be even worse company. The strange nations have been getting worse and worse ever since we left Phaiaxia. Ah, that was a fine land! Are you sure about these Gamphasantians? They're said to be unfriendly to strangers."

"I'm not worried. I met one in Sedarado who

seemed decent enough, even if he did try to murder me, and if I can warn them of the attack by the Gwedulians, I should earn their gratitude."

Fual shuddered. "If the Gwedulians haven't got there before us. Why not go straight home, sir? We have that lump of star-metal . . ."

"Because I'm minded to have this lump made into rings and things, and the smiths of Tartaros are the only men who can do it. Are you thinking of that promise of freedom I made you?"

"Y-yes, sir," said Fual, mopping his forehead.

"Don't worry; I keep my word . . . These Gamphasants keep good-looking fields, don't they?"

They had left the sands of the Tamenruft behind them and were cutting into the meadowlands of Gamphasantia. Vakar sweated in the August heat, though he had stripped down to mantle and loincloth. In the middle distance, a tall naked brown man hoed his patch with a stone-bladed hoe. Ahead, a hamlet of mud huts took form out of the haze.

"Hé!" cried Vakar.

As they entered the hamlet, people rushed out of the huts and surrounded the three ponies in a jabbering mass. All were tall and slender, with curly black hair and narrow aquiline features, and all were nude and burnt nearly black by the sun. Dogs ran barking around the edges of the crowd.

"Stand back!" shouted Vakar, drawing his sword. He repeated the warning in all the languages he knew. "Get away from those animals!"

When they paid no attention, he whacked one with the flat to clear a path. With an outburst of yells, the mass closed in. Before he could strike again, Vakar felt himself seized in a dozen places and ignominiously hauled from his horse. Out of the corner of his eye he saw Fual being likewise dismounted. He gritted his teeth in rage; what a fool he was!

The Gamphasants hauled Vakar to his feet and wrenched the sword out of his hand, but did not strike him. A wrinkled, leathery-looking man, with a white beard and a melonlike potbelly, stepped in front of Vakar and spoke to him.

Vakar shook his head. "I don't understand."

The oldster repeated his inquiry in other languages and finally in broken Hesperian:

"Who are you?"

"Vakar of Lorsk."

"Where is Lorsk?"

Vakar tried to explain, but gave up with a vague gesture towards the northwest.

"You come with us."

The old man gestured, and a couple of younger ones slipped a noose over Vakar's head and another over that of Fual. These nooses formed part of a single rawhide rope, whose ends were held by several husky Gamphasants. Under the old man's direction, these now started along the road towards Tokalet, dragging the travelers with them. Others led the horses. Vakar, masking his fury, asked the old man why they were being so treated.

"Foreigners no live in Gamphasantia," was the reply.

"You mean you will kill us?"

"Oh, no! Gamphasants good people; no take life. But you no live."

"But how—"

"Is other ways," chuckled the patriarch.

Vakar wondered if that meant that they would toss Fual and himself into a cell to die of starvation, thereby achieving their end without personally slaying their guests. He tried to tell the old man about the Gwedulians, but the latter either had never heard of the desert raiders or did not care about them. They walked all day until Vakar's feet were sore, spent the night in another mud-hut village, and the next day set out with another escort. Thus they were passed from village to village until they came to Tokalet.

Tokalet, on the marge of sparkling Lake Kokutos, was a sprawling unwalled town, essentially a mud-hut village on a larger scale. Vakar shambled down a broad street in his noose, eyeing blank walls of sun-baked brick. Few of the folk were abroad in the heat of the day, and those few looked stolidly at the prisoners.

Vakar was dragged into some sort of official building. He listened uncomprehendingly to a colloquy between the leader of his present escort and a man who sat on a stool in a room, and then was stripped and shoved into a cell with a massive wooden door, closed by a large bolt on the outside. The door slammed shut, the bolt shot home, and they were left in semidarkness.

The door had a small opening at eye level with wooden bars; a similar opening served as a window on the opposite side of the cell.

"Well, sir, now you have got us in a fix!" said Fual. "If you'd only—"

"Shut up!" snapped Vakar, cocking a fist.

But then he relaxed. Their energy had better be put to uses other than fighting each other, and he had resolved not to hit Fual any more over petty irritations. He prowled around, scratching at the soft bricks with his thumbnails and wondering how long it would take to claw one's way through the wall. The window gave a restricted view across the main street of Tokalet. All that could be seen was another mud-brick wall opposite, and occasionally the head of a passing pedestrian. (The Gamphasants seemed neither to ride nor to use chariots, and Vakar had seen no metal among them.) The window also revealed that the wall was at least two feet thick.

At the other opening, that through the door, Vakar started back with a grunt of surprise. Another cell stood opposite this one, and through the grille in its door a fearful face looked into Vakar's. It was huge, apelike, and subhuman, and at the same time vaguely familiar.

"Ha!" said Vakar. "Look at that!"

Fual got up from where he crouched and looked, raising himself on tiptoe. He said:

"My lord, I think that's the ape-man we saw in Sederado, or another just like him."

Vakar called: "Nji!"

A low roar answered.

"Nji!" he said again, then in Hesperian: "Do you understand me?"

Another roar, and the thump of huge fists against

the door. Vakar tried various languages; but nothing worked, and he finally gave up.

Vakar Zhu had seen enough nudity in his life not to be impressed by it, but he still found the sight of the nation's highest court meeting in that state incongruous. It was the morning after his arrival in Tokalet.

His interpreter said in Hesperian: "You are accused of being a foreigner. What have you to say to that?"

"Of course I am a foreigner! How can I help where I was born?"

"You may not be able to help where you were born," said the judge through the interpreter, "but you can help coming to Gamphasantia, where it is illegal for outlanders to trespass."

"Why is that?"

"The Gamphasants are a virtuous people and fear that commerce with barbarian nations would corrupt our purity."

"But I did not know about your silly law!"

"Ignorance of the law is no excuse. You could have inquired among the neighboring nations before you so rashly invaded our forbidden land. We will therefore stipulate you are a foreigner. Next, you are accused of carrying weapons in Gamphasantia. What do you say?"

"Of course I carried a sword! All travelers are permitted to in civilized countries."

"Not in Gamphasantia, which is the only truly civilized country. As no Gamphasant ever takes life, there is no reason why anybody should go armed, save when a farmer in an outlying region is allowed a spear to drive off lions. We agree, then, that you are guilty of carrying this murderous implement I have here before me. Next, you are accused of wearing clothes. What say you?"

Vakar tugged at his hair. "Do not tell me that too is illegal! Why can you not let folk do as they please?"

"If such a shocking anarchistic suggestion were followed, we could never maintain our standard of ethics. Clothes are worn for three reasons: warmth, vanity, and false modesty. Gamphasantia is warm enough to make them unnecessary, and vanity is such an obvious sin that we need not discuss it. As for the third motive, found in some barbarous nations, the gods made the human body pure and holy in all its parts, and it is therefore an insult to them to cover any part as if it were shameful. We will therefore agree that you have worn clothes. But we are just people. If you object to this trial or the conduct thereof, speak before sentence is passed."

Vakar cried: "I do indeed have something to say! I could have skirted your country, but chose to enter it instead to warn you of a deadly danger."

"What is that?"

"Do you know of the Gwedulians?"

"A barbarous tribe, I believe, who live far to the east around Lake Lynxama. What about them?"

"A great army of Gwedulians is nearing Gamphasantia across the Tamenruft on camels, to assail and plunder you."

"How do you know this?"

Vakar told of his séance in the throne room of King Awoqqas. The judge pulled his scanty beard and said:

"It might or might not be true, but it makes little difference."

"Little difference! The difference between life and death!"

"No; you do not understand us. We deem it unethical to oppose aggression by force; why, we might cause the death of one of these Gwedulians! If they come, we shall show them there is nothing worth stealing—no gold or jewels or fine raiment or such gewgaws—except food which they might have for the asking. Then we shall courteously ask them to leave, confident that, faced by our greatness of soul, they will do so."

"Oh, is that so? Judge, the usual wont of such robbers is to kill first and discuss ethics afterwards. If you do not—"

"The gods will take care of us. Once previously raiders came out of the eastern deserts, and before they reached our land a sandstorm overwhelmed them and killed the lot. Another time an army of Gorgons marched up the Kokuton River to attack us, and a plague smote them in the marshes so only a few fled back to the Gorgades. However, we cannot continue this interesting discussion because I have other cases to judge. I find you guilty and sentence you both to be placed in the arena this afternoon with the ape-man Nji, and then that will happen which will happen. Take them away."

"Ha!" shouted Vakar. "You speak so virtuously of never taking life, but if you shove me into a pit with that monster it is the same thing—"

The attendants dragged Vakar, still shouting, out of the courtroom and back to his cell.

XV

The Arena of Tokalet

"HELLS!" GROWLED VAKAR AS THE BIG BOLT SLAMMED home again. "This time it looks as though they had us."

Fual said: "Oh, my lord, say not that, or I shall die of despair even before the ape rends us! You've gotten us out of worse fixes . . ."

"That was mostly luck, and any man who presses his luck too far will at last run out of it." Vakar kicked the wall, hurting his toes. "Ow! If this were a civilized country, the door would have a bronze lock to which you might steal the key, but I have no idea of what to do about that great stupid bolt."

They settled down to a despondent wait, but before they had sat staring for long, Vakar heard the bolt drawn back. In came a young Gamphasant.

"Master Vakar!" said this one in Hesperian. "Do you not know me? Abeggu the son of Mishegdi, in Sederado?"

"I am glad to see you," said Vakar. "I did not know you without your clothes. What brings you here?"

"Hearing two foreigners were to be tried today, I came to watch and recognized you. I tried to catch your eye, but you were otherwise occupied."

"You find us in a sad state indeed, friend Abeggu. What is your tale? How goes it with you?"

"Far from well."

"How so?" asked Vakar.

"My travels unsettled many of the ideas with which I started out, and when I returned home I imprudently went around telling people how much better things were done abroad. As any such talk is frightful heresy to a Gamphasant, I was ostracized, and for months nobody would have anything to do with me. If my family had not let me have access to their food stores, I should have starved. Now, though folk are beginning to ease up, they still look down upon me as one corrupted by foreign notions. But what brings you to this doom?"

Vakar outlined his travels since leaving Sederado, adding: "What happened in Sederado after Thiegos's body was found?"

"I do not know, for like you, I went into hiding and fled at the first chance after my wound healed."

A rumble came from the cell across the corridor. Vakar said: "That thing across the way looks like the giant servant of Qasigan, that wizard who tried to kill Porfia and me—"

"It is indeed Nji! Not many days ago, Qasigan and his ape-man came to Gamphasantia in a chariot. They were not stopped when they first appeared, as you were, because they raced through the villages and because the peasants were afraid of the chariot, most of them never having seen a wheeled vehicle. However, as they entered Tokalet, their way was blocked by an ox-drawn sledge, and the people seized them. The ape-man slew three with his club before they threw a net over him. It was intended to expose them in the arena to the attentions of a lion we kept for the purpose, but the next day there was a great hole in the wall of this cell and the wizard was gone, no doubt with the aid of his magic. You can see where the wall has been closed up with new bricks.

"When the ape-man was thrust into the arena, he

wrenched the door out of its sockets and broke the lion's back with it. Then it was decided that as Nji was more beast than man, it would be more just to keep him as the national executioner in place of the lion he had slain."

Vakar said: "Why do you kill people in this unusual manner? For such a peaceful people it seems like a bloodthirsty amusement, watching men eaten by lions."

"It is no amusement! We are required to attend as a salutary moral lesson. Since our principles forbid us to kill undesirables ourselves, our only alternative is to let a beast do it."

"Quibbling!" said Vakar. "If you force a man into a pit with a lion, you are as responsible for his death as if you had sworded him personally."

"True. We Gamphasants, being an honest folk, admit it, but what can we do? Our ethical standards must be maintained at all costs, or at least so think most of my people."

"What happened to Qasigan's other servant, the one with the ears?"

"I visited Qasigan in his cell—did I understand you to say he had tried to kill you and the queen?"

"Yes; he brought the serpent throne to life with his damned piping. But go on."

"I did not know that and supposed him merely an old acquaintance. Besides I do not often get a chance to converse with foreigners, and after my travels I find my own folk dull.

"Qasigan told me he had been following you—he did not say why—with the aid of this Coranian, whose ears served not only to hear sounds of the usual sort but also to hear men's unspoken thoughts—even though the men were miles away. Thus so long as he followed you closely enough, Yok could always tell what direction you were in. You left Huperea at such a clip that for a while you were out of Yok's range, but the King of Phaiaxia had told Qasigan you were bound for Tritonia—"

"Curse the old rattlepate!" cried Vakar, but then remembered that he had no cause to blame Nausithion, whom he had not sworn to secrecy. Abeggu continued:

"They had a hard time getting to Tritonia. First you stole a wheel from their chariot, which took them many days to replace, and then the vehicle kept breaking down and getting stuck. Qasigan may be a mighty magician, but he is no wainwright. In Tritonia, the Amazons captured this odd trio and took them to Kherronex.

"The warrior women had just chosen a new queen to replace the old, who had died in some confused sea battle wherein the king of the Tritons had also perished. Now, the Amazons extend the ultimate in female hospitality to any male they catch. Nji performed nobly, serving the queen herself; Qasigan begged off on grounds of loss of his magical powers; but poor little Yok succumbed under the strain of so much love-making and died."

"I can see how he might. What then?"

"Without the Coranian, Qasigan lost the trail, as nobody among the Amazons knew whither you had gone. Therefore he escaped from the Amazons by magical means and started homeward."

"How did he do that?"

The Gamphasant's melancholy face lit up with a rare smile. "He cast upon them the illusion that an army of lovers came to visit them: tall beautiful men with great—ah—thews. These phantoms told the Amazons they loved them but would not consummate their love until Qasigan were safely ashore on the mainland, and so he set out for our land."

Vakar grinned. "I imagine the girls were in a rare rage when their promised gallants faded away. Go on."

"Well, Qasigan came hither as I have told you. When I saw him he was in a gloomy state, fearing that, even should he escape his present predicament and win back to the Gorgades, King Zelund would take off his head because of his failure.

"However, let us concern ourselves with methods of saving you, for I have no wall-shattering magic like that of Qasigan. I have a plan, though. If, when you enter the arena, you take three paces straight out from the door and dig in the sand, you will find two broadswords. These I brought back from my travels, but I had to hide them or the magistrates would have had them thrown into Lake Kokutos."

"Why are you helping us?" asked Vakar.

"Because you once spared my life in Sederado when, by your principles, you were entitled to take it."

"If we beat Nji, what then?"

"It will give us time to plan something else while the consuls send men to catch another lion. This is a hard land to escape from, being flat treeless country with few places to hide; and horses are not tamed here."

Vakar mentioned the impending attack of the Gwedulians. Abeggu shook his head, saying:

"The judge's action is what I should have expected. Even if he had wished to defend the land by force, what could he have done? The folk have no weapons and would not know how to use them if they had, for they have been taught weapons are accursed things."

"Could you not appeal to the king?"

"We have no king. There is a hereditary senate of big landowners—my father is a senator, which is how I could travel—and every year the people elect two consuls. As these consuls are men of conventional Gamphasantian outlook, it would do no good to appeal to them."

Vakar said: "I believe some free cities like Kernê are governed like that. Judging from your people, the masses are not enough aware of their own interests for the scheme to work."

Abeggu shrugged. "It might work if they could all read, and if papyrus were so common every family could own a scroll containing the wisdom of the race. But here writing is deemed an evil foreign innovation, and all knowledge is handed down by word of mouth. However, I must go now to bury those swords, or it will be too late."

He called to the jailer, who came with his assistants to unbar the door. Vakar, watching Abeggu's departing back, said:

"It's nice to know we have one friend in this hog wallow of a country. Cheer up, Fual; we're not dead yet ... Yes?"

The jailer had placed his face against the grille and was saying: "What is this?"

Vakar took a look. The fellow had the Tahakh in one hand and held Abeggu's arm with the other. Using the latter as interpreter the jailer explained:

"We have burned your clothes and thrown your weapons into the lake, and your other possessions we have placed in the common store, but we do not know what to do with this. What is it?"

"Tell him," said Vakar, "it is a talisman—you know, a good-luck piece."

The jailer went off, staring at the heavy blackish mass, and Abeggu departed likewise. Then Vakar had to put up with Fual's nervous chatter. One minute the little man was boasting of what such puissant heroes as they would do to the monster; the next he was giving garrulous tongue to abysmal despair:

". . . last night I dreamed of a goat that ate three blue apples while reciting poetry, which undoubtedly means we shall be slain, sir. Ah, why didn't you let me go when I asked you in Gadaira? Never shall I see the golden spires of the Temple of Cuval in Kerys again . . ."

Vakar was tempted to cuff his man about to silence him but forebore, thinking how sorry he would be if he did and then Fual did die in the arena after all.

Under the blazing tropical sun, the sand of the arena glared whitely in Vakar's eyes. He put a bare foot upon it, then hopped back with a yelp.

"That's hot!" he said.

"Out you go," said the jailer behind him. "Or must we push you?"

"Come, Fual," said Vakar, setting his teeth against the heat of the sand. "We should have toughened ourselves by walking barefoot on hot coals, like the devil-dancers of Dzen."

A door opened in the far end of the arena, and Nji slouched in with the same old brass-bound club over his shoulder. Vakar took three paces quickly and started to dig.

"Help me, ass!" he snarled at Fual as his sifting fingers met nothing solid.

Nji swaggered closer. Vakar was too busy scrabbling in the sand to notice the elliptical plan of the arena, the tiers of mud-brick benches, and the silent brown crowd.

"Ha!" His fingers struck metal. An instant later he and Fual were on their feet facing the ape-man, each with a broadsword in hand. A murmur of surprise came from the spectators.

"Remember," said Vakar, "our only hope is a head-long attack. If we run in under his club quickly enough, one of us at least may get home before he knocks our brains out. Ready?"

Vakar tensed for a dash. Nji took hold of his club with both hairy hands and opened his great mouth.

"Go!" cried Vakar, sprinting.

Nji gave a roar and charged—but not at Vakar. He ran at an angle, in pursuit of Fual, who in a spasm of panic had dropped his sword and run towards the side of the arena, apparently with the idea of climbing up among the spectators.

Vakar struck at the ape-man as the latter lumbered past him but missed; then doubled, leaning for the turn and cursing his servant's cowardice under his breath. Fual had almost reached the wall when Nji caught up with him and brought the club down in a mighty blow. Fual's skull crunched and his brains spattered. And at the same instant, Vakar came up behind Nji.

With no time for a survey of the towering hairy back, Vakar bent and struck a powerful backhand draw-cut at the monster's leg just above the heel, then sprang back just as Nji started to turn. As the creature put weight on his hamstrung leg, the member buckled under him. He fell with a ground-shaking thump. Vakar sprang in again to slash at the ape-man's throat. The great teeth snapped and an arm caught Vakar's ankle and hurled him to the ground, almost dislocating the attached leg.

Vakar rolled over in an effort to twist free, but the bone-crushing grip held fast. Feeling his foot being drawn towards the ape-man, Vakar looked and saw that the creature was about to stuff the appendage into his gaping mouth. The Lorskan doubled and twisted, planting his other foot against Nji's chest to give him a purchase and, getting a grip on Nji's shoulder-hair with his free hand, hacked at the hairy hand that held his ankle.

Nji screamed shrilly and let go the ankle but instantly caught Vakar's right arm in one hand and his hair with the other. This time the monster began to pull Vakar's head towards his jaws while it scratched and kicked at his body with its great splay feet.

Vakar grasped Nji's thick throat with his right hand, not to choke the ape-man (a task far beyond his strength) but to hold off the slavering fangs, which wanted to tear off his face. Meanwhile his left arm was furiously driving the sword into Nji's chest and belly. Again and again he stabbed, but the ape-man's immense strength seemed undiminished.

Although the muscles on Vakar's lean arms stood out like iron rods, little by little his right arm bent as the ape-man drew him nearer. Blood and spittle ran over his gripping hand, and the creature's foul breath blasted into his face. The tusks gaped closer.

At last he drove the sword into the gaping mouth itself, and up through the crimson palate—and up—and up . . .

Nji relaxed with a shudder as the bronzen point broached his brain. For an instant Vakar, battered and worn, lay panting on the baking sand, his blood and that of the ape-man running over his skin in big red drops. The front of Nji's body was covered with wounds, any of which would have killed a man.

Then Vakar staggered to his feet. He was covered with blood and dirt and some of his hair had been pulled out. His ankle was swollen and discolored where Nji had wrenched it, and the scratches from Nji's toenails on his belly and legs stung like a swarm of hornets. When a glance showed him that Fual was patently beyond help, he turned towards the exit.

He found himself facing a crowd of Gamphasants with nets and ropes in their hands. For an instant he considered trying to cut his way through, but gave up that idea. Though he killed two or three, the rest would overpower him and then things would only go harder with him. A similar crowd had issued from the other entrance, the one through which Nji had come.

"All right," he said in his rudimentary Gamphasantian. "I will come quietly."

The jailer, scowling, asked: "Where did you get that sword?"

Vakar smiled. "The gods visited me in dreamland and told me where to dig. Does this make me the official executioner?"

"No. Nji was made executioner because he was more beast than man, and the Gamphasants, being a just people, do not punish dumb brutes for breaking laws beyond their comprehension. You, however, are not only a man but also an intelligent one, and must therefore pay the full penalty as soon as we can get another lion."

Vakar limped back to his cell feeling forlorn. Poor Fual would never see the silver beaches of Aremoria again. The little fellow may have been a snob, a coward, and a thief, but he had been faithful in his lachrymose and unreliable way. Vakar would keenly miss a man to tote his burdens and listen to his jokes and songs. He regretted the beatings he had given Fual because of the latter's incurable thievery; for all his faults, Fual had saved his life in Torrutseish, which counted for more than a bookkeeper's balance of virtues and vices.

The tears were running freely down Vakar's own face when his cell door opened and in came Abeggu lugging a ewer and a towel. The Gamphasant said:

"You did a great deed, and I am sorry your servant was slain. I cannot spend much time with you, for I think I am suspected of having a hand in this affair. I asked my father if he would intercede to free you, but he said he had got in enough trouble by letting me travel abroad contrary to the traditions of the Gamphasants and would do nothing."

"I hope," said Vakar, "you can think of something before the next lion arrives."

"I will try, but I am not hopeful."

"How about a tool to dig through the wall?"

"No good. The jailer comes into your cell every day, and since Qasigan's escape, one of his assistants walks continuously around the outside of the prison. But we shall see."

And off he went, leaving Vakar feeling let down. He thought some bitter thoughts about fair-weather friends; but then he reflected that Abeggu had already saved his life once at some risk, and he had no reason to expect the man to do it over and over.

In the morning, Vakar was awakened by a distant murmur. Still stiff and sore from the previous day's ape-handling, he called the jailer:

"Ho there, Nakkul! What is happening?"

The prison seemed deserted. Vakar went to his window but could see nothing. The murmur grew and the heads of several Gamphasants shot past Vakar's window, going at a run. Now Vakar could distinguish shrieks of pain and terror.

If anyone were here to bet with, he thought, I'd wager ten to one the Gwedulians have come. And then the bolt of his cell door thudded back and the door creaked open. Abeggu, standing in the doorway, cried:

"The Gwedulians are slaying us! Flee while you can!"

"Good of you to remember me," said Vakar, hurrying out.

"The consuls went forth unarmed to welcome them, and these fiends slew them with javelins . . ."

In the jailer's office, Vakar paused to glance around on the slim chance that some of his belongings might still be there. It was no easy thing to flee forth in a strange country without clothes, arms, or trade goods. He saw none of these, but in one corner lay a dark lumpish thing: the Tahakh. He snatched it up by the knob at one end and turned down the short corridor that led out.

At that instant, a Gwedulian stepped into the entrance, a few paces away. The intruder wore the usual head cloak and face veil. On his left arm was strapped a small round ostrich-hide buckler, which left his left hand free, and in both hands he carried a long copper-headed spear. Before he could do more than stare at the newcomer, Vakar heard a shriek beside him and saw that the Gwedulian had thrust his spear deep into the brown belly of Abeggu, who seized the shaft with both hands.

Vakar took three long steps forward, swinging the Tahakh down, back, and up in a circle at the end of his straight left arm. The Gwedulian tugged on his spear, but Abeggu still gripped it. Then the Gwedulian released the shaft with his right hand to fumble for a hatchet in the girdle of his breech-clout. Before he could pull the shaft free, the Tahakh descended on his head with a crunch. Down went the Gwedulian.

Vakar looked back at Abeggu, who lay huddled against the wall of the corridor, still clutching the spear shaft, though the Gwedulian's tug had pulled the head out of the wound.

"Can you walk?" asked Vakar.

"No. I am dying. Go quickly."

"Oh, come along! I will help you," said Vakar, though in his heart he knew that men seldom recovered from a deep abdominal stab.

"No, go. It will do you no good to drag me, for I shall be dead soon, and you will merely get yourself killed if you try."

Muttering, Vakar tore the head-cloak and veil off the dead Gwedulian and put them on. Under them the nomad was a lean dark man, physically much like the Gamphasants, with his head shaved except for a scalp-lock. Vakar also took the man's sandals but left the corpse its breech-clout, feeling squeamish about putting so foul a garment against his own skin. He appropriated the buckler, the ax with the head of polished stone, and the spear. Then he took Abeggu by the arm and tried to drag him down the corridor, but the man shrieked, crying:

"Go on, fool! You can do nothing for me!"

Vakar gave up and hurried out the door, feeling a mixture of guilt at leaving Abeggu and relief at not having to haul the wounded man to safety.

In front of the entrance knelt the Gwedulian's drom-

edary. Vakar glanced up and down the street. Gamphasantian corpses lay here and there, and other Gwedulians rode hither and thither in pursuit of live victims,
riding them down with their lances or hurling javelins
into their backs. A swirl of pursuers and pursued raced
past Vakar while the camel sat placidly chewing its cud.
A hundred paces upstreet, a knot of dismounted
Gwedulians was raping a woman *seriatim*.

Vakar approached the camel in gingerly fashion.
The beast looked at Vakar from under long eyelashes,
its jaw moving with a rotary motion. A wooden frame
fitted over the hump on its back, with a foot-long piece
of wood sticking up in front. A kind of blanket was
fastened over and under this frame, and from the sides
of this saddle hung a quirt, a quiver of flint-tipped javelins, a large goatskin booty bag, and smaller bags containing food and water.

Vakar gathered up his meager booty and climbed on
to the camel's back, trying to assume the Gwedulians'
posture. The Tahakh and the ax he dropped into the
large bag. But how to make the creature go? Several
commands produced no result; he knew no Gwedulian.
Finally he unhooked the quirt and struck the camel on
the rump. Nothing happened, so he punched the beast
with his fist.

The camel's hindquarters rose with such suddenness
that Vakar was pitched off its back on to his head in
the roadway. He saw stars and wondered for an instant
if his neck were broken. When he rolled over and got
to his feet the camel was standing beside him, still chewing. Its legs were hobbled with a tackle of braided
rawhide to keep it from running away.

Now how should he mount the creature without a
ladder? He tried speaking to it and tapping it here and
there with the whip, hoping to persuade it to kneel
again, but the camel stood masticating while the wrack
of conquest and massacre swirled past it.

At last Vakar untied the hobble, planted the Gwedulian spear in the ground, and hauled himself up hand
over hand, kicking and straining. He took hold of the
spear and whacked the camel with the whip, whereupon it grunted and started up with a jerk that nearly

unseated him for the second time. He found that a camel did not trot: it paced, jerking its rider from side to side until Vakar thought he would fly to pieces. In his present bruised and battered state, the motion was torture. He clung to the post in front of the saddle, and by sawing on the reins got his mount headed out of Tokalet.

The sounds of massacre died away behind Vakar as the camel racked along the road that followed the shore of Lake Kokutos southward.

XVI

The Wizard of Gbu

VAKAR ZHU RODE ALONG THE MARGIN OF LAKE KOKU-tos, seldom seeing a living person. Sometimes he passed through a village, but either it was deserted or Gamphasant corpses lay about, showing that the Gwedulians had arrived before the inhabitants had time to flee. In the stifling heat, the bodies became noisome in a few hours, so that Vakar learned to detour such settlements.

The few live Gamphasants he saw fled screaming at the sight of his head cloak. Bands of camel-riding Gwedulians paid him no heed save to call an occasional hail. When he came upon a group of them in a sacked village, he stopped to watch them manage their camels. When he rode on he at least knew the tongue clicks used to make the animals kneel and rise.

When the food in the Gwedulian's provision-bag ran low, Vakar killed an abandoned cow and, using the copper head of his lance and his stone ax, cut the more accessible portions of the meat into narrow strips across the grain. After hours of sweaty work, he hung a hundred pounds of these strips on the camel's saddle to dry. Thereafter, until the beef was jerked at the end of the following day, he rode amidst an opaque cloud of buzzing flies and blessed the voluminous head-cloak for keeping most of them off his person. He would have preferred a nice compact pig, but the Gamphasants did not seem to keep them. In fact, he had not seen a pig, barring the big wild tuskers of the inland savannas, since leaving Phaiaxia. When the beef was dried, he scraped the flies' eggs off it with his nails and stowed it in his bags.

Vakar had always been accustomed to travelling with a lavish equipage of spare clothes, toilet articles, weapons, and trade metal, and one or more menials to carry the stuff. Now that the Gamphasants had stripped him down to fundamentals, he learned that one can live on a much simpler level, with practically no worldly goods save a supply of food or means for getting it. He never learned to like it, though. He missed Fual keenly.

Because of the terror incited by his costume, he had less trouble on this leg of his journey with men than with his mount. Though a tame and tireless beast, able to eat anything in the plant line, it was also stupid and unresponsive, quite apt unless watched to stop short in the middle of a morning's run, fold its long legs (pitching Vakar over its head) and settle down to a placid session of cud-chewing.

By painful experiment, Vakar mastered the art of camelitation. To make the camel go, one waved the whip where the animal could see it; to stop it, one pulled the reins and hit the beast over the head with the butt of the whip. Its racking pace was hard enough; its walk was worse, bouncing less but jerking the rider back and forth and from side to side in a labyrinthine pattern; while its gallop was impossible to endure for any time.

Vakar missed Fual and somberly pondered on the bloodshed that had dogged his track. Surely the gods had it in for him. Nearly everybody who had been friendly to him—Queen Aramnê, Fual, and Abeggu of Tokalet—had come to a violent end. What curse lay upon him? He was not a bloodthirsty man, but one who only asked to be allowed to go about his business in peace . . .

As Vakar neared the southwest end of Lake Kokutos, the farms thinned out and the signs of Gwedulian violence ended. Vakar took off the stifling face veil and stopped the camel within earshot of a goatherd, who did not seem to have heard of the invasion, for he did not run away. With their few words in common and much sign-language, Vakar learned that beyond the end of the lake, a track continued across the sandy wastes to the Oasis of Kiliessa, and beyond that one came to the Akheron River, which flowed to the sea. The goatherd had never heard of Tartaros and its black craftsmen, but Vakar was sure that he could find that region once he reached the Western Ocean.

Two days later, Vakar rode over a rise into sight of the Oasis of Kiliessa. A glance showed human beings moving among the palms. Tired of hearing no voices but the yap of jackals, the laugh of hyenas, and the gargling groans and grunts of his camel, he rode rapidly down the slope with a hail on his lips.

As he neared the oasis, there was a stir of activity and mounted figures came out towards him: three men on asses, beating their beasts along. As they came nearer, the leading rider nocked an arrow and let fly just as he passed the camel. The shaft grazed Vakar's face, tearing a two-inch gash in his cheek at the edge of his beard.

Vakar was so caught by surprise that he did not even try to dodge the arrow, but then he moved quickly. The second and third men each held a bundle of javelins in one hand and poised a single such dart in the other as they came closer. The second man's javelin struck the saddle-frame. Vakar, holding the saddlepost with one hand, leaned over and drove his lance into the third man just as the latter threw. The javelin went wild, and the man's ass continued its rocking gallop, the man clawing at the spear so that the shaft was wrenched out of Vakar's hand.

Vakar turned the camel around, slipped the ostrich-hide buckler over his forearm, and started back towards his assailants, pulling Gwedulian javelins out of their quiver. The first two attackers had turned also. As they came close again each loosed a missile as Vakar threw two in quick succession. Vakar caught the arrow with his shield; the other foe's javelin struck the camel. One of Vakar's javelins missed while the other struck the archer's donkey, which bucked with such violence that it pitched its rider off into the sand.

The man whom Vakar had speared had now fallen off his ass. The remaining rider took to flight, galloping off into the desert. The archer got up and started to run. The Lorskan followed him, throwing flint-headed javelins until the man collapsed with five of the things sticking in his back. Then Vakar knelt his camel, walked over to the man, and brained him with the stone ax.

Vakar took stock. The man he had speared lay dying with bloody froth running from his mouth. The wounded ass was disappearing over the sky line, while the unwounded one had fallen to nibbling on a desert shrub. Vakar examined the camel and found the stone-pointed javelin stuck into the shoulder-muscle. He pulled the dart out; the camel bled a little but chewed its cud without appearing to notice the wound.

Vakar picked up his spear and cautiously approached the palm-trees. The other human occupants of the oasis comprised twelve naked Negroes: nine men and three women, fastened together by means of a set of wooden yokes strung together like a chain. One named Yoju spoke some Hesperian, the universal trading-language of the coasts of the Western Sea. Yoju explained:

"We are from between the Rivers Akheron and Stoux, but inland from that land you call Tartaros. The chief of the Abiku (may his wives bear scorpions) enslaved us and sold us to these traders, who were taking us to Kernê. We hope your lordship will not slay us."

Vakar asked: "Why did the traders attack me?"

"Because they greatly fear Gwedulians, who slay all who come across their path. Thinking you a scout for a party of raiders, they thought their only chance was to kill you before you could fetch your fellows."

More useless bloodshed! Vakar leaned upon his spear in thought. He could use a couple of stout slaves and would have had no great compunction about so employing these people. But as a practical matter he could not use all of them, for being afoot they would slow him to a walk. They would be of little use chained, and if he unshackled them they would likely murder him in his sleep and flee. Even if Vakar had been willing to butcher all but one of the Negroes in cold blood (which he was not), that one might still stave in his skull with a stone some night.

"What," he asked, "would you do if you had your choice?"

"Return to our homes!"

"Then hear me. I am no Gwedulian, but a traveler on his way to Tartaros. I am minded to free you. Have you enough food to take you back to settled country?"

"Yes."

"In addition I need a servant to accompany me to Tartaros. If *you*" (he indicated Yoju) "would like to ride home instead of walking, you may come with me, earning your food and fare. If I release you and carry you as far as Tartaros, will you swear by your gods to serve me faithfully until I find the man I am seeking there?"

The man swore. Vakar freed the Negroes, stripped the corpses, and rounded up the unwounded ass. He found that he had acquired a good woolen tunic to cover his nakedness, several gold rings and a fistful of copper torcs, and a bronze sword: a two-foot chopper with a double-curved blade like a Thamuzeiran sapara.

As his own wound had begun to sting abominably, he looked at his reflection in the water of the oasis. The luxuriance of his beard, now all matted on one side with dried blood, startled him. He thrust his face into the water, to wash away some of the blood and dirt, and pinned the edges of the wound together with a small golden pin that he had found among the effects of the dead traders.

One of the Negroes spoke to Yoju, who translated:

"He says that as whites go you are a good man, and if you ever come to his village you need not fear being eaten."

"That is kind of him," said Vakar dryly. "If you are ready we will set out."

He mounted the camel and signaled it to rise. Yoju mounted the ass and together they started southward. The remaining Negroes waved after them.

Twenty days later, Vakar arrived at Tegrazen, at the mouth of the Akheron, and once again heard the boom of the surf. The town was formidably walled against a possible Gorgon raid. The language was similar to Gamphasantian and Belemian, but many of the people spoke Hesperian. The houses were mixed: some of the mud-brick Gamphasantian style, some stone Kernean-type dwellings, and some beehive thatched huts like those of the Negroes to the south. The population was equally mixed: tall brown Lixitans, bullet-headed yellow-skinned renegade Gorgons, bearded Kerneans, Tartarean blacks, and all intermediate shades.

Vakar thrust through the teeming tangle, towing his camel. The town boasted an inn, where Vakar took a place on a bench with his back to the wall. (He had made a habit of doing so ever since his experience in the house of the Ogugian witch Charsela.) The innkeeper set down big blackjacks of tarred leather and filled them with barley beer from a gourd bottle. Vakar was setting down his mug when he observed a curious expression in the eyes of Yoju.

"What is it?" he asked.

Yoju pointed. Vakar craned his neck and saw, on the end of the bench, a man dressed as a Kernean trader, a horny-skinned fellow with a full black beard speckled with gray—but the man was less than two feet tall. This midget was drinking barley beer too, but out of a child's cup.

When the innkeeper came to refill Vakar's blackjack, the latter jerked a thumb, saying: "What on earth is that?"

"Him? That is Yamma of Kernê. When his accident happened, he did not dare return home but settled in

Tegrazen as a dealer in metals. Would you like to know him? He is a friendly little fellow."

"I should indeed," said Vakar.

The innkeeper picked up the midget by the slack of his tunic and set him down upon the table in front of Vakar, saying: "Here is a traveler named Vakar Lorska, Yamma, who would like to know you. Tell him the story of your life: tell him what happened to you when you told that witch-doctor he was full of ordure."

"I should think it was obvious," said Yamma.

"What witch-doctor is this?" asked Vakar.

"Fekata of Gbu, the greatest smith of Tartaros. If I had known who he was and had not been drunk, I should have been more careful."

"Tell me more of Fekata. He sounds like the man I seek."

"It is said he can pull down a star from heaven with his tongs and hammer it into shape on his anvil. He is headman of Gbu, in the middle of the peninsula of Tartaros, halfway to the Abiku country. When you find him, spit in his soup for me, though he will probably turn you into a scorpion for your trouble."

Gbu was, like all Tartarean towns, a cluster of beehive huts, whence came the barking of dogs, the yelling of children, the tinkle of the bells hung round the necks of a Kernean trader's asses, and the buzz and clang and clatter made by the craftsmen of Tartaros as they plied their trades. Vakar threaded his way among the stalls of woodcarvers, bead-drillers, jewel-polishers, shield-makers, and goldsmiths until he found the premises of Fekata, headman of Gbu, smith, and wizard.

Fekata had his smithy in an open shed alongside the clump of huts that served him and his wives for a home. A fresh leopard skin hung at the back, drying in the sun. A young Negro tended the furnace, while in the middle of the shed Fekata himself hammered a bronze axhead into shape with a stone-headed sledge hammer. He was a middle-aged Negro of about Vakar's height, but much broader, with a prominent potbelly and the most massive and muscular arms that Vakar had ever seen. One eye was blinded by a cataract, and a short grizzle of gray wool covered Fekata's head.

As Vakar approached, the smith looked up and stopped hammering. The buzz of flies became audible in the quiet. Vakar identified himself and asked:

"Are you he who made a ring from the metal of a fallen star?"

"That is true, and if I ever catch the blackguard who swindled me out of my price on that job . . ."

"What happened?"

"Oh, it was long ago, though I, Fekata of Gbu, do not forget such things. There was a beggarly trader from Tritonia, one Ximenon, who had been in the Abiku country when the thing fell with a great flash and roar and buried itself, and he had tracked it to the spot and dug it up. He promised me enough ivory and gold to break the back of that camel of yours if I would make him a ring of the metal of the star.

"I did, though it took a crocodile's lifetime to learn how to work the stuff. Then when he had the ring he started off on his ass as jaunty as you please. 'Ho,' said I, 'where is my price?' 'Come to Tritonia when I have made myself king and I will pay you,' said he, and away he galloped. I threw a curse after him that should have shriveled him to a centipede—not knowing then that the star metal was a protection against all magical assaults. Later I heard he had become king of the Tritons by the help of this ring, but I did not see fit to travel half-way across the world on the slim chance that Ximenon would honor his promise. What do you know of this?"

"King Ximenon is dead, if that pleases you," said Vakar. "As for the fallen star, is this it?" He produced the Tahakh.

Fekata's eyes popped. "That is it! Where did you get it? Did you steal it from Ximenon?"

"No, from another king: Awoqqas of Belem. How he got it I do not know, though I should guess Ximenon gave it to him in return for help in making himself king of the Tritons. Could you make more rings from it?"

Fekata turned the lump over in his huge hands, his good eye gleaming. "For what price?"

"I have several ounces of gold, and some copper . . ."

"Pff! I, Fekata of Gbu, have little need of gold and copper. I make enough from my regular work to keep myself and my six wives and twenty-three children in food and drink. But to work on a new metal . . . I will tell you. I will make one article for you—one only— from this piece, and in payment you shall give me the rest of the piece. How is that?"

"What? Why you damned black swindler—"

The smith shot out a hand and gripped Vakar's arm. The great fingers sank in and in, and Fakata pulled and twisted until Vakar thought his arm would come off. Though a wiry and well-muscled man, he was like a child in the hands of this giant.

"Now," said the smith in a deadly-soft voice, "what was that again?"

"I said I thought your price was a little high," grunted Vakar, "but perhaps we can agree."

The crushing grip relaxed. Vakar, massaging his arm and inwardly cursing the cross-grained temper that got him into these tiffs, said: "Will you agree before witnesses to make one article, anything I demand, in return for the rest of the star?"

"I agree." Fekata spoke in his own tongue to the youth, who trotted off.

"What did you say?" asked Vakar.

"I told my son to fetch the heads of the Ukpe, our secret society, to act as witnesses."

In time four men with ostrich-feather headdresses and faces painted with stripes and circles, wrapped in buckskin blankets and an immense dignity, showed up. Vakar and Fekata repeated their engagement before these. Fekata asked:

"Now, how big a ring do you wish?"

"Who said a ring? I will have a sword blade, made to my measurements."

The smith stared blankly; then his face became distorted with rage until Vakar feared the fellow might spatter his brains with a hammer blow. But then Fekata's expression changed again and he burst into a roar of laughter, slapping his paunch.

"You damned whites!" he bellowed. "How can an honest craftsman make a living with you rascals cheating him? But I will make your sword. I, Fekata of Gbu, keep my word, and the biggest sword an insect like you could swing will take less than half the star. Give me that thing. Angwo, fetch a few of your brothers; we shall need all the lungs we can get on the blow pipes. You see, Vakar, the trick in working the star metal is that it must be forged at a bright-red heat, where copper or bronze would shatter, and with a hammer of double the normal weight . . ."

XVII

The Grip of the Octopus

VAKAR BID FAREWELL TO YOJU AND RODE BACK TO Tegrazen, where he found little Yamma of Kernê drinking barley-beer in the same tavern. Yamma was telling the story of his life to a shaven man with the yellowish skin of a Gorgon.

"Hail," squeaked Yamma as Vakar sat down. "You are that fellow who was on his way to see Fekata, are you not? Did you spit in his soup?"

"No; he and I did a bit of business."

"It is always like that! Nobody will take up the cause of poor Yamma, who is now too small to fight his own battles."

"You know what Fekata looks like," said Vakar. "I should want a small army at my back before I crossed him. But who is your friend?"

"Wessul, late of the Kingdom of Gorgonia."

"Why late?"

Wessul spoke: "A slight difference of opinion with my captain, which developed into an exchange of knife-thrusts. He wished to demote me from mate to ordinary seaman, claiming I was too popular with his wife. I left him holding his spilt guts in both hands and weeping into them as he waited to die, and came away, for Gorgonian law is hard in such cases." The Gorgon sighed. "Now I am out in the great world with nobody to order me about, and I do not mind telling you gentlemen it is a lost and lonesome feeling. Worst of all, I shall miss the great raid."

"What raid?" said Vakar sharply.

"Have you not heard? The mainland has been buzzing with it. King Zeluud has gathered all the forces of Gorgonia and its tributaries for an assault upon some northern land."

"What land?"

"He is not saying, though some rumors name Euskeria, some Poseidonis, and some far Aremoria."

"When will he sail?"

"He may have done so already for all I—ho, where are you going?"

"Kernê," Vakar flung back. "Innkeeper! The scot, quickly."

Five days later, Vakar jounced into Kernê, haggard from hard riding with mere snatches of sleep. He led the weary camel along the waterfront, where the great stone warehouses looked down upon the picket fence of masts and spars. Men of all nations and colors jostled him; horses and asses shied from the smell of camel, and their owners cursed him in many languages. Vakar, sunk in thought, paid them no heed. It was time, he thought, to make use of his connections.

He inquired until he learned where Senator Amastan dwelt and presented himself at the door, giving his name as Prince Vakar of Lorsk. After a long wait, a eunuch beckoned him in.

Even after all his travels, Vakar found the ostentatious wealth of this house overpowering, with palms standing in pots of solid gold. Amastan was a big stout man, with rings on all his pudgy fingers. He smelled strongly of perfume, wore multicolored silken robes, and said:

"Welcome, Prince Vakar. Have you brought the other half of Drozo's medal?"

"No. The damned Gamphasants stripped me to the skin."

"Indeed?" Amastan tapped the fingers of one hand on the palm of the other. "That may be true. But—ah—we really must have some means of identification, you know."

"Hells!" blazed Vakar, then controlled his impatience, remembering that to Amastan he was just a wild-looking, sun-baked wanderer. "Find somebody who knows Lorsk and I will answer his questions till Poseidonis sinks beneath the Western Sea. Meanwhile, assuming that I am who I say I am, I should think my credit would be good."

"The credit of the heir to the throne of Lorsk would certainly be good," murmured Amastan, and turned to a scribe. "Fetch Suri. Prince—ah—Vakar, what do you wish with me?"

"I want to get to Amferé, quickly."

"Well, if you have the fare, ships still leave for Amferé every few days, though this is near the end of the trading-season."

"Too slow! I am likely to be stuck in Sederado a month waiting for a fair wind. Do you know about the Gorgons' raid?"

"We have heard of their collecting an armament, but not of their having yet put to sea."

"Well," said Vakar, "I must get home to warn my people."

"What can we do? Though we have some passable magicians, I know of none who can give you fair winds all the way."

Vakar made a rude comment as to what Kernê could do with its sailing merchantmen. "I want a galley! One of your precious battleships. Lorsk will pay you well for the service."

"Ah, but unfortunately the Free City must keep its navy close to home while the Gorgon threat overhangs us. Much as we hate to let a good profit go, I fear we can do nothing for you."

Vakar argued some more but got nowhere. When the mariner Suri came in, the Lorskan said:

"Oh, never mind the inquisition, as you will not make a deal in any case. Perhaps you know a captain sailing for Amferé soon, who will not cut my throat as soon as we are out of sight of Kernê?"

Suri said: "Jerro of Elusion sails in two days; it is his last trip of the year."

Vakar found Jerro's ship, engaged passage, sold his camel, got a much-needed haircut—and then waited three days for an easterly wind. They coasted along the south shore of the peninsula of Dzen. Then, as the wind turned southerly enough to carry them north towards Meropia, Jerro headed in that direction across the blue Sirenian Sea.

The wind held fair, keeping the sail taut and creaking on its yards as one blue crest after another heaved against the high stern and slid underneath. For a day and a night, they drove northward, and then a sailor cried:

"Ships aft! A whole fleet!"

Vakar's heart sank, for the horizon was pricked by a score of mastheads, and every minute the number grew. Soon the low black hulls of a great fleet of war galleys could be seen.

Another sailor cried: "It is the fleet of the Gorgons!" and fell to praying to his Hesperian gods. Jerro cursed.

Vakar said to Jerro: "What do you mean to do?"

"To run as long as I can. You might as well be dead as a Gorgon's galley slave. If they are in haste, they may not stop for us."

All the sailors were now weeping and praying, crying out the names of their women and homes. Vakar kicked the gunwales in frustration. He toyed nervously with his hilt, realizing that if the Gorgons sent a ship after them, there was little that he, the captain, and four terrified sailors could do.

The fleet of galleys came closer, crawling across the smooth sea like a swarm of centipedes from under a flat stone. All their sails bore the octopus of Gorgonia, a symbol which ignorant landsmen sometimes thought to represent a human head with snakes for hair—which it did somewhat resemble. One galley detached itself from the rest and angled towards Jerro's ship.

Vakar interrupted his fuming to say: "If we are taken alive, pray say I am Thiegos of Sederado."

"Aye aye," said Jerro. "But what in the seven hells is that?"

Vakar looked. On the forward deck of the galley stood a man in the garb of a Gorgonian priest. He held one end of a golden chain, the other end of which was linked to a golden collar, which encircled the neck of a creature whose like Vakar had never seen. It was a little smaller than a man and vaguely human in shape. It had a tail, pointed ears, and a hooked beak, and was covered all over with reptilian scales, something like a Triton in his snakeskin armor. It squatted on the deck like a dog.

"That must be a medusa," said Vakar.

"A what?"

"Creatures said to have strange powers of fascination, though I see nothing fascinating about that overgrown lizard. Watch out, there!"

The approaching galley swerved to avoid running down the little merchantman. Somebody shouted across the water. Jerro shifted his steering yoke to send the ship angling away from the galley, but a sailor in the bow of the latter threw a grapnel over the rail of the merchantman. Several sailors pulling on the rope began to draw the two vessels together.

Vakar leaped to the rail of the merchantman, drawing from his girdle the curved sword-knife that he had taken from the Kernean at Kiliessa, to chop the grapnel rope. Before he could complete the action, the priest on the galley pointed at him and spoke to the medusa. The latter reared up against the rail of its own ship, extended its scaly neck, opened its beak, and gave a terrific screaming hiss, like steam escaping from a hundred cauldrons.

In mid-stride, Vakar's muscles froze to stony rigidity. His momentum toppled him forward so that his head struck the rail. He saw a flash of light and then nothing.

When he regained consciousness, he was already lying aboard the galley, still in his rigid statuesque posture, gripping the bronze sword in his fist, on the poop in front of a chair of pretence, in which a bearded man sat wearing a bronze helmet inlaid with gold and crested with ibis plumes. This man was examining Vakar's sword of star metal, turning it over, squinting along the blade, and swishing the air with it. He said to another Gorgon:

"Strip the others and set them to the oars when they recover. This one, however, seems to be something else. He looks like a Pusadian but is clad like a Kernean and carries a sword like nothing I have ever seen. We will save him to show to the king."

"Aye aye, Admiral," said the other man, and pushed Vakar's body over to the rail out of the way.

Vakar found himself facing the gunwale a few inches from his face. Since he could move neither his neck nor his eyes, he was forced to stare at the weathered wood by the hour as the ship plowed on. His paralysis had not diminished his capacity for discomfort, and after a few hours of lying on the heaving deck, his body was one vast ache. He could barely breathe, and his mind ran in futile circles trying to figure what course he should have followed instead of the one he had.

The sun rose to the meridian, though Vakar was fortunate in that the awning over the poop shaded him as well as the admiral. The sun went down. Vakar, suffering torments of thirst, lay where he was. The Gorgons must be in haste, he thought, for otherwise they would not have driven their rowers to make the two-day jump straight across the Sirenian Sea with no chance for the crews to sleep. No doubt they wished to get their great raid over before the storms of winter set in.

Towards morning, Vakar's paralysis wore off sufficiently for him to blink and swallow. His mouth tasted foul and his eyeballs were dry and scratchy.

When the sun came up again, there was much trampling and talking behind him, though he could not follow much of what was said. At length, a change in the motion of the galley told him that they were drawing into a quiet cove. They stopped with a lurch as the galley's bow grated on the sand, and there were sounds of men running about. Hands seized Vakar's body and half-carried, half-dragged it over the rail of the bow and down to the beach. As the sailors carrying Vakar turned him this way and that, his rigid eyeballs took in a wooden shore that looked like that of one of the Hesperides.

The men carried him shoulder-high down the beach, past the noses of more galleys. They hoisted him up over the bow of another beached ship, the largest of all. He was carried along the catwalk between the rowers' benches to the poop. Here he was stood upright leaning against the rail, facing a dark paunchy man who sat on a chair like that on the other ship but more ornate. The admiral, who had followed Vakar, told the paunchy man of Vakar's capture. The paunchy man said:

"The effect should have begun to wear off. You there, can you speak?"

With a great effort Vakar forced his vocal organs to say: "Y-yes."

"Who are you then?"

"Thi-thiegos of Sed-sederado."

"A Hesperian, eh? Well . . ."

Just then another man thrust his way forward. Although Vakar could not yet turn his head or eyes, he was able to see that this was his old acquaintance Qasigan.

"King!" said Qasigan. "This is no Hesperian or Kernean, but our main quarry himself: Prince Vakar of Lorsk! I know him despite the whiskers."

The paunchy man, thus identified as King Zeluud, gave an exclamation. "Let us slay him quickly, then, and go on with the rest of our mission. Khashel, take this sword. Lean the body of the prisoner so that his neck lies across the rail, and strike off his head."

"No-no!" murmured Vakar, but they paid no attention.

The man addressed as "Khashel" seized Vakar's body and pulled it inboard so that Vakar's neck lay across the rail. He spit on his hands, spread his feet, and grasped Vakar's own iron longsword, the one Fekata had made for him, in both hands for a full-strength downward cut. He extended the blade in front of him and made a half-swing, sighting on the neck and checking the sword before it reached its target. He lowered the blade so that it just touched Vakar's skin, then raised it high above his head . . .

The instant the blade touched Vakar's neck, before Khashel raised it for the definitive blow, the paralysis departed from Vakar's muscles. Suddenly relaxing, he fell into a huddle against the gunwale. Khashel's blow, descending with terrific force, drove the blade into the rail where Vakar's neck had just been.

Khashel, eyes popping, tugged the hilt as Vakar rose to his feet, still clutching the curved Kernean weapon he had in his hand when the medusa had petrified him. Khashel still had both hands on the hilt of Vakar's longsword when the Lorskan stepped forward, bringing his arm around in a backhand cut that laid the bronze blade across Khashel's throat below his short beard.

As Khashel slumped into the scuppers, blood streaming from his severed throat, Vakar hurled his bloody blade at King Zeluud, who ducked. In the same movement Vakar seized the hilt of the longsword, yanked it out of the split rail, and vaulted over the side.

He lit with a splash in waist-deep water. As an uproar arose on the ship, he bounded shoreward, half falling as a wave tripped him, then sprinted across the beach, ignoring the stares of Gorgonian soldiery scattered about taking their ease. He plunged dripping into the woods and raced up the slope, away from the sea, dodging trees, until pounding heart and panting breath forced him to slow down. After him came sounds of turmoil: shouts, trumpet blasts, and the clatter of armament as the Gorgons rushed about like a disturbed ant city and organized a pursuit.

Vakar continued straight inland for a while, then angled to the right to lose his pursuers. Bushes scratched at his bare shanks as he fled. Up and up he climbed.

A patch of blue sky ahead drew him to a ledge of rock on the hillside, from which he could look out over the treetops at the shore below and the Sirenian Sea beyond. Here he collapsed, drinking in air in great gasps, and lay while beetles ran over his unprotesting limbs.

When his vision had cleared, he sat up and looked towards the landing place of the Gorgons. Their search-parties should still be streaming inland. Should he climb a tree? Would they have hounds? Could medusas follow a trail like a dog, or locate him by occult means?

Then he realized that the scene was not what he expected. Trumpet blasts, thin with distance, were recalling the searchers to the ships, and the Gorgons were swarming up over the bows of the beached galleys, some of which were pushing off.

Raising his eyes, Vakar saw why. Out in the Sirenian Sea lay another huge fleet, crawling towards the Gorgonian armada. This, Vakar guessed, must be the united navies of the Hesperides. He cracked his knuckle joints with nervous anticipation. Was he to have an arena-seat at the greatest naval battle of history?

But as time passed, the new fleet halted, while the Gorgons, instead of sallying out to meet them, rowed off to Vakar's right, parallel to the shore and away from the Hesperians. Vakar got up and climbed until he found a better lookout. Thence he could see that the shore curved around northeastward to his right, and beyond a wide stretch of sea, on the horizon, he could see the blue loom of another land-mass to the northwest. If he were on Ogugia, that would be Meropia; if on Meropia, the continent of Poseidonis.

The Gorgonian fleet was swinging northward to pass through this wide strait, the Hesperians following at a respectful distance. Evidently the Gorgons were not heading for Amferé, to march through Zhysk to attack Lorsk. Then what? North on the coast of Poseidonis lay the smaller Zhyskan city of Azaret, after which there was not a decent harbor until one came to Diöprepé, a mere village in rocky Lotör. As there was nothing in Lotör worth stealing, what then? Did the Gorgons mean to fall upon Avalon, or the Saturides, or fare even farther north to Aremoria or the coasts of wild Ierarné?

If they did land at Azaret, Lorsk would have little to fear, for the road thence to Lorsk led through lofty mountains, where a resolute squad might hold up an army.

Vakar Zhu watched for over an hour while the Gorgonian fleet, growing smaller and smaller, crept away northward. Then, seeing that the sun was near its apex, he turned back towards the beach.

Several days later, Prince Vakar trudged into Sederado—for, as he had soon learned, he was on Ogugia. He had lived by stealing from farmers and now was looking for means of subsistence, with no assets save the naked sword thrust through his girdle. He felt that he could relax as far as the Gorgons were concerned, as they evidently did not mean to assault Lorsk. Queen Porfia might still have it in for him because of Thiegos, but he hoped that between his beard and the prominent scar across his left cheek he would pass unrecognized.

What had he to offer? Though rated a scholar in Mneset, a provincial princeling like himself could hardly capitalize on his modest learning in the City of Philosophers. On the other hand, while no great warrior or athlete at home, being bigger than most Ogugians, he might be valued for his modest attainments in those lines here.

He found his way to the barracks of the Royal Guard, Ogugia's only professional, permanent force of fighting men. Like the other Hesperian nations, the Ogugians put most of their trust in their navy. Most of the Guard were foreigners, because the native Ogugians were more concerned with philosophy and their creature comforts than with martial glory.

Viahes, the commandant of the garrison, asked: "Who are you, and where do you come from, and what do you want?"

"I am Znur, a Lorskan." Vakar had given some thought to his alias; it would not have done to call himself Thiegos of Sederado again. "I have been travelling for months on the mainland, which explains the sunburn and the garb. Now I seek a livelihood, and thought the Guard might use me."

"What can you do?"

"Ride, and use this." Vakar touched the sword.

"Let me see that. Look at it, Gwantho. What is it?"

Vakar replied: "Something I got in Tartaros. The black smiths have a magical method of treating bronze."

"How did you get to Ogugia, with all ships hugging their harbors for fear of the Gorgons?"

"The Gorgons brought me."

"What?" cried Gwantho, Viahes's legate. "Are you a spy for them?"

"Not at all. They caught me, but I escaped when their fleet stopped on your shore to rest men and take on water."

"It could be," said Viahes. "We will have one of our Lorskan troopers question you in his own language to see if you are genuine, and then if you can demonstrate your skills, we will take you on at three pounds of copper a month plus food and quarters. We will issue you a shield, helmet, and spear, which you shall pay for at one-and-a-half pounds a month for six months."

"That is agreeable to me," said Vakar.

"Fine. You may have a chance to show your skills this afternoon, when the queen will make a short inspection." Viahes flashed a grin at his legate.

While Vakar was wondering how to get past the Queen's inspection without recognition, the Lorskan trooper came in: Raizh of Lezôtr, who looked sharply at Vakar and said:

"I'm sure I've seen you."

"Maybe. Though I'm of Mneset, I've often passed through Lezôtr. I usually stop at Alezu's inn."

"He is a Lorskan," said Raizh to the officers in Hesperian. "I should know that affected accent they use in the capital anywhere."

The guardsmen were lined up with helmets and spearpoints gleaming from their morning's polish. Vakar, whose arms had not yet been issued to him, stood to one side as Queen Porfia walked down the line—not exactly lurking, but trying to keep out of the queen's immediate range of interest. As she came close he felt his blood run faster; what a woman! Fantasies crossed his mind, of sweeping Porfia up in his arms, covering her with kisses, and bearing her off to the nearest couch. But much as he esteemed the queen of Ogugia, Vakar valued his head still more and so kept quiet.

The queen finished her inspection, pudgy Garal jerking along in her wake, and turned away. Viahes said something to the queen, then called: "You there! You with the hatchet-face, whatever your name is, Znur!"

"Who, me?" said Vakar in a meek voice.

"Yes, you. Since you claim to be an expert rider, you shall show your skill by riding Thandolo."

"A horse?" said Vakar, realizing that the queen and Minister Garal were looking at him with that same expression of puzzled near-recognition that he had seen earlier on the face of Riazh.

"And what a horse! Here he comes."

Two grooms were dragging in a big black stallion, who rolled his eyes ominously. Vakar, with an inaudible little sigh, walked towards the animal, pulling up his long Kernean jelab through his girdle.

Thandolo wore a bridle but no saddle pad, not even the girth just back of the forelegs with which the Hesperians equipped their horses. He made a set of teeth at Vakar as the latter came close.

"Behave yourself!" barked Vakar, and cuffed the animal's nose, jerking his hand away in time to avoid a riposte with equine incisors. "Give me the reins," he said.

He got a firm grip on the reins and vaulted aboard. As he came down, he clamped his knees on the beast's barrel and got a fistful of mane in his free hand just as Thandolo bucked.

Vakar clung with all his might, hauling on the reins to bring the angry animal's head up. It seemed to have a mouth of iron. Up came its back in another stiff-legged buck jump. Vakar felt his knees slip a little on the glossy hide, but as the beast came down he dug his toes between Thandolo's forelegs and body to keep from flying off at the top of each jump. Up—down; up—down; Vakar vaguely realized that he was yelling Lorskan curses and beating the horse with the slack of the reins. Up—down. The watching guards, Commandant Viahes, and Queen Porfia fled past in saw-toothed jerks . . .

Then Vakar missed his timing by a fraction of a second and felt the horse's barrel slide out from between his legs. He saw the ground come at him with a circular motion, and landed on his left hip with jarring force.

Thandolo trotted off shaking his head, while the grooms began the weary business of rounding him up. Vakar got shakily to his feet. No doubt the grinning Viahes had cooked this stunt up to have a laugh at his expense. While Vakar had never seen anything very funny in jokes on himself, he would not have minded so much if the commandant had not arranged that he be disgraced in front of Queen Porfia. He thought of challenging Viahes to a fight, but then told himself not to be silly. He was unarmed, and lame and battered from his fall, and Viahes would probably order his troopers to fill the Lorskan full of spears at the first hostile move.

His only course was to hobble out (since he had evidently flunked the test) with such dignity as he could muster. Perhaps he could work as a longshoreman . . .

He was limping towards the gates when Viahes's bellow came after him: "Ho there, Znur! Where are you going?"

As Vakar looked back blankly, the commandant bawled: "Come back! What is the matter with you?"

Vakar walked back to where Viahes stood with fists on hips, wondering if he were to be offered another chance. "Well, sir?" he said.

"Why were you running away? You are the best rider in Ogugia!"

"What?"

"Of course! No man has ever stayed on Thandolo's back for more than three heart-beats!"

"We can use men like you," said a familiar female

voice, and there was Porfia: green eyes, black hair, and figure to drive men to madness.

"Did you hear that?" cried Viahes heartily. "Now get back to barracks, where Gwantho will give you your arms."

Vakar bowed and departed. He was thoughtfully shining his new helmet until he could see his narrow, scarred face in it when a man came in. Vakar recognized Dweros, one of Porfia's lackeys.

Dweros said: "Prince Vakar, the queen asks that you come with me to the palace."

XVIII

The Philosophy of Sederado

VAKAR LOOKED UP NARROWLY. SO SHE HAD RECOGnized him! Was she trying to lure him to his death? If she were, wouldn't she more likely have sent a squad of soldiers to seize him?

He pulled his mustache in perplexity. Strike down Dweros and flee? This time he had no ship waiting, and on such an island it was only a matter of time before he was hunted down . . .

He made his decision, told Dweros: "Wait here," and a few minutes later was back with his magical sword (in a borrowed scabbard) at his side. Now let somebody try to disarm him!

He followed Dweros through the streets, scowling somberly. At the palace gates he saw no sign of ambush: only the usual bored-looking guards leaning on the helves of their zaghnals, and the thin traffic of petitioners and officials going in and out. Inside, Dweros led him through the anteroom ahead of his turn, so that he was conscious of sour looks from those who waited. He tensed as Dweros pushed the curtains aside, ready to whip out the star-sword . . .

And Porfia's arms were around his neck and she was pressing her lips to his. Then she thrust him back, saying:

"Well! By Heroé's eight teats, when I kiss a man, he does not usually stand like a statue with his hand on his sword!"

Vakar smiled, his eyes darting around the chamber, ready to seize Porfia for a hostage if need be. He said:

"Excuse my caution, dear madam, but I thought you might have cause to kiss me with sharpened bronze."

"So that is why you skulk about my kingdom under a false name with that bush on your face! Why should I kill you?"

"Thiegos," he said dryly.

"Oh, him! I was disturbed by his taking-off, true, but you did the only thing you could. Anyway I had ceased to love the cowardly jackanapes, with his airs and his sneers."

"Well then?" said Vakar, making a movement towards Porfia and raising his arms.

She held out a hand. "Not until you are cleaned up, Elbien! Take Prince Vakar . . ."

In the chamber he had occupied on his first visit, he found a fine Ogugian tunic laid out: a knee-length garment of sky-blue linen embroidered with sea-monsters. There was also a razor, with which he removed the beard, leaving the luxuriant mustache. In the silver mirror, the pallor of his newly-exposed jaw contrasted oddly with the swartness of the rest of his face, which bore a lean, worn look, like an old and oft-whetted knife blade.

He dined alone with a radiant Porfia. When she saw him she said: "I wonder I knew you, you look so much older."

"Oh, is that so? The things I have experienced in the last seven months would age a god."

"Where did you get that great scar?"

"I forgot to duck." He entertained her with a slightly censored account of his adventures. She commented:

"I always thought those Pusadian epics to be mere barbarous bombast, but here we have such an adventurer-hero in the flesh."

"I am neither hero nor adventurer, but a quiet bookish fellow who would like to settle down in Sederado and study philosophy. In all these fights and flights, I have never known that mad joy of battle of which the epics speak. Before the combat I am frightened, during it I am confused, and after it I am weary and disgusted."

"Well, if that is what you can do when you are frightened, confused, and disgusted, I hate to think of the slaughter you would wreak if you really took to the trade. Are you sure King Awoqqas tried to net you before the headless woman's temptations had time to take effect?"

"Quite sure, madam, though I do not claim any special virtue. I have merely been fleeing my ill-wishers for the past few months too fast for dalliance." Vakar thought it more tactful to say nothing about Tiraafa the satyr. "But now that we are being frank, who is the lucky successor to Thiegos?"

As he spoke, Vakar tried to keep the glitter of interest out of his eyes and the pant of passion out of his voice. He could not look at Porfia without feeling the blood rush to his face. Though he had as a matter of course been introduced to the arts of love early, he had never met a woman who affected him like this.

She said: "In truth, I have the same tale to tell as you. For seven months I have slept in a cold bed; I have forsworn all light loves and resolved to hold myself inviolate until I find another consort, as Garal has been plaguing me to do. But I will not have that grasping Shvo; I will have none of your Pusadian polygamy."

Vakar nodded sympathetically. Although in Poseidonis the male ruled the roost absolutely, Vakar's detachment enabled him to appreciate a different point of view. Porfia continued:

"Besides, it is time I produced some heirs, lest I die and leave my cousins to fight for the throne and rend the kingdom in their struggles."

"Can you?"

"Surely. I bore a girl to Vancho, who died, poor thing. Thiegos was my only other. But enough of me.

Tell me of your plans. You will be off to Lorsk on the first ship, I suppose?"

"That depends. What have you heard of the Gorgon fleet?"

"When our combined Hesperian fleets broke off following them, they were still headed north."

The servants had taken away the food. They faced each other across a single small table supporting a jug of wine. Porfia sat on a new carven chair of pretence, replacing the serpent throne, while Vakar sat on an ivory stool. The flames of the lamps made little highlights in her green eyes.

"Then," he said, "they cannot intend to attack Lorsk, and I need not hasten home." He set down his goblet and stretched. "Do not worry about having to keep me, Porfia darling. I will send home for funds to live on while I study philosophy under your Ogugian masters and tame that stallion Thandolo."

"Really?" She gave him an eager smile.

"Yes." He rose and stepped around the table and took her hands and gently raised her from her throne.

With an easy fluid motion their arms went around each other and their lips met. After a while he sat down on the chair of pretence and pulled her down upon his lap, marvelling again at her lightness. Vakar rapped the oak of the chair with his knuckles, saying:

"Let us hope this chair does not act in the uncanny manner of the other, the last time you sat in my lap."

Porfia giggled. They kissed. Vakar slid one hand over her shoulder and down inside the thin robe, but she snatched it out and gave it a slight slap.

"No," she said. "I told you I had foresworn light loves, and that includes you, Vakar dear, even though those big black eyes of yours almost turn my will to water."

"Who said light? I, madam, am heir to the throne of Lorsk, and do hereby most solemnly propose myself as your consort and wedded spouse."

"Oho! That sheds another light upon the matter. But what should we do when you are King of Lorsk? Where should we dwell?"

"Let us ford that stream when we come to it. Perhaps we can spend our summers in Lorsk and our winters here."

"And how if we return to one of our kingdoms to find our regents have seized the throne in our absence?"

"That is a matter of choosing reliable surrogates. But think of the advantages: The bronze and brawn of Lorsk wedded to the philosophy and fleet of Ogugia! Who would dare molest such a combination?"

"You bring weighty arguments to the conference-table, sir. But we should take into account one other slight matter."

"Yes?"

"Whether our personal natures are such as to ensure the growth and endurance of love and affection between us."

"Do we not love already? I, at least, burn for you with white-hot passion."

"I speak of the other kind of love, not mere carnal lust, which for all its delights both of us know for a sly deceiver. Oh, I know you would give me a tumultuary time beneath the drugget; but how about the long pull, when teeth decay and skins wrinkle and sag and tempers grow short?"

"I have thought of that too," said Vakar, who had not considered the matter at all until that moment. "Do you wish a quiet reliable husband, who would rather chase obscure tomes than lustful wenches, but who can if need be prove an adequate man of his hands?"

"You make it sound wonderful, sir. Could I but be sure ..."

"Wait to be sure of anything and you will find yourself looking out through the sides of a funerary urn, your quest unaccomplished. As it says in *The Death of Zormé:*

Death distrained all,   *the primly prudent*
And roistering reckless,   *the grimly grasping*
And squandering spendall, *with divine disdain*
Of dealing just deserts ...

He drew Porfia's face to his and kissed her some more. This time she did not object as he slid his hand over her shoulder, but pressed his hand against her with her own. After a while she gently disengaged herself and rose to her feet. As Vakar looked up, his bushy brows making a question, she held out a hand.

"Come," she said.

He stood up, picked her up as if she were a kitten, and carried her in the direction that she indicated.

Next morning, with a fistful of copper celts borrowed from the Ogugian treasury in his scrip, Vakar Zhu threaded his way through the streets of Sederado, gaily whistling a Lorskan lyric, until he found the house of Rethilio. Porfia had offered to send a lackey to fetch the owner of the house, but such was Vakar's respect for philosophy that he preferred to go in person. Besides, he was curious to see how a philosopher lived.

Like other Hesperian residences, Rethilio's house was built around a court, presenting a blank brick wall to the outer world. A porter let Vakar in, and presently the philosopher himself appeared, saying:

"Why, I know you! I met you some months ago ... Let me see, you are ..."

Vakar identified himself.

"Of course!" said Rethilio. "And what can I do for you, sir?"

"As I am likely to be in Sederado for an indefinite time, I should like to study your philosophy."

"Admirable! Do you wish to enroll in my regular afternoon class, or do you prefer special tutoring? The latter is more costly, but I suppose a prince would not care about that."

"This prince does," said Vakar, whose periods of destitution in the course of his wanderings had wonderfully sharpened his appreciation of the value of trade metal. "However, as I wish to cram as much as possible into a short time, I will undertake both."

The philosopher seemed delighted, and presently Vakar was listening ecstatically to Rethilio's theory of the world-egg. When the philosopher had brought his pupil up to date on the main points of his course, he began asking him about his travels and the peoples he had seen. Vakar in his turn asked about the Gorgons.

"Their origin," said Rethilio, "is lost in the mists of myth. An ancient race, and in many ways a strange and evil one. The story—and let him believe who will—is that thousands of years ago the Gorgades were inhabited only by medusas, who then were a civilized folk themselves, with cities."

"Those reptiles civilized?" said Vakar.

"Yes, it is said that they are really as intelligent as men. In that day, the present Gorgons were a nation of naked savages dwelling along the shores of Tartaros, barely come to full manhood from their apish ancestry. Well, the medusas, being not over-fond of toil, were wont to raid the mainland for slaves, until there dwelt in the islands several times as many Gorgon slaves as reptilian masters. And a hard servitude that was, for the medusas tortured their slaves for pleasure and ate them for food.

"An aristocracy of wizards ruled the medusas and would no doubt have continued to do so to this day, had not the president of this sorcerous senate been even lazier than most medusas. Not satisfied with compelling his human slaves to carry him about, dress and disrobe him, and put the very food (he preferred roast young woman) into his scaly mandibles, he became too indolent even to perform his own magical spells and taught a trusted slave his principal cantrips."

"I think I know what is coming next," put in Vakar.

"Quite so. The upshot was that the slaves rose and overthrew the masters, slaying all but a few. These they kept to be slaves in their turn; but, learning from their predecessors' error, they take care to rear each new medusa in solitude, allowing it to learn no more than is absolutely necessary for it to fulfill its functions. And their chief function is to hiss at those enemies whom their masters point out to them, striking them with paralysis."

Vakar sat rapt through the afternoon lecture. At its close he could hardly tear himself away—until he thought of Porfia. He grinned with pure happiness.

He was bidding farewell to the philosopher when the

porter announced: "Master, a man to see you. He says he is Ryn of Mneset."

Vakar gave a violent start as Rethilio said: "Show him in. I have heard of—what is the matter, Prince? Do you know him?"

"All too well. He is our court wizard, who sent me on this chase."

The hunched figure of Ryn scuttled in. "Well, well!" he cackled. "They told me I should find you here. So our young savior, instead of rushing home, is learning how to split a hair and cut blocks with a razor! Hail, Master Rethilio. I arrive just in time, before he becomes so entangled in your sophistical cobwebs that nothing will extricate him."

"Now look here," said Rethilio, "you may be the deadliest spell-caster in Poseidonis, but that gives you no license to condemn the divine art of philosophy, which is to your dark sorceries as day is to night."

"Who is insulting whom now? At least my magic accomplishes some practical good, as when by the help of the witch Gra I learned this lad was in Sederado. Come, Vakar, we can talk on our way to that gilded cage of yours. Farewell, Rethilio; I will tell the Lorskans you are the finest quibbler among the Ogugians, who are the greatest quibblers on earth!"

As they walked towards the palace, Vakar asked: "Why don't you like Rethilio?"

"Pff! I dislike him not, but I know his kind. They spend the morning combing their beards to present a specious appearance of wisdom, and in the afternoon they haul in gold with hoes by lecturing on the worthlessness of wealth. His world-egg theory is no worse than the others, to wit: utterly worthless, for no man knows how man and the universe originated. But now to more weighty matters: What are you doing here instead of hastening back to Lorsk in her hour of peril?"

"I stopped here because I saw the Gorgon fleet sail off to northward, having no intention of landing in Zhysk. I see no reason why I shouldn't settle here, wed Queen Porfia, and become a real scholar and not a brainless Lorskan bison-hunter."

"Oh, so you'd marry her green-eyed majesty! At least your taste in women is good. Does she know of this?"

"Knows and approves. So you may tell my loving family—"

"Young fool! Don't you know what the Gorgons are up to? They're sailing around the north end of Poseidonis, around Lotör, to come at us from the west!"

"Oh!"

"Yes, oh. They thought to surprise us by the maneuver and would have, save that one of our lords, Kalesh of Andr, happened to make a pilgrimage to the temple of Three-eyed Tandyla in Lotör and heard a rumor among the Lotris. He scouted the coast, saw the Gorgon fleet creeping along upon the sky line, and posted home as fast as his nag could bear him. Now, what's this magical what-not you were supposed to run down? Have you found it?"

Vakar told his tale and showed the sword of star metal.

"Ah!" said Ryn. "This all ties in together. Now I know what the gods most fear and why."

"What is it?"

"Before I took ship across the Sirenian Sea, I stopped in King Shvo's library in Amferé. You know, Shvo's a fanatical collector: of land, wealth, women, records, anything he can lay hands on. I suppose you know he's been trying to collect your pretty little Porfia?"

"What? Just let him try—"

"Easy, easy. Bear it in mind and be careful, for if he knows of your intentions, he might bribe somebody to poison your wine. Watch that fat Garal; he's less harmless than he looks. In this case, however, Shvo's greed stood us in good stead, for amidst that warehouse full of junk he calls a library, I found a tattered old papyrus from a ruined temple in Parsk that bore the legend of Kumiö."

"What's that?"

"It's a legend referred to in Oma's *Commentary*, of which only a fragment survives and which is itself so old it can no longer be dated. But here was the original, or at least a copy of a copy of a copy of the original."

"What did it say?" asked Vakar.

"It tells how a thief and blasphemer named Kumiö found a fallen star as your friend Ximenon did. He broke off a piece and wore it around his neck as an amulet, gradually discovering it rendered him proof against all supernatural influences. Witches could not cast spells upon him; demons could not harm him; even the gods could neither touch him nor communicate with him.

"Now, Kumiö lived in what is now the Bay of Kort, west of Lorsk. There stood the capital of the Kingdom of Kort, the great city Klâto with its towers of scarlet and black. The people were wont to rely for protection of their goods on spells and talismans they bought from the magicians, but with the advent of Kumiö and his amulet all was changed. A chest kept closed by the mightiest spell would easily open to Kumiö once he had touched it with his piece of star. He even got into the king's zenana, guarded by a three-headed fiend of anthropophagous tastes, who nevertheless could not come near him, and reveled among the king's concubines for six days and fled before the king learned of his visit. And thus the first locks and bolts were invented, to keep out the light-fingered Kumiö.

"In time the gods took counsel, for it occurred to them that, if knowledge of this metal became widespread, all men would seek to carry a bit of it. Then the gods would be unable to communicate with men, who would forget the gods and cease to worship them, which for a god is virtual death."

Vakar said: "Rethilio was explaining the *Fragments of Lontang* along those lines."

"So," continued Ryn, "the gods decided to do away with Kumiö. First they tried to take him off by sickness, but he was proof against plagues from any but natural causes. Then they incited another thief to steal his piece of metal, but the thief relied upon a spell of invisibility he bought from a wizard, and Kumiö saw him coming and knifed him. I won't tell you all the things they tried; but at last, growing desperate, they sank the whole Kingdom of Kort beneath the waters of the Western Ocean. Thus Kumiö was drowned along with all the other Kortians save a handful of survivors."

"Is this true?"

"Who knows? Probably not in all details. But it gives us the reason for the gods' fearing star metal."

"What is the stuff? Is it found on the earth's surface?"

Ryn shrugged his uneven shoulders. "How should I know? Of the five known metals, gold and silver are found in their native state, tin and lead are extracted from rocks, and copper occurs both ways. How do we know what other kinds of metal lurk in the rocks, could we but extract them? But nobody has yet so obtained star metal."

Vakar mused. "I see how the sword broke that spell the medusa put upon me, when the fellow who meant to cut my head off touched my neck with the blade first, as you do to aim your stroke. Now that we know how it works, what shall we do with it?"

"That will transpire at the proper time; I've never known Gra's prescience to fail. Meantime you must hasten back with me before the seas wax too boisterous."

"Hells!" Vakar kicked a clod. "Why should I, when I've just found what I really want? What's there in Lorsk save a perpetual bicker with my brother? Why can't you take the sword—"

"There's the kingdom to which you're heir. Your father is unwell, and if you're not there at the time ... I leave the inference to you."

Vacillating, undecided, Vakar marched gloomily back to the palace. He sent a footman in to interrupt an audience the queen was giving, and told her the news.

"No!" cried Porfia, a hand to her throat. "You shall not go! Our nuptials are in six days, and having found the one man to share my throne I will not let him be slain in some petty brawl on the edges of the world ..."

Her tone nettled Vakar enough to make him say: "Consort or none, dear madam, I shall make my own decisions. After all, I have my duty to my people as you have yours."

After further argument, she said: "Let us take counsel with Charsela. Will you abide by her advice?"

"I will take her counsel into full account," said Vakar carefully, "if you will let me send for Rethilio likewise."

"I see where I shall have to feed all the seers and sages of Sederado," said Porfia, "for the dinner hour draws nigh."

"Huh!" said Ryn. "As if my advice were not so good as that of that hairsplitter! He will wish you to stay here, so he can continue to milk the treasury of Lorsk by his lectures."

The old she-wizard arrived first, saying: "It is the young gallant who saved the queen and me! Though you did leave my house in a gory mess. And this, if I mistake not, is the great Ryn of Mneset?"

"Yes, yes," gruffed Ryn. "How is the love-potion business?"

"Poorly, your honor, for the maggots of philosophy have so far addled the brains of the people that they have little thought for love. I of course except our royal protectors here, who obviously have thought for little else at the moment."

Rethilio arrived, gravely greeting those present. Queen Porfia led them to a dark little chamber in the midst of the palace, lighted by a single lamp. Charsela filled her cauldron and went into her trance. After a long while she said:

"If Prince Vakar returns to Lorsk he will suffer great loss, but will not long regret it."

Porfia cried: "Do not go, my love! She means you will lose your life!"

"While I do not hold my life cheaply," replied Vakar, "yet after the perils I have lately escaped, I am not to be deterred from returning home by fear of a doubtful oraculation. What do you think, Rethilio?"

The philosopher said: "Most men possess an inner voice that informs them what is the righteous course to pursue. Some attribute this to a guardian spirit, some to a favorite god, and some to the soul of the man himself. Which is right I know not, but you disobey this voice at your peril, for it will have its revenge upon you. Thus if you steal despite the prohibitions of the voice, it will cause you to stumble when the watchman is chasing you and so bring you to justice."

"Then," said Vakar, "I will return to Lorsk forthwith. What transport is available, Ryn?"

"A galley of the navy of Zhysk awaits at the waterfront. We can be off tomorrow."

"So be it. We shall—why, Porfia!" Vakar started to rise.

For the Queen of Ogugia had dissolved in tears. She rose, saying between sobs: "I will have my servants bring you dinner, but pray excuse me. I wish to be alone—no, Vakar, you shall remain here to entertain our guests. Later you may come to me."

Vakar unhappily watched Porfia depart, fingering his mustache and wishing that he were better able to cope with such emotional crises. While he stood indecisive, the servants brought in food and wine. Over the tables, Ryn said to Rethilio:

"I owe you an apology; I had not thought you would give such disinterested advice."

"Oh, I claim no special virtue for it," said Rethilio blandly, breaking open his loaf of bread. "My livelihood depends upon my reputation for impartiality, and what would it profit me to urge the prince to remain in hope of collecting fees from him, if he then became bored and sought other amusements, leaving me with tarnished repute?"

"You wrong me, sir philosopher," said Vakar. "I would not leave you from boredom, but only if I learned of a philosopher more profound than yourself, for to me the pursuit of ultimate truth is the world's most fascinating pastime."

"Well, let us hope we shall all live for you to resume it. Master Ryn. it occurs to me that you, too, had better take up philosophy."

"Why?"

"Because if the knowledge of star metal and its properties diffuses widely, so that all men take to carrying fragments of the material, your profession would wither away to nought."

"A point I had not thought of. However, I am too old to learn a new bag of tricks and shall not live to see this change. Perhaps my successors, now young sprigs in the magical lycea of Torrutseish, will improve their art to counter the anti-magical qualities of the stuff."

Charsela spoke in her hollow voice: "There is more to it than that. The star metal will some day cast the very gods from their thrones, for with it men will be cut off from their gods, as to benefits, punishments, and mere communication."

"Then no more gods?" said Rethilio.

"No; there will be gods, but mere ineffectual wraiths, kept in being by their priests to enable these priests to live without toil on the offerings of the credulous. I have seen it in my visions."

"And then," said Vakar, "all men would be like me, who have never conversed with the smallest godlet. Which might not be a bad thing."

Later, Porfia clung to him with a violence that made his ribs creak, alternating spells of passion such as he had never known from a woman with periods of tempestuous tears.

"I shall never see you again!" she wailed. "I know Charsela meant you will be slain!"

"Oh, come, love. She did not say so, and we all have our time—"

"Nonsense! That is one of those philosophers' arguments, sounding impressive and meaning nothing. I love you to madness and cannot give you up. You know I am no blushing virgin, but never have I known a man so to stir me . . ."

He gave her passion for passion but stubbornly refused even to defer his sailing for a day or two. She was still asleep when he stole from the palace with Ryn before dawn. As the Zhyskan galley creaked and crawled out of Sederado Harbor, Vakar leaned on the after rail, staring somberly back at the graceful city, pink in the sunrise. Ryn at his elbow said:

"Cheer up, my boy. Just think of me; you may have loved and lost, but with my hump I never——"

"Shut your mouth, you old fool! No, I don't really mean that. But if I'm killed on this expedition I'll haunt you to your urn."

XIX

The Bay of Kort

AT THE GRIM CRAGGY WALLS OF MNESET, VAKAR reined up as the guards crossed their halberds and said: "I'm Prince Vakar! Let me through, fools!"

"What's that?" said one of the guards. "Everybody knows Prince Vakar went a-traveling over the earth and fell off the edge."

"He do look something like the prince," said the other. "Who can identify you, sir?"

"Oh, hells!" growled Vakar.

He had ridden on ahead of Ryn in his impatience to learn how things went in Lorsk, and now he had to sit his panting mount until Ryn's chariot rattled up. Then the guards were profuse with apologies, to which Vakar paid little heed as he spurred for the castle.

The first person of rank he met there was the chamberlain, whom he asked: "Where is everybody? Where are my father and brother?"

"The king lies sick, sir, and Prince Kuros has gone to the Bay of Kort with the army."

Vakar went quickly to his father's chambers. King Zhabutir lay on his bed, surrounded by servants and adherents and looking blankly up. Vakar pushed through them and said:

"Hail, Father."

The king's eyes looked out of their sunken sockets. He said faintly:

"Oh, Vakar. Where did you come from, dear boy? Have you been away? I haven't seen you lately."

Vakar exchanged glances with the people who crowded the room, and it seemed to him that they looked at him with pity. The king continued:

"How did you get that scar on your face, son? Cut yourself shaving?"

Then Ryn came in and steered Vakar out by his elbow. The old wizard said:

"He's been like this for a month, gradually sinking until now he seldom talks sense."

"Shouldn't I stay until he either mends or dies?"

"Nay. He might go any time and again he might last months more, while the army fights the Gorgons. We must set out for the Bay of Kort now, trusting to luck he'll still be alive when we return."

"Shouldn't I stop to sacrifice to Lyr and Okma, then, for bringing me through so many perils?"

"Not now. After all this time, they can wait a few days."

Vakar went to his chambers feeling shaken, for though he had never been very close to his father, the loss of a near relative is sobering. He armed himself with his jazerine cuirass of gilded bronze scales, his second-best helmet (not the solid gold one, which was too soft), and a bronze shield like that he had started his journey with. He kept the sword of star metal, which in odd moments he had honed down to razor sharpness. Then he and Ryn set out for the Bay of Kort, where the Gorgonian fleet was expected.

Four days later, they reached the pass through the hills around the bay, where from a bend in the road they could see the whole bay and the crescent of flatland between it and the hills spread out below like a dinner plate. The cool autumnal wind whipped their cloaks. In the foreground lay the Lorskan camp.

"Lyr's barnacles!" cried Vakar.

The Gorgon fleet was already drawn up along the beach in a line miles long, hundreds of vessels great and small with sails furled, oars shipped, and bows resting on the strand. The Gorgonian army had disembarked and was drawing up in a great rectangular mass, in regular ranks with big wood-and-leather shields and helms in exact alignment, bristling with spears, while clumps of archers gathered on the flanks. Over each unit floated its vexilla, hanging from a gilded crossyard.

A half-mile inland from the Gorgonian array, the forces of Lorsk were strung out in loose aggregations, each group comprising the followers of some lord or high officer.

"The damned fool!" croaked Ryn. "He told me he meant to attack while they were disembarking! A good enough plan, but it's gone somehow awry. Having failed to catch them with their kilts wet, he should withdraw into the hills to ambush and block them, meanwhile harassing them with cavalry, of which they have none. On the plain, that Gorgonian meat-grinder will make short work of our gallant individualists."

"We have an advantage of numbers."

"That'll avail us little. The headstrong fool . . ."

"Perhaps he's planned it that way," said Vakar, and told Ryn of the words of the dying Söl.

"Ye gods! Why haven't you told me before?"

"I left Mneset in such a rush I had no time, and so much happened later that it slipped my mind."

Ryn muttered something about the dynasty's ending in a litter of halfwits, then said: "Let's get on to the battle."

"It'll take us an hour," said Vakar, but started his horse down the slope. Ryn's chariot bumped behind.

As Vakar rode, he saw the course of the battle like a game played on a table-top. The shrill Lorskan trumpets rang out and the horsemen and light chariots moved out to harass the foe, dashing up to within a few feet of them to discharge bows or cast javelins, then wheeling away. A few such skirmishers swirled around the ends of the Gorgonian line, but the archers drove them off with flights of bone-tipped arrows.

Others galloped towards the ships drawn up along the beach beyond the ends of the Gorgonian army. As they came, these ships pushed off. Vakar saw the Lorskans catch one still beached. There was a scurrying of little figures and a twinkle of weapons in the sunlight, and then smoke rose from the ship as the Lorskans set it afire.

Now the deeper tones of the Gorgonian trumpets answered those of Lorsk. Vakar saw a ripple of motion go through the Gorgonian array as the phalanx began to advance. The Lorskan chariots and horses bolted back through the gaps in their own force to the rear, and the towering kilted Lorskan foot soldiers loped forward under their bison banners, yelling and whirling their weapons.

Then Vakar could see clearly no more, for he had reached the level of the plain. Now the battle was a dark writhing line of figures on the horizon, the plan and progress of the battle being hidden from view by the backs of the rearmost Lorskans and by the clouds of dust that now arose.

"I halt here!" called Ryn. "I'll cast a few spells; you go on and see what you can do."

Vakar rode forward, skirting the Lorskan camp, whence camp followers yelled unintelligibly at him. The roar of battle strengthened until he could make out individual shrieks. Behind the main battle front, the Lorskan cavalry and chariotry stood awaiting orders. As Vakar approached, he glimpsed the faces of foot soldiers, first a few, then here, there, and everywhere. That meant that they were facing the wrong way— were running away. Had the battle been lost already?

The fleeing foot zigzagged between the horses and chariots and ran past Vakar through the grass towards the hills: first one or two, then hundreds, most without weapons. Now the cavalry and chariots too began to move retrograde, sweeping past Vakar and overtaking and passing the infantry. Once Vakar glimpsed his brother Kuros, riding rearwards with the rest. Kuros would naturally be among the first to flee, knowing that his men would soon follow his example and that his secret pact with King Zeluud would thereby be carried out. It was a full-fledged rout.

Vakar caught one foot soldier by his crest. The chin-strap kept the helmet from coming off, and the jerk nearly broke the man's neck.

"What's happened?" roared Vakar into the dazed man's face.

"Magic!" gasped the man. "They had creatures like great lizards in front of their line, and as we closed with them, the lizards hissed at us and our men fell as if struck by thunderbolts. Let me go! What can mere men do against such magic?"

Vakar released the man, who resumed his flight. The bulk of the Lorskan army had now swept past Vakar, who almost wept with rage. Never in the memory of man had the proud men of Lorsk suffered such a disgraceful defeat. After the Lorskans came the Gorgons under their swaying octopus banners, the sun gleaming on their cuirasses. Most of them had dropped their heavy shields of wood and bull's hide to run faster after their foes. In their pursuit, they had abandoned their rigid rectilinear formation so that they now surged forward in a great irregular and scattered mass. From his height Vakar could see over the heads of the Gorgons the bodies of thousands of Lorskans lying stiff and stark in the grass. Off to his right, King Zeluud stood in the Gorgons' only chariot, trotting at the head of his men.

Vakar drew his sword and put his horse towards one of the gaps in the Gorgonian line. The Gorgons stared at the single horseman hurling himself into their midst. One or two took a few steps in Vakar's direction, but he went past them like a whirlwind. A plumed Gorgonian helmet appeared in front of him. The Gorgon swung a battle-ax, but before he could strike, Vakar drove his sword into the man's face. He felt the crunch of thin bones and wrenched his point out as the man fell. Then he was through the hostile array and pulled up to look around.

Back towards the hills he now saw the backs of the Gorgon mass, still running after the Lorskans. Their officers urged them on with hoarse shouts; nobody bothered with the lone horseman whose mount had evidently gone mad and carried him willy-nilly through the army.

Between Vakar and the sea, the victims of the medusa attack lay in long rows, in stiffly unnatural positions like statues toppled from their pedestals. Their heads lay towards the sea, for when the screams of the medusas had petrified them in mid-charge, their momentum had caused nearly all of them to fall forward.

Between Vakar and the fallen Lorskans, he saw what he sought: the medusas and their attendant priests of Entigta. There were nine reptiles, each on a leash. At the start of the battle, the priests had been spaced evenly along the Gorgonian front, but now that their part was over they were gathering in a single group in the middle of their line, a few hundred feet to Vakar's right as he faced the sea. Half a dozen of them had congregated there already, and the remaining three were walking towards this group.

Vakar spurred his horse and cantered in a wide curve that brought him up to the last of the priests from behind. Before he reached the Gorgon, the priest, aroused by hoofbeats behind him, looked around. The priest pointed at Vakar and spoke to the medusa, which opened its beak and hissed.

The horse shied, and Vakar felt a vibration run through him, but gripping the magical sword he plunged at the pair. So long as he gripped the hilt, the contact between his hand and the tang of the blade protected him. A downright slash sank into the medusa's scaly head and then he was past, sparing only a glance back to see the reptile writhing in the dust.

Then he was on the second. A sweeping backhand cut shore through the snaky neck and sent the medusa's head flying.

He swept past the clump of priests and rode towards the remaining individual who had not yet reached them. His swing missed a vital spot and sheared off one of the medusa's ears; he jerked his horse around in a tight circle and came back. This time another head flew off.

"Prince Vakar!" cried the priest, and Vakar recognized Qasigan.

But now he had no time to settle old scores with mere men. He rode at the remaining six priests, who stood in a group and watched uncertainly. At the last minute they grasped what he was doing. There was a flurry of movement as they tried to form a circle around the medusas, drawing knives from their belts to defend their beasts with their lives. Then Vakar crashed squarely into the group. There were screams of men and medusas as bones crushed under the horse's hooves and Vakar's sword flashed down on shaven polls and scaly crania.

Then he was through and wheeling to charge back, blood spraying from his sword as he whirled it, yelling wordlessly. Crash! A sharp pain in his leg told him that one of them had gotten home with a knife, but he kept on, slashing and thrusting ...

And he was chasing one surviving medusa over the grass. The reptile went in buck jumps like a rabbit, the golden chain attached to its collar leaping and snaking behind it. Vakar rode it down and left it writhing with its entrails oozing out. Four priests, including Qasigan, were running for their ships, hiking up their robes to give their legs free play.

Back towards the hills, the Gorgonian army still receded in pursuit of the Lorskans. Vakar knew that the road up to the pass would get jammed and the Gorgons would have a holiday massacre. And now what? The sword that had destroyed the medusas would also revive the fallen Lorskans, whom the Gorgons had not taken time to bind or slay.

Down at the waterfront, among the beaks of the beached ships, men were pointing at Vakar and shouting, but seemed undecided what to do. Most of them were mere unarmed servants.

Vakar rode down to one end of the windrows of stricken Lorskans and turned back. Holding his horse's mane with his shield-hand he leaned down as he passed the bodies and slapped them on faces and hands with the flat of his blade. As he did so they lost their rigidity and scrambled up. Vakar shouted:

"Get up! Get in formation! Pick up your arms!"

There seemed to be no end to the process. He had to keep looping back to touch men whom he had missed, hundreds and hundreds of them. It was as tiring as a battle. But the crowd of recovered Lorskans grew and grew. For want of other guidance they obeyed him. Down at the shore the Gorgonian galleys, alarmed by the springing to life of an army of corpses, were putting to sea.

Time passed. Vakar's arm ached. Only a few score more bodies to go ... Vakar speeded up, careless of slicing off an occasional nose or ear. And then they were all on their feet. He rode back to the middle of the line and waved the sword, shouting:

"Get in line and follow me! The magical powers of the Gorgons have been destroyed. We can take them in the rear and wipe them out!"

He harangued them and got them into motion across the plain at a fast, mile-eating walk: tall bearded Lorskan yeomen with their miscellany of weapons. As they neared the edge of the coastal plain, Vakar could see what was happening ahead. Many of the Gorgons had abandoned the pursuit to sack the Lorskan camp, where they were amusing themselves by butchering the cooks and sutlers and raping the women. The rest had caught the fugitives funneling into the road leading up to the pass and had fallen upon them with spear and sword. The slaughter of the mixed mass of Lorskan soldiers and camp-followers had been terrific, checked only by the fact that the front ranks became so jammed up that they had no room to swing a weapon.

As Vakar neared the Gorgon rear with his force, he could see Gorgonian officers rushing around trying to get their men faced about to receive the new attack. Vakar, judging the distance, yelled: "Charge!"

Forward they went at a run with deep roars, stumbling over bodies. They plunged through the camp, sweeping the plunderers before them and trampling them down, and then the lines met with a crash and a crush that lifted men off their feet and snapped the shafts and spears and halberds. Weapons rose and fell like flails. Behind the Gorgonian array, the Lorskan fugitives picked up courage. Instead of trying frantically to elbow their way up the road or to scale the steep hillsides to safety, some turned back, picked up discarded weapons, and plunged into the fight. As most of the Gorgons now lacked shields, their advantage in equipment was neutralized.

Howls of dismay rose from the Gorgons as they realized that they were trapped. Vakar, caught in the melée, hewed at every plume-crested head he saw until he could scarcely swing his blade. A spear point gashed his leg again; another drove through the chest of the already wounded horse. With a scream the animal died, but such was the press that it could not fall, but gradually subsided on to a struggling knot of fighters. Vakar, exhausted, dragged himself clear and then was knocked over and buried under a welter of bodies.

He dragged himself out from under the pile of wounded and dead, battered and bruised and covered with his own and others' blood, to find that the Gorgons had been split into several small groups being ground to nothing. In the midst of the largest knot rose King Zeluud's chariot. The horses had been killed and the king stood in the vehicle, swinging over his followers' heads with a long two-handed sword at any Lorskan who tried to break through to reach him. Vakar began to push through the press towards the chariot. The Gorgons around the chariot fought like fiends until a huge Lorskan burst through to climb up behind the king, seize him by the neck, and drag him over the side. King Zeluud disappeared.

Now the Gorgons began to lose heart. Some cast down their arms and cried for quarter. Most of these the infuriated Lorskans struck down without mercy, but Vakar managed to save a few from slaughter. There was much about Gorgonia that he wished to know, and dead men could tell him nothing.

The sounds of battle died away, leaving several thousand Lorskans leaning on the shafts of their weapons and panting. Those who had the breath to do so raised the shout of victory. Some cut the throats of the Gorgon wounded; others dragged their own wounded out from the piles of dead to see if they looked salvageable or whether they too should, as an act of mercy, have their throats cut. The ground was carpeted with bodies and severed members and with helmets, shields, swords, spears, daggers, axes, maces, halberds, trumpets, and all the other paraphernalia of war. Tattered battle standards lay among the litter, some so bloodstained that the bison of Lorsk could hardly be distinguished from the octopus of Gorgonia.

Where the ground could be seen, it was dark red-brown with blood. Clouds of flies were settling upon the cadavers, and vultures circled expectantly overhead.

Vakar Zhu sheathed his blade and tied up his leg wounds with strips of cloth from the garments of fallen men. He found Lord Kalesh (he who had brought word of the Gorgons' circumnavigation to Lorsk) astride a blood-spattered horse. Vakar put Kalesh in charge of the army with instructions to secure any Gorgonian ships that had not gotten away and to camp on the plain that night. Then he borrowed Kalesh's horse and set off up the steep road for Mneset. At the top he picked up Ryn with his chariot. Vakar slid off his horse, saying:

"Mind you if I ride with you? These wounds in my legs will heal faster."

"Get in, get in."

They creaked slowly homeward, learning that nearly everybody they met thought that the Lorskans had lost the battle, such word having been spread throughout the land by the early fugitives.

Nine days later, they reached Mneset in a drizzle, with several hundred men trailing behind them. They found the gate shut and signs of preparations for a siege. Vakar shouted:

"Ho there! Open for Prince Vakar! The Gorgons are beaten!"

An armed man stuck his head over the wall. "What's that, sir?"

"I said, the Gorgons are beaten. Open up!"

"Just a minute, my lord." The man disappeared, but others appeared in his place, looking down silently and fingering their bows and spears.

Vakar fidgeted with impatience. The stragglers from the army came seeping along the road, afoot and on the backs of horses and mules, until a crowd of them was gathered in a semicircle around the gate.

Vakar fumed: "I don't know what ails those fellows. They've had plenty of time to open."

He shouted, but without effect; the armed men on the wall stared down silently. After a while the head of his brother Kuros appeared, saying:

"What's this lying tale of the Gorgons' being beaten?"

"Lying!" cried Vakar. "Come out here, coward, and I'll show you what's a lie!"

"What? No man speaks to a king like that and lives!"

"King?" yelled Vakar. "What do you mean, king?"

"Just what I said. The old man died while you were gone, first naming me his successor. He agreed it was high time we dropped the absurd old custom of ultimogeniture."

It took Vakar a few seconds to gather his wits after this shattering news. Finally he said:

"That's illegal and unconstitutional, and you know it. Even if it's true, which I have only your worthless word for, the king may not change the succession without the Council's approval."

"Well, I'm king in any case, with several thousand soldiers to make it stick. What are you going to do about it?"

"Murderer! Traitor! Usurper!" screamed Vakar, foaming in his rage. "You slew Söl the spy when he'd have revealed how you'd sold Lorsk to the Gorgon king! You tried to destroy your own army at Kort by fleeing as the battle started, and now you've seized the throne after no doubt hurrying our poor father into his next incarnation by smothering him with a pillow! Come out here with your sword, now, and we'll settle the succession man to man!"

"Do I look stupid?" replied Kuros. "Here!"

As he spoke, Kuros snatched a bow from a man beside him, nocked an arrow, and let fly. Vakar ducked as the missile whizzed past, missing him by inches and piercing the foot of one of the spectators, who yelped. The stragglers scattered in all directions, the wounded man limping after them with the arrow in his foot. As Kuros reached for another arrow, Vakar cracked his whip, wheeled the chariot around, and drove back out of range, snarling:

"I'll back-track and pick up the rest of the army! I'll take Mneset by storm and hang that traitor from the gate towers until he rots . . ."

Ryn shook his head, clawing at his goatish beard. "That would be hard on the city, no matter who won."

Vakar leaned against the side of the chariot, staring somberly into space. The stragglers stood about in little clumps, looking from Vakar to Kuros, who stood on the wall with his second arrow nocked but not drawn, waiting to see what Vakar would do. Ryn added softly:

"And is that what you really want? Think now."

Vakar straightened up with a laugh. "Now I see what Charsela was driving at! And I also know what Rethilio meant when he said I should have to make a choice of destinies; I couldn't encompass them all in one lifetime. Why should I fight that oaf for a drafty old castle and the right to boss a mob of yokels, when I have a much pleasanter berth awaiting me in Ogugia?"

"Why indeed?"

"I'm no conqueror, but a quiet fellow who asks only to be let alone to acquire true scholarship. Say farewell to Bili for me and lend me some trade metal. I'm for Sederado!"

Vakar filled his scrip and, his legs now healed, vaulted on to Kalesh's horse. He raised his voice to the stragglers and the men on the wall:

"You have all seen and heard what has happened here. If you wonder why I'm not pressing the fight against my brother, 'tis for two reasons: first, I'm not so avid of the duties of kingship as he seems to be, and second, our land has suffered enough of late without plunging it into civil war. I'm going into exile, without renouncing any claim to the throne. If at some future date, you tire of the rule of a murderer and traitor . . . Well, we'll let that take care of itself when the time comes. Farewell!"

Vakar waved, threw an ironical salute to Kuros, and galloped off toward Lezôtr, singing:

Vrir the Victorious   *rode to the river*
His scabbard of silver   *shining in sunlight . . .*

The gods, gathered in their place of assembly, all yammered at Drax: "Fool! Why told you us not that the center of this malign influence would shift to Tartaros, Vakar Lorska being but one minor link in the chain of causation . . ."

Drax writhed uncomfortably. "Pray be patient, divinities. I gave you all that my science had revealed to me. Perhaps all is not yet lost. By speeding the sinking of the western regions, we can submerge not only Poseidonis but Tartaros as well."

"What matters it," said Lyr, "whether we perish by the spread of the star metal or by the extermination of our worshippers? Why could you not leave well enough alone? If we had not caused Entigta to stir up his Gorgons, the Tahakh would still be a mere lump of meteoric iron, a harmless curiosity in the hands of Awoqqas of Belem."

"No doubt all this was fated from the beginning," said Okma.

This started a furious argument over free will versus predestination, in the course of which Asterio, the bull-headed forest god of Ogugia, pulled Entigta's tentacles cruelly.

But Vakar of Lorsk rode happily towards Amferé to take the last ship of the season for Sederado.

Lester del Rey

Available at your bookstore or use this coupon.